GUNMAN'S
Song

Also by Ralph Cotton
in Large Print:

Ralph Compton: Death Along the Cimarron
Vengeance Is a Bullet

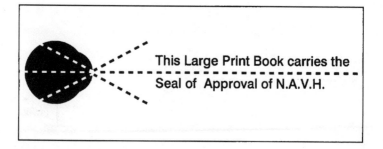

This Large Print Book carries the
Seal of Approval of N.A.V.H.

GUNMAN'S
Song

RALPH
COTTON

Thorndike Press • Waterville, Maine

Published in 2004 by arrangement with
NAL Signet, a member of Penguin Group (USA) Inc.

Thorndike Press® Large Print Western.

The tree indicium is a trademark of Thorndike Press.

The text of this Large Print edition is unabridged.
Other aspects of the book may vary from the original edition.

Set in 16 pt. Plantin.

Printed in the United States on permanent paper.

Library of Congress Cataloging-in-Publication Data

Cotton, Ralph W.
 Gunman's song / Ralph Cotton.
  p. cm.
 ISBN 0-7862-6925-1 (lg. print : hc : alk. paper)
 1. Shooters of firearms — Fiction. 2. Vigilantes — Fiction. 3. Revenge — Fiction. 4. Large type books. I. Title.
 PS3553.O766G86 2004
  813'.54—dc22   2004053728

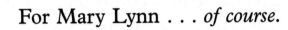

For Mary Lynn . . . *of course.*

As the Founder/CEO of NAVH, the only national health agency solely devoted to those who, although not totally blind, have an eye disease which could lead to serious visual impairment, I am pleased to recognize Thorndike Press★ as one of the leading publishers in the large print field.

Founded in 1954 in San Francisco to prepare large print textbooks for partially seeing children, NAVH became the pioneer and standard setting agency in the preparation of large type.

Today, those publishers who meet our standards carry the prestigious "Seal of Approval" indicating high quality large print. We are delighted that Thorndike Press is one of the publishers whose titles meet these standards. We are also pleased to recognize the significant contribution Thorndike Press is making in this important and growing field.

Lorraine H. Marchi, L.H.D.
Founder/CEO
NAVH

★ Thorndike Press encompasses the following imprints: Thorndike, Wheeler, Walker and Large Print Press.

PART
One

Chapter 1

Lawrence Shaw hailed from West Texas and was widely known as the fastest gun alive. But being known as a fast gun offered him no comfort at all when he got word all the way up in Arizona Territory that his wife, Rosa, had been brutally murdered by a gang of cutthroat saddle tramps who had come to their hacienda near the town of Somos Santos searching for him. By the time Shaw had ridden back to Texas his beloved Rosa lay in the ground and all of her family except for her younger sister, Carmelita, had gone back across the border and faded into the endless Mexican hill country. Carmelita had arranged to hire a buggy for the day, and when Lawrence Shaw arrived she drove him out to the Mexican cemetery behind the old Spanish mission where the silent ones had lived, the old missionary priests for whom Somos Santos had been named.

Carmelita didn't ask Lawrence Shaw why his left arm was in a sling. She could see the bullet hole in the shoulder of his shirt and the bloodstain that a stiff washing in a nameless creek had failed to remove. It was not her place to question her dead sister's husband. "A young man arrived in town three days ago," she said. "He was asking about you." She looked at him to check his response. Shaw only nodded slightly, gazing straight ahead.

"There have been other men come looking for you . . . they are gunmen who want to kill you, *si?*" she asked, careful not to appear to be prying into his personal affairs.

"That is likely," Shaw said flatly.

"They wish to kill you, and have people know they killed you, so men will fear them." She shook her head slightly, considering it. "That seems so cruel, so senseless," she said.

"It happens," was all Shaw offered.

"*Si*, it happens," Carmelita whispered almost to herself, thinking of the cruel, senseless killing of her sister Rosa by these same such men. They rode on in silence.

At the cemetery Carmelita stood back and watched Shaw slump in grief and helplessness, his shoulders shuddering quietly until at length he flung himself to his knees, his left arm coming out of the sling as he clenched his fists in the dry, loose dirt. "Oh, God, Rosa!" he pleaded, first to

10

the mound of fresh earth, then to the hot, windblown Texas sky. "Why her, God? Why not me? Why my precious Rosa? She never harmed a living thing!"

Shaw cursed aloud and shook his dirt-filled fists at the heavens, raging at God with such fury that Carmelita was certain that if God had shown his face right then, Lawrence Shaw would have tried to strike him down. Carmelita waited patiently. When at length Shaw's blasphemy turned to bitter weeping, Carmelita crossed herself as if to guard from the terrible anger that filled the air. She had held herself back as long as she could, and now that Shaw had spent his rage and sunk farther to the ground, she stepped forward and knelt and wept beside him, embracing the hardened gunman as she would an injured child.

"Oh, Carmelita," Shaw said, purging himself of layer upon layer of grief and guilt as the two emotions came upon him, "I have been such a fool . . . such a hopeless, blind, ignorant fool!"

"No, no," Carmelita said tightening her embrace. "Do not say these things; it lessens the memory of my sister to say she married such a man as you call yourself."

"But it's true, Carmelita," Shaw said. "I had received two letters from her in a

11

week, each one urging me to come home." He took a deep breath and let it out slowly. "I kept waiting, putting it off, telling myself just one more day . . . one more day of drinking, playing table billiards . . . telling gunfighter stories. Oh, Rosa, I should've been here for you," he said down to the mound of earth. "May God never forgive me for being the rotten, no-good —"

"Stop it, Lawrence," said Carmelita, slipping her arm around his waist, drawing him to her. "My sister loved you very much. You must know this and tell yourself this from now on, so that you can forgive yourself as she has already forgiven you."

"Do you . . . do you really believe that, Carmelita?" Shaw asked. "I mean that Rosa is looking down on us right now, and she knows how sorry I am . . . and how much I loved her?"

"Of course I believe that," said Carmelita, "and you must believe it too. Rosa would not want you blaming yourself. She would want you to go on living, and to find whatever happiness you can find without her."

"There is no happiness without her," said Shaw. Yet even as he spoke he collected himself gradually, reached inside his

12

coat, and took out a bandanna. He gave it to Carmelita, then wiped his own eyes when she had finished and given it back to him. After a while Shaw freed himself from her arms and stood up, dusting his trouser knees. "I need to go to town and talk to the sheriff. I want the men who killed her to pay for it."

"You mean you want to see them *hang?*" Carmelita asked, choosing her words.

"No," Shaw said, the strength coming back into his voice, "I don't want to see them hang." He picked up his dusty Stetson from where he had laid it on the ground and leveled it atop his head. He rubbed his eyes briskly with the bandanna.

Without another word, he walked toward the buggy while Carmelita stood in silence for a moment, watching him go. She wondered if even her dead sister Rosa had ever seen this man weep. She shook her head and pushed back a strand of her dark hair that had crossed her face on the wind. Well . . . his tears were a secret she would never reveal. With a parting look at her sister's grave, she made the sign of the cross and walked away.

Shaw sat stiff and silent all the way back to town, and Carmelita noted to herself how much she must look like her sister

Rosa, sitting there beside Lawrence Shaw. If anyone didn't know about this terrible thing that had happened they might have easily mistaken her for her sister Rosa. *The Shaws,* she thought, seeing the two of them as someone else might see them, crossing the flat stretch of sand, the horse holding its head high, her scarf licking back in the hot wind. She smiled softly and adjusted the riding scarf lower around her neck as she gave Shaw a glance.

"What?" Shaw asked, surprising Carmelita, who didn't realize his peripheral vision was wide and alert.

"Nothing," she said softly. "I am just glad to see you are feeling better."

"Feeling better?" he said quietly, taking a deep breath. "I don't think I'll ever feel *anything* again as long as I live."

"I mean just for this moment," she said.

Shaw considered it for a second. "For right now . . . I suppose I feel some better."

"Yes, for this moment," said Carmelita, "that is all I meant."

When Shaw offered no further conversation but only stared out across the endless wavering stretch of sand, mesquite, and creosote, Carmelita gazed ahead and said nothing more the rest of the way into town.

When they arrived in Somos Santos, Carmelita said, "I will take the buggy to the livery barn and ride the horse back to the hacienda. Will you be coming home tonight?"

Shaw's gloved right hand rested on the stripped-down bone-handled Colt resting in a one-piece tied-down Slim Jim holster. His expression was flat, yet it implied that she should know that this was no question to ask a gunman, particularly one who had had a stranger asking questions about him in his hometown.

"I mean, so I will know whether or not to prepare a dinner for you," she added quickly.

"I don't know," Shaw said. He stepped down from the buggy into the rutted dirt street and looked back and forth searchingly. "But don't worry . . . I doubt if I'll be hungry." He walked away toward the sheriff's office.

"But you must eat," Carmelita said. She stared after him for a second, wondering how she had said the wrong thing, or even *if* she had said the wrong thing. What kind of man was this her sister Rosa had married? Was he evil? she wondered, watching him walk away. Even with all the whiskey he had drunk throughout the day he moved like a man with great personal power and confidence, yet with a wariness and a conviction about him, like a man carrying a cross. No, this man was not evil, but dark and complicated, she answered herself — a man who had seen and touched much evil, and now had been touched upon by much evil. But she sensed no evil in him, not a part of his spirit, at least, she thought . . . or not in his heart.

When she realized he was not going to respond to her Carmelita coaxed the horse onward to the livery barn. She did not have to ask herself what her sister had seen in this man. She already knew. Her sister Rosa saw in him that thing that all women saw in all injured wild creatures that needed to be saved, either from the wilds or from the wildness of themselves. Carmelita knew that Lawrence Shaw had made Rosa ache inside for him. Rosa had never told her, but Carmelita knew it was so, because this was the same way Lawrence Shaw had always made her feel. She crossed herself quickly at thinking such a thing, hoping that she had not just brought some terrible fate upon both her dead sister's husband and perhaps herself as well. But it was true, wasn't it? She hastened the horse toward the barn, not wanting to think about it.

Shaw walked on. Out front of the sheriff's office a man stood leaning back against the building, rolling a smoke, with his head lowered just enough to hide his face beneath his hat brim. Instinctively Shaw knew as he walked closer that this was not the young gunman Carmelita had told him about. Shaw looked him up and down, recognizing something familiar about him in spite of time and distance. "Cray Dawson?" Shaw said, stepping onto the boardwalk and stopping.

"Yep," said the voice, but only after running the cigarette in and out of his mouth to wet it and firm it up. Then he raised his head slightly, giving Shaw a little better look at his face. "It's been a long time, Fast Larry."

Shaw started to tell Dawson then and there that "Fast Larry" was not a name he went by anymore. There had been a time, a few short years ago, when Shaw had gotten a real boost out of hearing people call him Fast Larry. But no longer, especially now. Yet Shaw decided to let it pass for the moment. "It has at that," Shaw replied. He watched Dawson raise his head more, bringing up a sulfur match, striking it, then touching the fire to the end of the cigarette. "Sheriff Bratcher's at the Ace

High Saloon," Dawson said, staring into Shaw's eyes. There was more to be said between them, and they both knew it. But each saw by the other's demeanor that anything that needed to be made right would keep until another time. There was no bad blood between them, only things that men needed to clear up in order to face one another as men. "He figured you'd be coming to see him."

"Obliged." Shaw nodded.

As he stepped back down from the boardwalk and headed for the saloon, Dawson called out to him, "Fast Larry?" And when Shaw stopped and turned to face him, Dawson said, "She was a good woman, Rosa."

Shaw only nodded and touched his fingertips to his hat brim.

Cray Dawson pushed himself forward easily from against the building. "Mind if I walk with you? I was fixin' to go there anyway."

Shaw only nodded again, but he waited until Dawson walked down from the boardwalk in the same slow, sauntering style Shaw remembered from childhood. When the two walked toward the Ace High Saloon, Shaw asked, staring straight ahead, "How long you been back here?"

"Oh . . . a couple of months, maybe more," said Cray Dawson, "You know there's a kid in town been looking around for you."

"Yep, I heard," said Shaw, acknowledging the matter, then dismissing it. "So you was here when it happened," said Shaw.

"Yeah, I was here," said Dawson. A short, stiff silence passed; then he said, "I saw them when they rode off down Comanche Trail."

Dawson's words almost stopped Shaw cold in his tracks. But he managed to stare straight ahead and change neither his voice nor his expression. "Recognize any of them?" he asked.

"Just Barton Talbert and Blue Snake Terril. Of course, you already know about them. The other weren't from these parts." He looked Shaw up and down. "You're going after them, I know."

"Yep," said Shaw.

"Want some company?" Dawson asked, letting go a stream of smoke onto a hot breeze.

"Was you with Sheriff Bratcher?" Shaw asked without answering his question.

"Yep, but everybody give out before we made the border," said Dawson.

"There'll be no 'give out' riding with me," said Shaw, as if in warning.

"I know it," said Dawson. "That's why I'm offering."

"I usually ride alone, Cray," said Shaw.

"But this ain't *usually*," said Cray Dawson. "I remember their faces."

Shaw only nodded. "How eager was Sheriff Bratcher to find the killers?" Shaw asked.

Dawson caught the implication in Shaw's voice and said, "He's old, Shaw. He couldn't have handled this bunch anyway." They paused on the street out front of the Ace High Saloon and Cray asked, "Can I say something?"

"Say what suits you, Cray," said Shaw.

"I believe your reputation kept Bratcher and his posse from going any farther. For all anybody knew this bunch could have been aiming to kill you. Once the posse realized these men were bold enough to come looking for a big gun like you, it more or less took some of their bark off."

"So the posse men were afraid of them," said Shaw.

"That, and the fact that it looked like they were headed for the border," said Dawson. "Not many lawmen want to cross that water. You know how that goes."

"Yep," said Lawrence Shaw. "I know how that goes."

They started to step onto the boardwalk out front of the Ace High Saloon when a voice called out twenty yards away, "Shaw! Fast Larry Shaw! I've been looking for you."

Shaw and Cray Dawson turned, facing the young gunman who stood taking off a pair of leather gloves by loosening one finger at a time. Beside him stood a shorter young man wearing a tattered brown bowler hat. He took the young gunman's gloves and backed away.

"Want me to go get Sheriff Bratcher?" Dawson asked.

"It never changes anything," Shaw said absently, keeping his eyes on the gunman, at the same time looking past him and from side to side, making sure nobody was hidden with a rifle just for backup. "The sheriff can't stop it."

"No," said Cray Dawson. "I meant to witness it, make sure you don't get accused of any wrongdoing."

"Wrongdoing . . . I never get accused," said Shaw, raising a hand slowly, pressing Dawson farther away from him. Dawson took the hint and moved back on his own.

"What is it, mister?" Shaw replied to the

gunman, already stepping slowly sideways to the middle of the street.

"You know what it is, Shaw," said the man. "It's five thousand dollars. That's what it is."

"Dang!" Cray Dawson whispered, "five thousand dollars?"

Shaw answered the young gunman. "That'll get you into the ground real proper with a lot left over. But it's your call."

From inside the Ace High Saloon the old sheriff had heard the young gunman call out Shaw's name. He stepped out through the saloon doors with his hand on a big Walker Colt holstered on his hip. Beside him stood a young deputy with a tin badge drooping down from his sagging shirt pocket. The deputy raised a sawed-off shotgun with his thumb lying across the hammer. "I know what it is too," Sheriff Bratcher called out to both gunmen, "And I ain't having it. You want to get Shaw to kill you, take it somewhere away from Somos Santos." As soon as Sheriff Bratcher spoke, he turned to the deputy and said in a lowered tone, "Freddie, get out from under me. Spread out along that boardwalk where you can do me some good. I hate for one shot to kill us both."

"Howdy, Sheriff Bratcher," Shaw said from the middle of the street without taking his eyes off the gunman.

"Howdy, Shaw," said Sheriff Bratcher. "I see you've brought more trouble to my town."

"I didn't bring it, Sheriff; it was here waiting for me," Shaw said.

"I notice you didn't try talking him out of it, though," said Bratcher.

"I figured that was your job, Sheriff," said Shaw. "I won't kill him here in Somos Santos if I can keep from it."

"I got news for you, Fast Larry," the young gunman called out, "you ain't killing me nowhere, nohow. So let's get 'em pulled."

"You heard the sheriff, mister," said Shaw. "He said no gunfighting here."

"To hell with him," said the young man. "He can't stop it."

"Whoa, now that's not using your head," said Shaw. "We pull iron, the sheriff here and his deputy are going to be pulling iron too. When the smoke clears it won't matter what kind of showing you made against me . . . you'll never know about it."

"I ain't going to be talked out of this, Shaw!" the gunman shouted. "I'm here to kill you, and nothing's going to stop me."

He cut a quick glance to where Freddie the deputy had hunkered down behind a wooden barrel. "You've got no right shooting at me . . . that's like you're taking his side!"

Freddie rose up with the shotgun hanging slack in his hands and looked along the boardwalk at Sheriff Bratcher. "Is that right, Sheriff?" he asked, looking confused. "Are we taking sides?"

"No, it ain't right, Freddie!" Bratcher barked at him. "Now get down and stay put!" The sheriff directed his next words to the young gunman. "I'm on the side of whoever is defending himself. I know Shaw here ain't going to draw first . . . so you're starting off in the wrong. If you was to kill him, which I know you won't, then I'll see to it you get tried for murder and hanged, or else you'll make a move on me, and we'll kill you where you stand. Now that's where you've put yourself today. It ain't working out quite like you had it figured, is it?"

The young gunman bristled. "I'm doing it! Shaw, come on, you ready?"

Shaw didn't answer. He only stared.

"I mean it, Shaw! It's time!" he shouted.

Shaw stood silent.

"Don't you want to know my name

first?" the gunman asked.

Shaw only shook his head slowly.

"Son of a . . ." the gunman raged. His hand moved fast, as fast as any Shaw had seen lately. But not fast enough. Shaw's shot hit him dead center of his forehead before the young man got his pistol up level enough to get an aim. The gunman's shot went straight down in front of his boot. Shaw's Colt didn't stop even for a split second. It cocked toward the man in the bowler hat.

"Don't shoot!" the man pleaded, throwing his hands up. He backed away, stumbling a bit.

At the hitch rail a spooked horse had reared, causing its tied reins to snap the crossbar from the rail. Shaw's pistol swung toward the horse, then lowered and un-cocked as someone appeared with his hand raised in a show of peace and settled the animal.

"My God, Shaw!" Cray Dawson said, stunned by Shaw's speed, "that ain't like nothing human!"

Shaw didn't answer. He looked down at the gun. Gray smoke curled upward around his hand as if being caressed by a serpent's tongue. He raised the gun and let the spent smoking cartridge shell fall to the street. He replaced it with a fresh round from his holster belt, keeping his eyes searching back and forth along the empty dirt street.

"This happens everywhere I go. Are you sure you want to ride with me, Cray Dawson?" he asked sidelong in a solemn tone of voice, clicking the Colt chamber shut and out of habit giving it a spin.

"Yeah, I still want to ride with you," said Cray Dawson gravely, "right up until I see Rosa's murderers dead."

Chapter 2

It was past midnight when Lawrence Shaw walked through the door of the hacienda and placed his Stetson on one of the hat pegs along the wall. He carried a newly opened bottle of rye in his right hand, having already emptied a bottle drinking shot after shot in the Ace High Saloon while talking to Sheriff Bratcher, Cray Dawson, and Freddie the deputy. There were a couple of others there but Shaw couldn't recall who they were in his present condition. Shaw was drunk, but not nearly as drunk as a man should be given the amount of raw rye he had poured down himself. He was still in control of his faculties, he thought. Yet, in the flickering glow of a candle Carmelita had left burning inside a glass globe, he weaved a bit before catching himself with one hand on the back of a tall wooden chair. The chair legs made a scraping sound on the stone floor and brought Carmelita up from the darkness where she had been lying on a deep wooden-framed sofa with a woolen Mexican serape around her.

"Lawrence? *¿Esta usted?*" she asked, her voice not sounding like that of woman awakened from sleep.

"*Si, estoy yo* . . . I mean yes, it's me," Shaw said, for a second speaking as he would have to Rosa, then catching himself quickly. Not that it should have mattered, his speaking Spanish to Carmelita. But it did somehow. There was something to it that he could not explain, but somehow it mattered.

"Are you hungry?" Carmelita asked. "I prepared some food. I can warm it." Her eyes moved across the bottle in his hand, then moved away.

"No, I'm good," said Shaw, sobering a bit now that he had to in order to speak clearly.

"Is there anything I can get for you? If there is, tell me," said Carmelita, stepping in closer, picking up the candle and holding it up for better light.

Lawrence Shaw looked into her dark eyes, so overcome by the resemblance to his Rosa that he resisted the aching need to hold her to him. "I'm not hungry," he said, averting his eyes from her, turning and walking through the darkness toward the bedroom at the end of the long hallway. Carmelita followed him with the candle, holding it up to light his way. Shaw avoided looking over at the broad hearth across the room. When he had arrived off the trail earlier that day, Carmelita had just finished scrubbing the hearthstone with a coarse brush and a bucket of soapy water. Shaw had pretended not to notice the pinkish color of the water or the two bullet holes in the hearthstones.

In the bedroom, Carmelita set the candle on a table inside the door, then raised the globe of an oil lantern, lit it, and trimmed it to a soft glow. "Let me help you," she said. Yet, turning toward him, she saw he had set the bottle on a nightstand and stood unfastening his gun belt. She watched him loop the belt, rebuckle it, and hang it on the corner of the bed within reach. She gazed at the gun and holster, at how they seemed so at home hanging there. When she looked back at Shaw he had seated himself on the side of the bed. He dropped a boot to the floor. She hesitated for a second, wondering if her offer of help was welcome, or even needed.

"I talked to the sheriff," Shaw said, reaching down, struggling with his other boot. "He told me the details."

"Please," Carmelita said softly, "let us

not speak about it any more tonight." She raised his foot and helped him take off the other boot. "You have had much to drink; let me help you."

"I'll be leaving tomorrow, first light," Shaw said. "Cray Dawson is coming by. He's riding with me."

"Oh," she said matter-of-factly. "Then I will prepare some food for you to take with you." She stepped in close and began unbuttoning his bib-front shirt as she spoke.

"That's not necessary," he said. Feeling her stop, he added, "The food, I mean. It's going to be a long ride . . . a day's food won't matter much one way or the other." He thought about what he'd just said, and corrected himself. "Unless you don't mind doing it, that is?"

"No, I do not mind." Carmelita finished unbuttoning his shirt and peeled it up over his shoulders, taking care with his healing wound. She dropped the shirt beside him and touched the tender flesh for a second as if examining it. Then she stepped around the bed and turned down the covers. "Finish undressing," she said quietly, fluffing the feather pillows. "Will you need a nightshirt?"

"No, I've grown unaccustomed to them," he said. Feeling a bit awkward with her in the room with him, Shaw took off his socks, dropped them, then stood up and waited for her to leave before unfastening his trousers.

"Good night, Lawrence," Carmelita said, stepping away from the bed and to the door. She reached down, turned out the lantern, and left the room with the candle in her hand.

Shaw crawled beneath the cover and lay barechested, wearing only his knee-length summer johns. He stared at the dark ceiling, feeling the emptiness beside him where once his wife had lain, the emptiness compounded by his knowing he would never feel the warmth of her beside him again. His cheeks were wet with tears — Fast Larry crying shamelessly in the dark — and he thought about his last day in Wakely, after he'd learned of Rosa's death and of the bodies of the men he'd left lying in the dirt street. He had delivered death so easily, he thought — too easily to be lying here taking death so hard.

"Rosa," he whispered, as if she were there in the darkness, or at least someplace unseen but where she could hear his voice. "Rosa," he whispered even more softly as sleep overtook him.

But sleep abandoned him shortly and he

31

awakened with a start to the sound of his own voice crying out. For a moment he lay shivering as if suffering a fever, unsure if he had really cried out aloud or if it had happened only in the throes of a tortured dream. The effects of the rye whiskey had all but worn off, and he felt the terrible pain of reality close around him like a tight fist. He wanted to reach for the bottle on the nightstand. He wanted to pour the whiskey down himself and feel the shivering, the hurt, and the emptiness dissipate in a warm surge. But as he lay there drawn up into a ball, he saw the door to the room open in a soft glow of candlelight.

"Lawrence?" Carmelita whispered, slipping into the room and closing the door behind herself. "Are you all right?" She moved to the side of the bed and looked down at him, her free hand holding her robe closed at her throat.

"I . . . I went crazy when I got the telegraph," he said, his voice blurting it out as if releasing something that had been building up like a storm inside him. "I killed some men in Wakely who had been dogging me, wanting a gunfight. That's how I got the wound." As he spoke, he reached out from under the cover for the bottle of whiskey.

Carmelita reached down, picked up the bottle, uncorked it, and handed it to him.

"Thanks," he said. "I know I've got to stop drinking whiskey. But right now, it helps some."

"Do what you must do," she said without judgment. "In such a time as this we must all do whatever helps our pain." She turned slightly back toward the door as Shaw took a long drink, let out a long sigh and held the bottle close to his chest for a moment in silence. Then, seeing her start across the room, he said before he could stop himself, "Don't leave, Carmelita. . . . Stay."

She stopped and turned back to him, facing him in the circled glow of candlelight. "Stay with you? Are you sure?" she asked softly.

"Yes . . . I mean, no," he said shakily. "I mean, it wouldn't be right." As he spoke Carmelita stepped forward and set the candle on the nightstand.

"Is it right, is it wrong?" she whispered with a shrug. "I do not know. But this is not a night for deciding what is right and what is wrong." She took the bottle from his hand and set it down beside the candle.

"But you're her sister. . . ." Shaw's words trailed off.

"*Si*, and I cherish her memory . . . and I miss her," said Carmelita. She untied the sash on her robe, slipped the garment from her shoulders, and let it fall down her body. She stood naked in the flickering candlelight. Shaw gasped slightly at the sight of her. When she leaned down over him, raised the edge of the covers, and slipped into the bed beside him, he caught the scent of her hair, familiar, yet slightly different from that of his wife's.

"Jesus," he moaned, "I can't . . . I know I can't. This is crazy." But even as he said it, he felt the heat of her against him, the steamy heat of her as she opened her legs and drew him to her, the piercing heat of her as she pressed her breasts against his chest.

"Shhh," she whispered. "Yes, you can. I will help you." Her hands traveled down his stomach, and Shaw knew she was right. He felt her mouth warm on his chest, his stomach, then lower as she moved down beneath the cover.

When he was ready for her, Carmelita seemed to engulf him, and they made subdued, gentle love in her sister's bed until the two became less and less aware that this was once Rosa's home, her bed, her husband, and more aware of the need their bodies summoned from one another. "Hold me," Carmelita whispered afterward as Shaw lay with his face buried in the fragrance of her long dark hair. "Hold me and fall asleep inside me."

"*Si*, I will," Shaw whispered, still catching his breath.

He fell asleep in her arms and for a while felt only the warm darkness embracing him, until he soon awakened again in the night with the same aching hollowness returning to his mind and body. At first he did not recognize his own bedroom in his own home. But soon, as the shroud of sleep lifted and realization crept into him, he sank into the deep sense of dread he had lately come to know. In their sleep they had changed position, and now he ran his hand along the slim arm lying across his chest, following it up to Carmelita's face, where he felt her breath on his skin. "Oh, Jesus," he whispered to himself as his recent memory came back to him. For a full moment he wanted to lie frozen in place forever, as if to move in any way and perhaps feel Carmelita's nakedness against him would further violate whatever degree of reverence he held for Rosa's memory. Yet something compelled him to touch her. He caressed her warm, slender back to satisfy himself that she was real, and that she was Carmelita, not his wife come back to him through some indiscernible process known only by the dead. Carmelita moaned beneath his touch and snuggled closer against him.

Suddenly he was moved by a smothering sense of guilt that forced him up from the bed, making careful moves in order not to disturb Carmelita. In the dark he climbed into his trousers, hooked the gun belt over his shoulder, picked up the whiskey bottle, and crept silently from the room. On his way through the house he picked up a blanket from the wooden-framed sofa and draped it around himself. He stepped out the front door into the chill of the night and found a seat for himself on the edge of the wide porch. He took a drink from the bottle and sat waiting for the fresh surge of whiskey to calm his belly and dull his pain. She had planned this, he told himself, coming into his room wearing only the robe, nothing beneath it.

He took another drink, thinking about it. So what? He was a man of the world . . . his wife had known that about him. He had not been a faithful husband, or a very *good* husband, as far as that went, he reminded himself. With his and Rosa's life together over and done, the best he could say for himself was that he had loved her. He took another drink. Perhaps that was as much as any man or woman could ever say about another. And now he had slept with her sister. Well, Rosa was gone, as gone now as she would ever be. A warm, naked woman had come to him in the midst of a bad night and he had taken no more than what was offered. It wasn't about Rosa. It wasn't about the dead. It was about Carmelita . . . and about him. It was about those still living, and the comfort they had to take. *So be it. . . .*

Behind him he heard the door open and close. Without turning or looking up, Shaw held his blanket open and draped it around her with his arm as she sat down beside him. She wore nothing but his bib-front shirt she had picked up from beside the bed, and she shivered a bit against him until the warmth of the blanket and his naked chest warmed her.

"Are you feeling better?" she asked, burrowing against him.

"Yes, I am," he replied. And the two sat in silence until they drifted back to sleep.

The next time he opened his eyes, it was to the sound of a horse blowing out its breath no more than a few feet from him.

He sensed someone standing there, and when he heard a man clear his throat, his hand instinctively snatched the big Colt out of its holster and from beneath the blanket, cocked and ready, in one swift stroke.

"Whoa, now!" said Cray Dawson, raising his hands chest-high.

Carmelita's eyes snapped open. *"¡Santa madre!"* she whispered, startled, pulling the shirt closed across her bare breasts. Seeing Dawson standing before them and seeing Shaw's pistol pointed at his chest, she slipped quickly from beneath the blanket and hurried into the house, the bib-front shirt concealing very little.

"Damn it," Shaw said in a growl, standing, letting the blanket fall as he lowered his pistol, let the hammer down, and slipped it into his holster. "What are you doing here, Cray?"

Cray Dawson tried to let the whole scene pass as if he hadn't seen a thing. He adjusted his hat atop his head, looking away for a second. "I said I'd be here . . . remember?"

Shaw let out a breath, pushing his hair back out of his eyes. "Yeah, I remember." He looked at the door as it slammed shut behind Carmelita. He started to say something to Cray Dawson, make some denial, offer some explanation. But deciding against it, he said, "Come in. I'll make us some coffee before we leave."

Cray looked at the nearly empty bottle of rye sitting on the edge of the porch. "Might just as well, I reckon," he said as he hitched his big bay to the hitch ring and stepped up onto the porch. "We're getting a late start anyway." In the east a streak of early sunlight mantled the horizon. He looked again at the bottle, then at the discarded blanket and Shaw's bare chest.

"Something you want to say, Dawson?" Shaw asked, reading disapproval on the man's face.

"No, not a thing," said Cray Dawson.

"All right then," said Shaw. "Let's get some coffee and get going." He turned and walked toward the door.

"Can I say something?" Dawson said, still standing on the same spot, his thumbs hooked in his belt.

"I thought you had nothing *to* say?" said Shaw.

"Not about this I don't." Cray Dawson shrugged, gesturing a hand toward the bottle and blanket. "But we was talking last night about Talbert and Blue Snake? Which way they might be headed?"

"Yeah?" said Shaw. "I remember."

"Well, I didn't want to mention it last night in the shape you was in, but Talbert's brother Sidlow is in jail up in Eagle Pass. I didn't see him with them, but you can bet he was somewhere not far away when they came through here. I figure we might squeeze something out of him."

"Why didn't you tell me this last night?" Shaw asked, a bit irritated.

"Because you were drunk, and I knew you'd want to fly right out of here and go to Eagle Pass," said Cray.

"I wasn't that drunk," said Shaw, letting his guard down a little.

"Nobody ever is," said Cray. "But anyway, he's there. Think we ought to go there?"

"Yep, that's where we're headed," said Shaw. "Let me get my boots and clothes on."

"What about that coffee?" Cray asked, seeing Shaw disappear into the house. Cray shook his head and walked in behind him.

Swinging three miles wide of Somos Santos they headed north toward Eagle Pass on the old Spanish missionaries trail. At noon they stopped in the dark shade of a wide creekbank. The water source had depleted to a thin trickle no wider than the back of Shaw's hand, but the high creekbanks provided shade for both man and animal alike. Riding down off of the burning stretch of bare flatlands where they had spent all morning without seeing a single traveler, Shaw and Dawson saw three Mexican goatherders resting in the creekbed amid a dozen milk goats. With the goatherders stood a tall gray gelding, and on the ground sat the man with the brown bowler hat who had held the gunman's gloves for him in Somos Santos.

"There's our friend from town," Cray Dawson said quietly to Shaw, the two stopping their horses ten yards away and looking the situation over. The goatherders called out a welcome in Spanish and motioned for the two to step down and take shade and water. Shaw and Dawson tipped their hats.

"*Gracias*," Shaw replied loudly enough for them to hear him. Then to Dawson he said, "Well, it is a main trail from Somos Santos." He stepped down from his horse, taking his rifle from the scabbard and cradling it in his arm as he took down his canteen and let the big buckskin drink from the thin stream.

They didn't venture any closer to the goatherders, but rather sat leaning back against the tall creekbank, allowing the horses to stand near them in the shade when they had finished taking their fill of water. "Can I ask something?" said Cray Dawson, after a moment of silence.

Shaw just looked at him.

"Last night . . . that gunman said, 'For five thousand dollars.' What was he talking about?"

"It's nothing," said Shaw.

"All right." Dawson nodded. "Sorry I asked."

A silence passed as a hot wind whirred across the open cut of the creekbed in the belly of the flatlands.

"It's a price some big gamblers have wagered on who'll be the one who kills me," Shaw said.

"You mean a bounty?" said Dawson.

"No, but it just as well be," said Shaw. "Except this is more of a pot. The pot keeps getting bigger every time I shoot another man." He looked at Dawson. "Hell of a life, huh?"

"Sounds like it," said Dawson, leaning forward a little and looking along the creekbank at the man in the bowler hat. "How do you suppose this man fits into it?"

"I figure he's just another flunky the oddsmakers have hired to come along and see how it's going. I've seen a few of them along the way this past year."

"That's too bad, Fast Larry," said Cray Dawson.

"Do me a favor," said Shaw. "Don't call me Fast Larry, all right?"

"Whatever you say. Lar— I mean, Lawrence," said Dawson, correcting himself. "Used to be that was the only name you'd go by."

"Yeah, well . . . I've changed a lot since then," said Shaw. "The truth is, I was a young, proud fool back then. I thought being a gunman amounted to something. But it doesn't. It's a dirty, bloody way to live."

"From the looks of that kid last night," said Dawson, "it's a dirty, bloody way to *die*."

"It's that too," said Shaw. He leaned forward now and looked toward the man in the bowler hat.

"I learned that dead man's name," said Dawson. "Want to know it?"

"No," Shaw said flatly. "Far as I'm concerned he quit having a name the minute he decided to put himself in front of me."

"Well, it's Hollis," said Dawson.

Shaw just stared at him.

43

Dawson went on, saying, "The barber found a letter on him while he was cleaning him up to bury. . . . He told Sheriff Bratcher his name was Dan Hollis. Does it sound familiar?"

"No," said Shaw. "There's a Red Hollis up in the hill country, prides himself as some sort of outlaw. Goes by the name Montana Red."

"Might be kin, I reckon," said Cray Dawson. He gazed at the ground for a moment, then said in a quiet tone, "I reckon we ought to get it talked out between us, about how much I cared for Rosa."

"I know how you felt, Cray," said Shaw, as if not wanting to talk about it.

"I would have married her," said Dawson, "that is, if you hadn't married her. That is, if she would have had me. That is, if things had been —"

"That's a lot of 'would have ifs,' Cray," said Shaw, cutting him off. "Are you going anywhere with this?"

"I just thought I ought to tell you . . . so you'd know," said Dawson. "That's why I wanted to come along with you. I want her killers too."

"I think I knew that, Cray," said Shaw. He uncapped his canteen, sipped from it, and passed it to Dawson, who turned it up and took a deep swallow before he realized it was rye whiskey. He made a harsh wheezing sound, then said, "Jesus! Lawrence!"

Shaw smiled at his reddened face. "I never knew you couldn't push down a mouthful of whiskey, Cray."

"I wasn't expecting it, is all," Dawson said, his words sounding raspy. "You might warn a fellow."

Shaw took the canteen back, capped it, and laid it beside him. "When this runs out, it's no more whiskey for me . . . least-wise not on the trail."

"That's a good policy," Cray Dawson rasped, getting up and going to his horse for his own canteen. When he came back, he sipped the tepid water, then said, "So we're squared up on where I stood? How I felt about Rosa?"

"We're squared up," said Shaw. "Let's not talk about it any more." He gazed at the canteen of whiskey for a moment, then said in a lowered tone, "I expect as it turned out, Cray, I wish to God she'd married you myself."

"Do you mean that, Shaw?" Dawson asked.

Lawrence Shaw dropped his head. "Hell . . . I don't know. She'd still be alive, wouldn't she?"

Chapter 3

As Shaw and Dawson stood up, dusted their trousers and prepared to mount their horses, the man in the brown bowler also stood amid the goatherders and pulled his horse along by his reins, walking toward them at a brisk pace. "Look who's coming here," said Dawson.

"I saw him," said Shaw, without turning his eyes to the man.

"Can I come over there?" the man called out, stopping fifteen feet away, holding both hands chest-high.

Shaw responded with a nod of his head.

"In case you're wondering, I'm not armed," the man said. He lowered his hand enough to lift the corners of his vest, revealing his belt line. "As you can see."

"What do you want?" Shaw asked, ignoring the man's smile of courtesy.

"Just got tired of the smell of goats over there," he said, expanding his smile.

"But you didn't mind sharing their shade?" Shaw asked bluntly.

"I'm only joking, of course, about the

goats," the man said. "Allow me to introduce myself. I'm Jedson Caldwell. My friends call me Jedson . . . I hope you gentlemen will do the same."

"What's on your mind, *Mr.* Caldwell?" Shaw said, letting the man know that his offer of friendship had been declined. He ignored the man's dirty outstretched hand.

His handshake rebuffed, Jedson Caldwell wiped his small, delicate hand on his side and said, "Certainly then, let me come to the point. Those herders were just telling me that there's a band of Comancheros running amok along the border. There's been a couple of settlers killed and burned! I was hoping perhaps I could accompany you gentlemen as far as Eagle Pass."

"What's in Eagle Pass?" Shaw asked. "Another gunman you want to see me kill?"

"Mr. Shaw, I want you to know I had no personal involvement with Hollis. He offered me ten dollars to be a witness that he had outdrawn you fair and square. I believe he felt that, this being your hometown, someone might claim he had cheated somehow."

"Maybe he should have," said Dawson. He gave Caldwell a half smile. "I hope you got paid in advance."

Caldwell looked embarrassed and said, "As a matter of fact, I did not, sir. That's why I'm traveling alone on horseback — Hollis's horse, I might add. I had counted on the ten dollars for stage fare to San Antone and rail fare to New Orleans."

"You backed the wrong gun, Caldwell," said Shaw, stepping up into his saddle, keeping his right hand free in case he needed to draw his Colt. "Better luck next time."

"Gentlemen, please, I beseech you!" said Caldwell, seeing Cray Dawson also step up into his saddle. "I didn't back Hollis against you, Mr. Shaw! I'm no gambler . . . and I'm certainly no gunman, let me assure you!"

"Then what are you?" said Shaw, staring down at him, ready to heel the big buckskin forward.

"By profession, I'm trained as an undertaker," he said quickly, "but I've been put upon by a rash of misfortunes and I fear if I can't get out of this godforsaken country I'll surely die here! I have no money to offer you at present, but if you'll allow me to ride along I promise to compensate you once I get on my feet in New Orleans —"

Cutting him off, Dawson said, "An undertaker," seeming not to have even heard anything beyond that, "and you couldn't make a living around here?"

"No," said Caldwell, "I'm afraid the barbers have monopolized undertaking, much the same way as they have dentistry. An undertaker can't compete with the barbers when it comes to burying the dead. Only a few weeks back I was threatened with a razor by the barber over in Hide City. Said if I didn't leave town I'd be burying an important part of *myself!* Needless to say, I left immediately."

Dawson gave Shaw a questioning look. "What do you say, Shaw? If there's 'cheros lifting scalps, three men riding together might be better than two."

Shaw considered it, then said to Caldwell, "Can you shoot?"

"No, sir, Mr. Shaw, not a lick," said Caldwell.

Dawson chuckled and shook his head. "You sure ain't got much to offer, Caldwell. Can you cook? Make coffee?"

"Cook, I don't think so," said Caldwell, "at least nothing that you'd want to eat unless you were near starvation. Coffee, I do all right with . . . I've never poisoned anyone . . . that I know of, anyway." Seeing the reluctance in Shaw's eyes, Caldwell added hastily, "But like he said, three men looks stronger than two. And in a desperate situation, you could always leave me behind and get away while the Comancheros are busy killing me."

"Now you're making sense," Shaw said gruffly, looking away across the flatlands. He heeled the big buckskin forward without another word.

"Does that mean I'm welcome to ride along with yas?" Caldwell asked Cray Dawson in a meek tone, watching Shaw ride away from them.

"Try not to say any more than you have to for the next twenty miles or so," said Dawson, gesturing for Caldwell to ride in front of him. "We hope to be in Eagle Pass day after tomorrow."

"Not a word," said Caldwell, "I promise." He hurried into his saddle and gave his horse a jerk forward, having to plant his hand down on his bowler hat to keep from losing it. Dawson smiled to himself and followed close behind, keeping an eye on him. Along the dry creekbed the old Mexican goatherders lifted their hands in farewell, watching the three horses file past them.

Shaw led the way on the dirt trail most of the afternoon. Caldwell kept his promise and didn't speak another word until after they had reached the end of the flatlands and began winding their way up and down across one low rise after another toward a string of low hills that stood purple and gray in the failing evening light. When Shaw stopped the big buckskin at the crest of a rise and halted Dawson and Caldwell with a raised hand, the undertaker craned his neck and stared in the same direction as Shaw as he asked Dawson in a nervous whisper, "Why are we stopped here? What's wrong? Are there Comancheros?"

But Shaw heard him and answered for Dawson, "I don't know if they're Comancheros or not . . . but there's a wagon and it's not moving. I've been getting a little better look at them each time we top a rise."

Dawson stood in his stirrups and gazed out through the evening shadows. "We could circle wide of it . . . but if somebody has slipped a wheel, I'd hate to leave them stranded out here with 'cheros on the loose."

"We'll ride in on them," said Shaw, raising his rifle from his scabbard, checking it, and laying it across his lap. "Be ready in case it's a trap."

"A trap?" Caldwell said, sounding shaky,

moving his horse closer to Cray Dawson. "Should you give me a gun or something?"

"Thought you couldn't shoot," said Dawson, looking pointedly at him.

"I can't," Caldwell replied, "but if you'll set it up for me I can keep pulling the trigger until it stops firing."

"Jesus," said Dawson, "just stick close to me for now. When we get past this, maybe I'll show you some pointers on shooting."

"Thanks," said Caldwell, his face ashen with fear. "I believe it's time I seriously learn to defend myself."

Dawson and Caldwell followed Lawrence Shaw until even in the closing dusk they could see the old Studebaker canvas-top wagon sitting with a rear wheel resting on a short pile of flat rocks. A few feet away stood four mules grazing on sparse clumps of grass.

At the rear of the wagon, a tall woman with long auburn hair saw the three riders coming across the rolling land and she said to the bald-headed man who worked feverishly on the broken wheel, "Dillard, someone's coming!" Then she walked around the side of the wagon, picked up the double-barreled shotgun, and walked briskly back and held it out to the man as he hurriedly wiped axle grease from his hands onto a dirty rag.

"If I ever get the hell out of this damn mess, I'll never leave the town limits again. I ought to have my ass kicked for ever coming along."

"Here, take this gun and try to act like a man," she said. "You were pretty keen on coming along when all you thought you had to help me do was claim that tavern and pick up any money the old man left me. Stop bellyaching!" She forced the shotgun into his hand, shoving him back a step. "If it's Comancheros, we're both going to die. Let's try to do so with some dignity."

"Dignity, my ass," Dillard Frome growled, checking the shotgun and raising it to his shoulder. "If they're not Comancheros, don't forget, we're Dillard and Della Frome, man and wife." He looked her up and down with contempt. "God forbid . . ." he added under his breath.

"Don't worry, Dillard; I know that little 'we're married' routine by heart." Della reached up under her dress, took out a short double-action Colt Thunderer, and held it down in front of her with both hands, her right finger on the trigger. "That's just about close enough," she called out to the riders when they had drawn closer. She raised the pistol and pointed it.

Shaw called out from fifty yards away, "Ma'am, I'd appreciate it if you wouldn't point that gun at us. We're on our way to Eagle Pass." His eyes went to Dillard and the shotgun, then back to the woman. "We saw your wagon and came to see if you need help," he continued. "If you do, we're here. If you don't, we bid you good evening and we'll be on our way."

"Wait," said Della, seeing the no-nonsense manner in which the man had presented himself and his colleagues. "Yes, we do need help. As you can see, our wagon had a busted wheel." She lowered the pistol a bit and nodded toward the rear of the wagon. "Pardon my lack of courtesy . . . we've heard there are Comancheros roaming about."

"Where are you men coming from?" Dillard Frome asked, lowering his shotgun as the three nudged their horses forward again. He waited for an answer but didn't get one until Shaw stopped his horse ten feet away and the other two closed up beside him.

"We're coming from Somos Santos," Shaw said. "We haven't seen any Comancheros.

But that doesn't mean they're not around here."

Cray Dawson tipped his hat at the woman and asked, "And who do I have the pleasure of speaking to?"

Dillard Frome cut in, saying, "This is my wife Della . . . Dillard and Della Frome, that's us."

"Bull, he's out of his mind!" said Della, disputing Dillard, ignoring Cray Dawson and staring into Lawrence Shaw's cool green eyes as he looked back and forth, studiously taking in the wagon, the broken wheel, and the campsite. "We say we're man and wife in case anybody might be inclined to take advantage. But the truth is, I'm a widow. I'm Della . . . Della Starks, the widow of Purvis Starks, deceased owner of the Desert Flower Inn in Eagle Pass. You may have heard of it?"

"I'm Cray Dawson, ma'am . . . and yes, I have heard of it," Dawson said, touching his hat brim. "In fact I've drank there."

Della Starks didn't even look at him as she said, "Is that a fact?" Instead she stared at Shaw as she said, "And what about you, mister? Have you ever been there?"

Shaw nodded, preoccupied with studying the rolling land, the dark hill line. "Sure,

55

I've been there. We need to get out of here and into the hills."

Della looked surprised. "Oh? Right now? It's almost dark."

"That's right, it is," said Shaw, "and anybody within miles has had all afternoon to spot you two out here and plan to do whatever suits them under the cover of darkness."

"We can't leave the wagon, mister," said Dillard Frome. "All Miss Della's things are in there."

"Then good luck to you both," said Shaw, backing his horse a step, ready to turn it and ride away.

"Is that it?" said Della, trying to sound outraged by Shaw, but still taken by his eyes, his demeanor. "Is that your so-called *help?*"

"Ma'am, you don't need our help to die . . . the Comancheros will oblige you on that matter."

Della cocked a hand onto her hip and said to Cray Dawson, "Is your friend here always so cross and rude?"

Having seen the way the woman was affected by Shaw, Dawson said, "No, ma'am, but while we waste time palavering . . . there could be Comancheros slipping up all around us. Do you have anything in that wagon you can't live without?"

"Well, not really . . . but I hate losing it," said Della.

"If we get unwanted company in the night, you'll be glad you left it . . . if we don't, it'll all be here come morning, won't it?"

Seeing that Lawrence Shaw was already leaving, Della tried to appear as if she were considering it. But then quickly she said, "Well, that does make sense." She said to Dillard Frome, "Grab the mules, Dillard; let's not keep these gentlemen waiting."

Hearing her, Shaw stopped his buckskin, turned it quarterwise to her, and sat leaning his forearm on his saddle horn, his rifle resting in his other hand propped up on his thigh.

"Do you men ever introduce yourselves?" Della asked. "Or do you leave a lady to wonder?"

Cray Dawson said, "I did introduce myself; you must've missed it." He touched his fingers to his hat brim again, saying, "I'm Cray Dawson, ma'am. This is Lawrence Shaw, and this is Jedson Cald—"

"Lawrence Shaw?" she said with a slight gasp, cutting Dawson off. She didn't even give a glance toward Jedson Caldwell. "Not Lawrence Shaw the gunfighter?"

Shaw turned a level glance to her,

saying, "Ma'am," with a touch of his hat brim. Then he looked away, more interested in what might be lurking in wait on the darkening land.

"Well . . . I certainly feel like I'm in good hands now," Della said, looking flushed all of a sudden. "Mr. Shaw, may I call you Lawrence?"

"Do what suits." Shaw shrugged, not paying any attention to her walking forward as Dillard arrived pulling the four mules along on a lead rope.

"Della, take your pick," said Dillard Frome, holding the lead rope toward her.

"Don't be a fool, Dillard," Della snapped at him, shoving his hand full of lead rope away. "I'm not about to ride a smelly bareback mule! Lawrence, would you be a dear?" she asked, reaching up to Shaw with both arms spread upward toward him.

"Amazing," Cray Dawson whispered to himself, marveling at how at the sight of Shaw and the mention of his name the woman seemed unable to keep her hands off of him.

Shaw looked around again, giving Dawson an embarrassed glance. Then he said grudgingly to Della Starks, "All right, ma'am, but just until we get inside the hills. I can't afford to blow this horse out."

Della started to climb up behind him, but Shaw swept down with his free arm, cradled it around her, and lifted her onto his lap. Dawson shook his head and nudged his horse forward, Caldwell tagging his horse right beside him, staring in disbelief at the woman on Shaw's lap.

"I've never been treated that way by a woman," Caldwell said between himself and Dawson.

"Neither have I," said Dawson. "I guess I just ain't killed enough people." They rode on, Dawson growing silent for a moment, then saying quietly, "I take it back, Caldwell . . . once, I met a woman who treated me real special like that. Only once in my whole life." He seemed to think about it for a moment, then turned his face to the dark hill line. "We better get on up there. Shaw's right: We're sitting ducks out here."

They rode across the rolling land for the next hour as night closed in around them. By the time they'd ridden upward into the hill line they heard distant shouting and whooping intermingled with gunfire coming from the direction of the wagon. "Oh, Lawrence!" said Della, tightening her embrace on Shaw. "You were right! You saved my life! How can I ever thank you enough?"

"Ma'am, you don't owe me a thing," said Shaw in earnest. "I'm just glad we came by when we did."

Hearing the two, Cray Dawson only nodded to himself with a wry smile. "It figures," he whispered to himself.

Beside Dawson, Jedson Caldwell looked back and said, "Do you suppose they will follow our tracks?"

"Probably not tonight," said Dawson. "They'll be satisfied with what they've found back there. It'll keep their attention until morning."

"But let's keep moving, just in case it doesn't," Shaw said over his shoulder to them, Della sitting in his lap with her arms around his neck.

They pushed on, and as soon as they rode higher and deeper into the shelter of the hills, Lawrence Shaw stopped the big buckskin and gently but firmly set Della Starks down from his saddle and turned the horse beside the narrow trail, watching as the others filed in behind him. "Give Miss Della a mule," he said to Dillard Frome.

Della said, "But I was so comfortable in your lap, Lawrence. And I feel so safe.

Can't I just go on riding —"

"I told you just until we reached the hills, ma'am," said Shaw, "I can't afford to wear this horse out."

"Oh, all right then," said Della, feigning a pout. "You men and your horses. Sometimes I think you prefer them over women."

Ignoring her, Shaw looked back across the land toward the constant shouting and shooting. "There it goes," he said, pointing back through the darkness. They all looked back into the night on the rolling land below and saw high, licking flames spring up where the wagon sat. Rifle and pistol shots grew heavier. Della held her hands to her mouth and sobbed. "All my beautiful dresses and gowns . . . all my hats! They're all gone."

Shaw looked around at the faces of Dillard Frome, Cray Dawson, and Jedson Caldwell. Frome stepped over and tried to put his arm around Della, but she brushed it away. Seeing that no one seemed able to console her, Lawrence Shaw stepped down from his saddle, walked over, and embraced her, drawing her against his chest. "You'll be all right, ma'am. You'll soon replace those things, maybe with something even better."

"Do you . . . do you suppose so,

Lawrence?" she asked, sniffling a bit, her cheek pressed firmly against him.

"Of course you will," said Shaw. He shot Dawson and the others a glance, almost shrugging. Dawson shook his head and looked away. "We'll go up a little farther, then make a camp for the night. No fire though — they might decide to hit us in our sleep."

"Won't it get awfully chilly without a fire?" Della asked.

"We have blankets, ma'am," said Shaw. "Don't worry; we won't let you get cold."

"Lawrence . . . ?" She paused, letting her words trail off.

"Yes, ma'am?" said Shaw.

"Will you stay close to me tonight?" Della lowered her voice, but Dawson and the others could still hear her.

"As close as I can, ma'am," said Shaw.

"But I mean *real* close, Lawrence," she whispered. "Will you stay *real* close to me?"

"We'll see how it goes," said Shaw, feeling a bit embarrassed, knowing Dawson was watching and listening.

"God almighty!" Dawson whispered to himself, turning away and watching the flames of the wagon lick high into the night. "He beats all I've ever seen."

Chapter 4

They made a dark camp beside the winding trail at the foot of an upreaching stretch of rock where jagged boulders — some as large as houses — littered the hillside and stood up like grave markers to some ancient race of giants. After sharing a sparse meal of jerked beef and tepid canteen water Cray Dawson and Shaw had brought with them, Shaw and Della stood up from the group and Shaw picked up a blanket from the ground. "We need to take turns standing watch," Shaw said. "Dawson . . . ?" His words trailed off.

"Sure," said Dawson, "I'll take the first." In the quarter-moon darkness he looked up at the black silhouettes of Shaw and Della Starks, seeing Della reach out and slip an arm around Shaw's waist and stand closer to him.

"*Gracias,*" said Shaw. Then, carrying the blanket with his canteen of whiskey over his shoulder, he disappeared with Della into the larger darkness surrounding them. Caldwell, Dawson, and Dillard Frome sat hunkered quietly for a moment, not knowing what to say.

Finally Caldwell broke the silence, saying, "Dan Hollis was the same way, I noticed, what little time I was around him. Women flocked for his attention . . . bartenders set him up drinks for free . . . restaurants didn't want to take his money. I never saw anything like it. I studied my head off learning the art of mortuary science, a respectable profession that serves a better purpose to the world." He spit and chuckled under his breath. "All I really needed to do was learn to shoot a gun, the way Hollis did."

"And don't forget," said Cray Dawson, "Hollis wasn't even the best. Imagine if a person's the best, like Shaw, I bet Shaw doesn't even pay for a shave and a haircut most places he goes."

"Same way with musicians," Frome said quietly and bitterly. "Had a wife once who left me for a guitar player — they never pay for anything either . . . sons a' bitches."

Dawson and Caldwell didn't know what to say. After a pause, Frome lowered his voice and said, "One thing's for sure: If Fast Larry ever paid for anything before, he'll never have to again, not if he cools Della's fire just right."

"I wouldn't get in a habit of calling him Fast Larry," Dawson said to Frome. "He doesn't like going by that name anymore."

"Oh!" said Frome, a bit startled. "Thanks for the advice. I meant no harm, that's for sure."

"I know," said Dawson, "that's why I warned you. What did you mean, he'll never pay for nothing again if he cools Della's fire?"

Frome scooted closer in the darkness. "All that malarkey she was dishing out about losing her dresses and hats," Frome said. "Ha! That woman goes through dresses, shoes, and whatnot like the queen of England." His voice lowered even more. "She's dirty-dog rich you know. She'll hand-feed Shaw like he's a lapdog."

"The queen of England?" Caldwell asked.

The two ignored him. "Her husband owned that Desert Flower, but he also owned a couple of copper mines and half interest in a stage line. Hell! He even owned part of a beef brokerage company in Chicago. He left it all to Della too." Frome stopped for a second as if letting it sink in, then said, "To be honest, I wanted to get my claws into some of it. Looks like Shaw has jumped my stake."

"Rich, huh?" said Dawson.

"Filthy," said Frome.

"My, my," said Caldwell.

"It just about figures," said Dawson.

A brief silence passed as each man pictured himself in Shaw's place. Then Caldwell said, "I guess I just don't understand it. What makes women so attracted to gunslingers anyway?"

"I don't know," said Dawson. "Power, I guess?" He shrugged. "I hate to think it's just because they're good at killing people. It sure looks like it at times, though."

"It's their fame, their *notoriety*," said Caldwell, as if the answer had just come to him in a flash. "That's it. Women want men other folks have heard of. Not some unheard-of undertaker like me."

"They all want men that other women want; that much I'll go along with," said Dawson. "I've never seen a woman want a man as bad as she does once she sees that some other woman will have him." He nodded. "I've had that happen to me, believe it or not."

"So have I," said Frome. "Being a bartender most of my life, I've had a string of wives that would reach hand in hand across Missouri. I've seen it all when it comes to women . . . not that I yet understand them . . . not that I yet understand why God ever made them."

"Oh, I understand why," said Dawson in wistful remembrance. He sipped from his canteen. "All I figured I'd ever need was one good woman. I figured I'd spend my life with her and never stray. But it wasn't meant to be," he said.

"How do you know it wasn't?" said Caldwell. "You're young; you might still meet that special woman."

"Oh, I met her already," said Dawson. "That's the bad thing of it. I met her, I fell in love with her . . . she fell in love with another man, and that was that. It wasn't meant to be, us spending our lives together."

Caldwell said, "Who knows, maybe someday she'll —"

"Naw, I don't think so," said Dawson, stopping him. As if he felt he'd revealed too much about himself, Dawson dropped the subject and said to Frome, "You've been a bartender; you tell us . . . why do gunfighters not have to pay for their drinks?"

Frome said, "I always set them up because I figured it might keep them pacified, so to speak. You never know when a gunslinger might take something the wrong way and commence blowing your head off. That's probably why other drinkers like to pay for their drinks too . . . to keep on their good side."

"Their good side," Dawson mused quietly.

"Well, not all women fall for gunfighters," Caldwell said. "There are some women who snub their noses at men like Shaw. They go for the kind of man who is settled and responsible and spends his life making something of himself and leaving something behind for his family. My father was that kind of man. I'm sure my mother respected him and loved him."

"Yep, you're right," said Dawson, "not all women fall for gunfighters. But they all seem to fall for the kind of man who has a gunfighter's nature . . . whether he is an actual gunfighter or not."

"That dangerous type," said Frome. "Or men with that kiss-my-ass attitude toward them, or toward the whole world, I reckon."

"Maybe," said Dawson, pondering Frome's words.

"Or," said Frome, "to get right down to the heart of the matter, I believe when all is said and done it's the size of a man's pecker that draws women to him."

Dawson and Caldwell just stared at him.

"It's a fact," said Frome. "All that don't-give-a-damn attitude comes from a man knowing he's ahead of the herd when it comes to women . . . that's what a woman senses in him, and that's what draws them to him." He jerked his head toward the darkness in the direction Shaw and Della had taken. "That's why he's got Della's feet stuck in the air and we're sitting in the dirt. Pecker size." He nodded. "That's what it's all about."

Another silence passed; then Caldwell said absently, "God, I hope not."

Dawson and Frome stared at him. He caught himself and said quickly, "I mean, that seems like such a minor attribute on which to judge a man."

Dawson spit and stood up and dusted his trousers. "Hell . . . it's as good a way as any, I reckon. At least it offers an answer where there seems to be no other." He picked up his rifle and walked to another rock a few feet away. "Frome, I'll wake you in a couple of hours, give you some time to study up some more wisdoms for us." He sat down and looked out toward the firelight that still glowed brightly in the black of night.

In a few moments Jedson Caldwell and Dillard Frome scooted closer together and leaned back against the same broad upthrust of rock. They shared a single threadbare blanket, each of them grasping a corner of it in his fist and hanging on, lest the other take it over in his sleep.

Pecker size, Cray Dawson thought. Behind him he heard the sound of the two men snoring, and the sound of Della Starks whispering something to Shaw in a gasping voice only a few feet away. Dawson offered a tired smile to the wide, empty night and ducked his hat brim down on his forehead. *All this time I've wondered why, Rosa . . . now I reckon I know.*

When it came time to wake Frome, Cray Dawson still sat watching the glowing wagon, only now he did so more intently, as if gauging the distance and studying something on the dark land lying between the hills and wagon below. There had been no gunfire for the past couple of hours. The night lay in dead silence without so much as a yelp from a coyote or the batting of a night bird's wings. Yet he sat stonelike, refusing to move, every fiber of his being concentrated on the silent land below.

There it was, he thought, his senses honing in on the sound of a horse's nicker in the distance. It stopped abruptly, but too late. It was nearly inaudible, but he'd heard it. It came from down the hill line almost at the base. The Comancheros had left the wagon ablaze and headed across the land, perhaps following the tracks, perhaps just running on common knowledge that whoever had been at the wagon had no safe way to run except for the shelter of the hills. He stood up and dusted his trousers again, feeling the chill of night tighten around him. He shook himself off and walked in the direction where he'd heard Shaw and Della in the darkness.

"Shaw, wake up," he whispered, reaching down and poking his rifle barrel gently into Shaw's ribs, barely making out his dark outline in the blanket that wrapped around the pair.

Shaw awakened quickly, Dawson hearing the soft click of his Colt muffled by the blanket. "What is it?"

"They're coming," said Dawson. "I heard them below us."

Shaw arose with the smell of whiskey about him. Della moaned and tugged at the blanket. "You heard them?" Shaw asked hoarsely. "How did you hear them this far up?"

"I was paying attention, listening real close," said Dawson. "They're coming, damn it! Take my word for it."

"All right," said Shaw, "I didn't mean to

doubt you . . . let me clear my head here." He blew out a breath, and Dawson heard the canteen cap come loose. He heard Shaw swig down a drink of whiskey.

"Jesus, Shaw, you said you were going to stop drinking," Dawson said.

"I am . . . as soon as this runs out. That's what I said, remember?" He rummaged around on the ground, found his trousers, and pulled them on. With his gun belt hung on his shoulder he found his boots and stepped into them. "I meant it too," Shaw said. "I never used to drink like this. It's just been since Rosa's death." He stopped and let out a sigh, then said, "I know that's no excuse. I've got to quit; that's all there is to it."

"Ain't judging you, Shaw," said Dawson, "I'll go get the others and gather the horses while you pull yourself together."

"Good idea," Shaw said with much effort, rubbing his temples as if to get his brain working.

"With a good start, we ought to be able to outrun until we reach the outskirts of Eagle Pass." That said, Cray Dawson turned to leave.

But Shaw stopped him, saying, "Whoa! Whoa! What are you talking about, outrunning them? We're not running from these cutthroat cowards. How would that look to the folks at Eagle Pass, us coming in out of breath, looking back over our shoulder?" Shaw shook his head. "Huh-uh . . . I've been taking a stand too long to start making a run for it now."

Dawson stared at him in the darkness. "Have you got any better ideas?"

"Any idea beats that one." Shaw's head seemed to have suddenly shaken itself free of the whiskey. He swung the gun belt from his shoulder and slung it around his waist and buckled it, all in one smooth motion. Dawson saw him bend slightly and tie his holster down. "We're going to back these horses off into the rocks the first place we find that looks right. Then we're going to build a fire and make ourselves some coffee. We'll be sitting on a ridgeline when they get here. We'll make sure we're looking down on the trail, where we see a good ways, and keep them from sneaking in on us. How does that sound to you?"

Dawson considered it and said, "I hope there's more to it."

Shaw chuckled under his breath. "You always was one for details." Then he said as he drew his Colt and checked and spun it back and forth in the darkness, "We'll tell them who they're up against and offer not to kill a bunch of them if they turn away and ride on."

"Damn it," said Dawson, "I was afraid you would say something like that. What are we going to do if they don't believe we can kill a bunch of them?"

As they spoke Shaw had walked away a few feet from where Della slept on the blanket. He lifted his gun belt enough to open his trousers. "Then I expect we will kill a bunch of them . . . the rest of them will get the point and ride on." He began to relieve himself.

Dawson shook his head, but reminded himself that this was the way Shaw had always done things — with bold deliberation. "I'll get the others," he said. "Think I ought to give Caldwell a gun?"

"Give him a gun," said Shaw, "but keep an eye on him."

"That goes without saying," said Cray Dawson, sounding a bit irritated that Shaw thought he had to remind him of something so simple.

"Then why did you ask?" said Shaw.

"Never mind," said Dawson, realizing this wasn't worth explaining and discussing right then. He turned and hurried back to where Caldwell and Frome lay snoring with the blanket pulled tight across themselves.

When he had awakened them and told

them what was going on, the two hurriedly arose and began gathering the horses and mules.

"I thought you said they would be satisfied with the wagon and wouldn't come after us," said Caldwell, as if Dawson had somehow let him down.

"I was wrong, Caldwell," Dawson said. "Do you want to stop and talk about it, or get ready to defend ourselves when they get up here?"

"Defend ourselves?" Caldwell said, both he and Dillard Frome stopping cold and looking at Dawson. "Aren't we going to make a run for it? Like we did last night?"

"Last night was different," said Dawson, finding himself defending Shaw's idea of making a stand. "We had no cover. Now that we've got some rocks for protection and have taken some higher ground, we don't want to let these Comancheros chase us into Eagle Pass with our tails between our legs, do we?" Dawson was surprised to hear himself talking a lot like Shaw.

"Well, yeah," said Dillard Frome, scratching his bald head in the darkness. "I don't care what the folks at Eagle Pass think of me. Far as I'm concerned, a good run beats a bad stand every time around the track."

"But we're not going to make a *bad* stand," Dawson heard himself say. "Now let's get these animals gathered and get going."

Shortly after dawn the first Comanchero scout rode slowly up the winding trail and had to visor a hand above his eyes to look up into the sun at the rise of smoke from the campfire. Perched atop a ridgeline twenty feet above him, Lawrence Shaw and Cray Dawson sat at the edge of the ridge with their rifles across their laps. Shaw sipped from a tin cup of steaming coffee in his left hand. Catching sight of Shaw and Dawson, the Comanchero started to back his horse and take cover, but before he could make a move, Shaw called out in a hearty voice, *"Buenos dias."* As the unsuspecting rider stopped cold in his tracks, Shaw called out, "What's your hurry? You just got here."

Turning his small paint horse slowly, the scout looked at Shaw and replied with his hand on his short-barreled rifle, "My hurry? I am in no hurry . . . not because of you, you foolish *gringos*." He offered a smirk and said, "There are fifty of us just around the turn in the trail. You should have run while you had the chance."

Beside Shaw, Dawson whispered, "Fifty? Jesus, Shaw!"

"Huh-uh," Shaw said sidelong to Dawson. "He's scared and lying. Divide what he said by at least ten. There's no more than a dozen, if that." He called down to the Comanchero, "There are five of us . . . that's all it's going to take. Where's your *honcho*? I only talk terms with the man in charge."

"Terms?" said the scout, looking amazed by Shaw's brassy attitude. "What do you mean, terms? We are the ones with the terms! You must pay to cross our land! I will wear your scalp on my saddle horn before the morning is over."

"Your land?" Shaw spit in contempt. "I'm through talking to a flunky," he said, setting the tin cup down beside him, standing up slowly, and handing Cray Dawson his rifle.

"Hold it, you," said another voice. Shaw and Dawson watched as another rider, then another and another came slowly into view around a tall rock beside the trail. The three spread out abreast beside the scout. Each of them wore some article of Della's clothing taken from the wagon before they had burned it. The one speaking was a white man with a thick crop of dirty red hair bushing out from under the brim of one of Della's fancy lady's hats. A crepe veil hung in front of his face. His ragged sombrero hung from his saddle horn. His red beard was a tangle of braids, feathers, and beads, with a tiny round bell plaited into the tip of it below his chin.

"What kind of fools are you that you sit here and wait for us to come kill you?" he asked, his pistol already out, cocked, and lying across his lap. He gazed up at Shaw but had to squint against the dazzling sunlight.

Shaw and Dawson heard the sound of unseen riders dismount and spread out into the surrounding brush back off the trail. Dawson tossed a glance over his shoulder at Dillard Frome and Jedson Caldwell. "We hear them," said Frome, re-assuring Dawson before he said a word.

"I'll say one thing though; you knew how to get the sun at your back," said the Comancheros' leader.

"You're not the first Comanchero roaches I've had to step on," said Shaw. "I'm going to give all of you one chance, and one chance only, to turn around right now and ride away. If not, I'm going to shoot all of you where you stand and get on back to my coffee while it's still hot."

The Comanchero leader offered a dark

laugh, and pointed his finger up at Shaw, saying, "You are one funny son of a bitch, you are. But we don't leave without the woman, the horses, and all your whiskey! You give us these things, we go. If not, we kill all of you!"

"Whiskey, huh?" said Shaw. Over his shoulder he said to Caldwell, "Undertaker, hand me my canteen."

Caldwell hurried to Shaw's horse, took the canteen from the saddle horn, and returned, pitching it to Shaw. Shaw called out as he threw it down from the edge of the ridge, "If it's whiskey you're craving . . . I'll oblige you."

"Ha!" said the leader, gesturing for one of his men to go get the canteen. A wiry young man with a face full of tattoos and beadwork jumped from his horse, ran over, and picked up the canteen. He uncapped it and sniffed the contents. Then he grinned and nodded at the leader.

"Hey, that's a pretty damn good thing you did. Now give us the woman and the horses, maybe we let you live."

"The whiskey's on the house," said Shaw. "Now turn and go if you want to live to enjoy it."

The leader laughed again. "I think I like you." As he spoke, the other two sat poised, their hands firm around the rifles in their laps. The third man ran back to his horse with the canteen, climbed into the saddle, and handed the whiskey to the leader. The leader sniffed the canteen, capped it, and shook it with a broad smile. "Who are you, anyway? How come I have never seen you crossing my land before?"

Shaw whispered sidelong to Cray Dawson, "Tell him who I am . . . impress the hell out of him."

Dawson called out to the leader, "This is Lawrence Shaw. Does that name ring a bell?"

"Lawrence Shaw?" said the leader, his horse suddenly stepping back and forth nervously. "You don't mean —"

"Yep, Fast Larry Shaw," said Cray Dawson, already seeing the worried look come onto the men's faces as they looked back and forth among themselves. "Now, ain't you glad you came?"

The leader recovered quickly, but Shaw still saw the look of doubt in his eyes. Rather than look bad in front of his men, he jerked his reins to settle his horse, then said, "Fast Larry Shaw means nothing out here! No matter how fast you are, you cannot escape what we will do to you. Neither can the rest of you!" He made a play to raise his pistol, calling out to his men, "Shoot him! Shoot them all!"

Without hesitation, Cray Dawson raised his rifle and drew a bead on the leader's chest. But just as he pulled the trigger a loud string of shots erupted from Shaw's big Colt and the leader was already falling back out of his saddle as Dawson's shot hit him. Before Dawson could lever another round into his rifle chamber, the other three Comancheros were also on the ground. Lawrence Shaw's blinding speed left Dawson shaken, but only for a second. He, Shaw, and the others turned their weapons toward the sound of men rustling hurriedly through the brush along the trail. They began firing as one into the brush and rocks, hearing screams and curses. But there was no return fire.

"Hold your fire!" shouted Lawrence Shaw. Beneath a gray rise of burned powder the four men and Della Starks stood listening intently to the sound of horse hooves beating a retreat down the trail toward the flatlands. Dillard Frome and Jedson Caldwell gave each other a look of amazement. Della let out a squeal of delight and ran to the ridge where Shaw stood reloading his Colt.

"Stay back, Della," said Shaw, but it was

too late. She stopped abruptly at the sight of the four twisted, bloody bodies lying on the trail below.

Her hands covered her mouth. "Oh, my God," she whispered through her fingers. She swayed weakly, but Shaw managed to catch her with his free arm and hold her in an embrace as he clicked his Colt shut and stood holding it pointed upward, studying the trail, the brush, and the surrounding rocks just in case. "You needn't look at them," Shaw whispered close to her ear. He raised a hand to her cheek and turned her face away from the carnage. Then he turned to Dawson and the others and said, "Get the horses; let's get going, before the rest of them get their courage up."

"What about these men?" Caldwell asked, gesturing down at the four bodies.

"What about them?" said Shaw.

"Shouldn't we bury them or something?" Caldwell asked.

"You can if you want to," Shaw said in an offhand manner. "We're heading to Eagle Pass. If you want to do something kind, gather those three horses down there. Either strip them and turn them loose or bring them with us for spares."

"Bring them as spares," said Dillard Frome, getting tired of riding one of the barebacked mules. He climbed down with Caldwell to gather the horses.

"Get Shaw's canteen for him," said Dawson, looking down where it lay on the trail.

"No, leave it," said Shaw, contradicting Dawson. He gave him a look. "I told you I was quitting," he said. He turned with one arm around Della and walked away from the edge.

Chapter 5

They rode nonstop until the noon sun beat down on them without mercy. When they did stop, it was at a water station where an old man and his German wife operated a waterwheel with the aid of a button-backed donkey. After watering the horses and the four mules, the party took shade beneath a large cottonwood tree at the edge of a low adobe-and-stone wall. As the others rested with their hat brims ducked low on their foreheads, Della sat down on a spread blanket beside Shaw and said, "Lawrence, that was the first time I've ever seen a man draw a gun and kill someone. I've heard of gunfights . . . but I've never seen one. When you three rode in on us at the wagon and I held the pistol on you? I was only bluffing. I don't know what I would have done if you were men out to do us harm. I like to pretend I'm fast and loose. But when it gets right down to it . . . I'm not."

Shaw looked at her, his green eyes much clearer now that he had sweated out the whiskey. "You would have done whatever it took to stay alive, is what I'm betting," he said.

Della shrugged. "Perhaps . . . at least I like to think so. But to be honest, after seeing those dead men today . . ." Her words trailed off.

Shaw tried to help her, saying, "You haven't settled it in your mind yet, have you? You haven't gotten rid of the picture of it."

"No, I haven't," said Della. "Seeing them, the way they lay there, their faces, all the blood, I don't think I'll ever get rid of it completely."

"Gunfights are not a pretty sight," Shaw said, looking almost ashamed.

"No, they certainly are not," said Della. But the picture she was having the most problem getting rid of was that of Lawrence Shaw drawing a gun so fast she saw only the blur of it. She kept seeing the deliberate brutality of him as he acted without the slightest hesitation in the killing of four human beings. This was the same man she had just spent the night with, wrapped in a blanket, their bodies naked and pressed together in the midst of a wide, dark night. He had been gentle with her, warm and loving, so much so that to awaken the next morning and witness firsthand the sort of terrible deeds that had brought him such notoriety had left her shaken. She feared this man. Yet, even as she feared him, she wanted him, perhaps even more than ever, if that were possible.

After a pause Della said, "Lawrence . . . what you told me last night about losing your wife . . . and how you're hunting her killers. Where will you go when that's done?"

Shaw nodded slightly, knowing there was an offer coming. "I haven't really thought about it, Della . . . I haven't had the time."

"Come back to Eagle Pass, Lawrence," she said. "You've lost your wife; I've lost my husband. Maybe we could take care of each other."

"We'll see," said Shaw, "I don't want to make promises that I don't know if I can keep."

They fell silent, Della snuggling against his chest for a few moments until Shaw leaned down and said in a quiet tone, "Get up now, Della . . . time to go."

Cray Dawson had looked over in time to see Della sit up and touch her fingers to her hair, straightening it. His eyes met Shaw's for a second and Shaw offered a tired, patient smile. Dawson shook his head and stood up, dusting his trousers, then walked to where the horses stood resting in the shade. The old man who ran the well and waterwheel said in a crackling voice, "Not to be meddling, but that feller looks familiar. . . . Who is he, anyway?"

Cray Dawson said in a flat, expressionless voice, as if he'd committed the line to memory, "That's Lawrence Shaw . . . known by some as Fast Larry . . . the fastest gun alive."

"Naw, it ain't!" said the old man, his eyes widening. "Is it sure enough?"

"It is sure enough," said Dawson, still with no expression. He picked his saddle up from the adobe wall and pitched it up onto his horse.

"A real honest-to-God living, in-the-flesh gunfighter," the old man said, looking over to where Shaw stood up and helped Della to her feet.

"Yep, he's *living*, all right," said Dawson with a wry grin, "better than most of us, anyway."

Having seen the way Dawson had looked at him and Della a few minutes earlier, Shaw came over to him and said, "Dawson, I know you don't approve of how I do, but I want to remind you that I've just lost the only woman I ever loved.

It hasn't been easy on me. I know I've done a lot of drinking and fooling around with other women. I reckon it's just my way of making up for missing Rosa. But I don't know what else to do to keep from losing my mind."

"I'm not judging you, Shaw," said Dawson stiffly as he cinched his saddle down and shook it, testing it.

"Then what are you doing?" Shaw asked in a level tone.

Dawson turned and looked him up and down, thinking about it, then said, "Hell, I don't know . . . envying you, I reckon." He shrugged. "Do you ever stop and see how easy it comes to you?"

"How easy what comes to me?" said Shaw. "Drawing a gun and killing a man? It just looks easy, Dawson . . . believe me, it's not."

"It's not just that, Shaw; it's everything," said Dawson. "But it ain't your fault; it's mine. We just see things different. And things just come different to us, that's all. I meant no offense looking at the two of you."

"I knew you didn't," said Shaw. "But I also saw that something was eating at you. I figured it better to ask than to keep wondering what it is."

"Then now you know . . . it's nothing," said Dawson, "just envy, wondering how it feels walking in your boots."

"Be careful envying a man's boots," said Shaw, turning away. "You could end up wearing them."

They finished preparing the horses and, rode on to Eagle Pass, arriving at the outskirts of town at midday in the boiling heat. Dillard Frome rode one of the Comancheros' little hard-boned barbs and led the four-mule string behind him. Della Starks also rode one of the Comancheros' horses. Dawson led the other two. The little desert barb horses drew curious looks from the adobes and plank shacks they passed going onto the main street. The horses wore feathers, beads, and scraps of bones and scalps woven into their manes and tails. Two wore coyote skins down onto their saddles and riding cushions that caused dogs to appear out from under boardwalks and porches and begin yapping with their hackles up.

"What the hell do we have coming here?" said the town sheriff, Earnest Neff, rising from a wooden chair out front of his office and stepping down onto the boardwalk.

"Looks like somebody got ahold of some Apache ponies," said the young telegraph clerk who'd been visiting with him in the shade of the boardwalk overhang.

"Naw," said the sheriff eyeing the ragged sombrero still hanging from the leader's saddle horn. "No self-respecting Apache would ride such a mess as that. Comancheros is what I make it to be."

"My goodness! They're *not* Comancheros, are they?" the clerk asked, growing apprehensive all of a sudden.

The sheriff squinted hard and recognized Lawrence Shaw at the head of the party, Della Starks beside him on the little barb. "No," he said, letting out a breath and adjusting his pistol out of habit, "but I might be wishing it was before this day is over."

Before Shaw made it to the sheriff's office, Sheriff Neff had hurried forward and met him in the street out front of the Big Spur Saloon. He kept his hands chest-high as he waved Shaw down. As Shaw and the others came to a halt, Sheriff Neff said in an even tone, "Mr. Shaw, I already know who you are and why you're here. I've got Sidlow Talbert in my jail right now. I don't want no trouble over him."

"I didn't come here looking for trouble, Sheriff," said Shaw, "but I did come looking for Sidlow. I want to know where his brother and the rest of that bunch are. You already know why."

"Yes, I do," said Sheriff Neff, "and I don't blame you for wanting to kill every one of them . . . just not in my town; that's all I ask."

Shaw stepped down and walked around to where Della sat atop the little barb horse. He helped her step down onto the dirt-and-stone street. "I'll do my best not to have any trouble here, Sheriff; you have my word. If you know who I am, then you also know that some hothead saddle tramp is going to pop up every now and then wanting to try me."

"I expect that," said Neff. "I hold no man to blame when it comes to defending himself."

"Then you and I are going to get along fine," said Shaw. He presented Della Starks, saying, "Sheriff, this is Widow Della Starks."

"Well, now, we've been expecting you, ma'am," said the sheriff, taking off his hat and running a hand back along his thinning hair. "We were all saddened to hear about Purvis's death. He hadn't been here for long, but we all still considered him one of our own. Hope you'll let us make you feel welcome here in our town, ma'am."

"Thank you, Sheriff," said Della, looking around for the Desert Flower Inn.

"Your inn is all the way down the street just before you reach the border road crossing. Albert and Fannie Jenkins are still running it, just the way they did before your husband's death. I'll be honored to escort you there right now."

"Thank you again, Sheriff," said Della. She looked up at Dillard Frome and said in a domineering tone, "Take those sweaty animals to the livery barn, Dillard. You can catch up to us afterward."

Jedson Caldwell and Cray Dawson stepped down from their saddles, stretched, and looked around the street.

"I'll accompany you and the widow Starks to the Desert Flower," the old sheriff said to Lawrence Shaw. "Then you and I can talk on our way back before you go in to see Sidlow." He raised a finger for emphasis. "You'll have to give me your word that you won't shoot him while he's in my custody."

"You're asking a lot, Sheriff," said Shaw, his jaw tightening. "But all right, you've got my word." Shaw turned to Cray Dawson, saying, "Dawson, I'll be back here shortly. See to our animals. I'll get us some rooms at the Desert Flower; that is, if Della here approves of our company."

Della only smiled demurely.

Caldwell looked at Dawson and said, "I'll tag along with you, help you with the horses, if you don't mind."

"No, I don't mind," said Dawson, sounding a bit dejected, watching Shaw walk away with Della and the sheriff. He shook his head and said jokingly, "Stick with me, Caldwell; you'll soon learn to be a top-rate stable hand."

While Shaw and his group broke off into separate directions, just inside the doors of the Big Spur Saloon two ne'er-do-wells looked at each other with knowing grins. The taller of the two said to his comrade, "You're right, Elton; that's Fast Larry Shaw, sure as hell."

"I knew it was, Sammy Boy!" said Elton Minton. "I can spot money on the hoof from a mile away. Our luck is just about to change."

"What do you mean, our luck?" said Sammy Boy White. "I'm the one who's quick enough to face him. I'm the one with the Colt." He patted the gun on his hip.

"Yeah," said Elton, thumbing himself on the chest, "but I'm the one with enough money to work up some bets on the fight. Now, are we still partners or not?"

"Hell, yes, we're still partners, Elton," said Sammy Boy. "Couldn't you tell I was just teasing with you?"

"All right, then, no more teasing," said Elton, raising his finger for emphasis. "I'm going to get Fat Man Hughes to back us financially. We'll get some wagers made, all very quietly so nobody will know what's about to happen until you're ready to meet Shaw on the street. Meanwhile, maybe you best go somewhere and practice getting that Colt out of your holster. Shaw ain't no easy play."

"Don't worry about my end of this deal," said Sammy Boy. "I'm ready for whatever comes at me."

"Good enough — just keep that kind of attitude and follow me," said Elton. He turned and walked to the crowded bar, shoving in between two of the drinkers at the right end of the bar, where a huge man wearing a black linen suit sat on a high wooden stool counting a thick roll of greenback dollars.

Seeing Elton and Sammy Boy move in beside him, he gave them a sharp glance, held his roll of money a little closer to his chest, and continued counting. "What do you want, Elton?" he asked gruffly.

Elton Minton looked taken aback by the

man's testy tone of voice. "Easy, Hughes," Elton said. "I came here to bring you a wagering opportunity. Of course, if you don't want it, I'll just mosey on."

"Yeah, okay," said Hughes, "you do that. I don't want to fool with you two saddle tramps."

"Saddle tramps?" Sammy Boy hissed, poising his hand near his pistol. "Nobody calls me a saddle tramp! You better fill your hand, Hughes!" Even though his voice was loud enough to be heard the length of the bar, nobody turned in his direction.

"My hands are already full, you idiot," said Hughes, nodding at the money. "Now both of you get out of here; I'm busy."

"Hold it, Sammy Boy," said Elton, giving his partner a slight shove to the side. "We came to talk business, remember?" He turned back to Hughes, who still concentrated on counting his money. "All right, Hughes, I'm going to tell you about this anyway, just because I want to see the look on your face when I win everybody's money."

Hughes gave up counting his money, and shoved the thick roll inside his linen suit coat. "All right, Elton, you've caused me to lose my count. Now tell me how you're going to win everybody's money."

"Lawrence Shaw just rode into town," said Elton, leaning in close to Hughes's ear.

"No kidding? Fast Larry, here?" Hughes looked surprised for a second, but then said, "So what's that to do with you winning everybody's money?"

Elton beamed and hooked a thumb in his dirty, ragged vest. "I've got the man here who can beat him with a gun."

"Yeah? Who?" Hughes leaned back and looked all around the saloon.

"Me, that's who," said Sammy Boy, looking angry.

Hughes gave Elton a dubious look. "Yep, that's who," Elton said, confirming it for Hughes.

Hughes fell silent for a moment. He looked Sammy Boy up and down. Then, unable to stifle his laughter, he let it roll, his huge belly bouncing as he slapped a thick hand on the bar top. "Lord God, Elton!" he mused, "have you been hearing banjos playing when there ain't no banjos around? Fast Larry Shaw wouldn't waste a bullet on this scarecrow! He'd stomp a foot and Sammy Boy would piss his trousers running!" He bellowed louder.

"Make this fat sumbitch shut up," Sammy Boy said to Elton with an embarrassed look on his face.

But Fat Man Hughes raised a hand toward them, got himself collected, blew out a big breath, and said, "*Whew* . . . all right, you've got my attention. Whatever odds you're offering, I'll take them." He reached inside his coat, snatched out the roll of dollars again, and slapped it down on the bar top. "Name your amount; I've got you covered."

"No, damn it," said Elton, "put your money away for now." He cut a quick glance around the saloon to make sure no one was listening. "I want to talk to you about you and me partnering up and taking all the loose money in this town."

"*Partner* with you?" Hughes started to laugh again, but this time he caught himself, shook his head, and said, "What you're wanting is a backer. Elton, I wouldn't back you selling ice water at the gates of hell. Now get away from me. I think you're both smoking opium!"

"Listen to me, Hughes!" said Elton. But before he could say another word, Hughes turned his back to him.

"Get out of here," Hughes growled over his shoulder.

Elton and Sammy Boy started toward the door, looking dejected. But before they had crossed the floor, a man wearing a pencil-thin mustache and tied-down Colt slipped in beside Elton and said in a guarded tone, "Did I hear you boys say Fast Larry Shaw just rode into town?"

Elton and Sammy Boy stopped and looked at the stranger. "Yeah, we saw him ride in a few minutes ago," said Elton.

"And you've got somebody you think can beat him straight up?" As he spoke he eyed Sammy Boy's Colt, then looked him up and down, evaluating him.

"Mister," said Elton, "you sure heard an awful lot for a man who wasn't being spoken to."

"I couldn't help overhearing you two talking to Fat Man Hughes." The stranger shrugged. "If you've got somebody and you're still looking for a backer, maybe I'm your man." Again he looked at Sammy Boy's Colt. "I take it this is the shooter you were talking about? He looks fit enough to handle the job," he added, getting on Sammy Boy's good side right away.

"Damn right I'm fit enough," said Sammy Boy.

"Well, all right." The stranger grinned and rubbed his hands together. "My name is Willie Devlin . . . business associates like to call me Willie the Devil." His grin widened; his expression grew crafty. "All in good fun, of course."

Elton nodded and jerked a thumb toward Sammy Boy. "I'm Elton Minton. This here is Sammy Boy White . . . soon to be known as the man who gunned down Fast Larry Shaw." He smiled boldly. "Willie the Devil, there are lots of sporting men in this town who would jump on this deal if I was to let it out. But the fact is, I want to keep it quiet until we're all set. Timing is everything, I always say."

"I agree," said Willie Devlin. "Now what's the deal? How much money do you need? How sure are you that our man Sammy here can get the job done?"

"Oh, Sammy Boy will get it done," said Elton. "I wouldn't have gone this far even thinking about it if I wasn't sure of that."

"Do I need to see Sammy shoot first or can I count on your word for it?"

"Count on it," said Elton, "this is the fastest man I've seen with a gun. I've seen him take a —"

"I've got three thousand dollars," said Willie Devlin bluntly, in order to get Elton to stop beating around the bush. "Am I in or out?"

Elton's jaw dropped, Devlin's words leaving him stunned for a second.

Sammy Boy looked at Elton and said, "Damn! Three thousand dollars!" He gigged Elton in his ribs. "Go on . . . tell Willie what you've got in mind."

Elton recovered, batted his eyes, and said, "Uh, sure thing, Sammy Boy. But I think you need to let Willie and me get together in private and handle the details. You go somewhere and practice your part in this thing. Keep that gun hand well oiled, so to speak."

Sammy Boy hesitated, but only for a moment. "All right," he said, "I'll go practice some . . . but I'm ready right now." He patted the pistol on his hip as he turned and walked out through the bat-wing doors.

As soon as Sammy Boy was out of sight, Willie the Devil said in a solemn tone to Elton Minton, "Tell me the truth: Do you really think that boy has a ghost of a chance against Fast Larry Shaw?"

Elton Minton looked slightly offended. "If I didn't would I be betting everything we have on him?"

"I don't know that we will be betting everything we have on him," said Willie. "For all I know you might be wanting to bet some on him and some on Fast Larry, just to hedge your bet."

"I wouldn't dream of pulling something like that on my old pal Sammy," Elton said, incensed.

"A smart man would," Willie the Devil suggested with a sly grin.

Elton's face reddened a bit; then he returned Willie's grin. "To be honest, I have to admit the thought did cross my mind."

"Good," said Willie, "because if it hadn't I wanted to be sure and mention it to you, make sure your mind is in the right place on this thing." The two shook hands; then Willie said, "Now back to what I asked you. Can that boy beat Fast Larry Shaw?"

"If we're going to bet it both ways, what do you care?" Elton asked, still grinning shrewdly.

"Because I know some people who want Fast Larry dead," said Willie the Devil. "If I tell them Shaw's as good as dead and then he *isn't*" — as he spoke he shaped his right hand into a pistol and poked his sharp finger firmly into Elton's stomach — "guess who *will* be?"

Elton's smile soured on his face.

"Now that he ain't standing beside you where he can hear you . . . tell me like your life depended on it," said Willie the Devil. "Is that boy going to be able to get the job done?"

"If my life depended on it?" Elton considered it for a second; then, not wanting to let Willie the Devil and his three thousand get away, he said with finality, "Damn right, Sammy will get the job done."

"Good then, partner," said Willie, throwing an arm up around Elton's shoulder, directing him back toward the bar. "Let's have a drink on that. I've got a friend I'd like you to meet."

Chapter 6

When the sheriff and Lawrence Shaw left Della Starks at the Desert Flower Inn, they walked back to the sheriff's office. Along the way, Sheriff Neff looked Shaw up and down and said, "If it's any consolation, Lawrence, I too lost a wife some years back. She was killed by a young drunken cowboy on a street in El Paso. I was out of town when it happened. I got back and found out about it three days later. I was so full of blind, killing rage I went straight to the jail. . . . I meant to kill him on the spot. Turned out he had sobered up and felt so sorry for what he'd done, he hanged himself with a wool blanket from the top crossbar of the cell."

"I'm sorry about your wife, Sheriff," said Shaw. He stared straight ahead. "But don't worry about me killing Sidlow on the spot. I gave my word . . . I never break it."

"I wasn't telling you that story to teach you any moral lesson, Shaw," said Sheriff Neff. "It just seemed fitting, is all, what with you losing your wife under similar circumstances."

"I understand, Sheriff," said Shaw, "and I appreciate it. I reckon we have something in common, you and me."

"Yep," said the sheriff, staring straight ahead of himself now. "There's very few people I've ever talked to about my wife's death, at least not in any personal way. I did notice that shortly after her death, it seemed like every available woman within miles wanted to do something to make me feel better . . . comfort me in my loneliness, so to speak." He looked at Shaw, noting Shaw's interest as he continued. "I know part of it was because of me being a lawman. It seems women have a powerfully high regard for lawmen and gunmen." He smiled and shrugged. "I've never known why, but being a gunman I reckon you know what I'm talking about." He nodded back over his shoulder toward the Desert Flower Inn.

"Sheriff, I'm not here with any designs on Della Starks, and nothing that belonged to her husband interests me in any way, especially his money."

"I admire a man not easily taken in by a dead man's fortune or a warm widow's charm," said the sheriff. After a second he said, "To tell you the truth I always had a soft spot for Della. When Purvis Starks died and I heard that his widow might be coming here to Eagle Pass, I had a wild notion that I might see how I fared with her." He rubbed his clean-shaven chin. "I even bought this new shirt and all. Now it looks like you've plumb swept her off her feet." He brushed a hand down the bib-front shirt. "Looks like I'm out thirty-five cents for nothing."

"Sorry, Sheriff," said Shaw.

"No need to apologize," said Neff. "She is a beautiful woman . . . you are a gunman." He sighed.

Shaw nodded. "I'm glad you understand."

"Now then," said Sheriff Neff, "let me tell you what I've got figured on Sidlow Talbert. The only charge I've got him on is public drunkenness and shooting out a string of windows along Front Street. There's already been a couple of men showed up and paid for the damage he did. I've got him serving thirty days for the shooting and disturbing the peace. Those two fellows who paid his damages offered to pay a fine to get him released. I figured it best to make him serve the time, make him think twice before shooting up my town again."

"Who were these two fellows?" asked Shaw.

"They said their names were Smith and Jackson," said Neff with a disbelieving expression. "Ha! I recognized one right off as Willie the Devil but I didn't let on right then. The other was probably Donald Hornetti. From what I hear they're always together."

"Are they part of Talbert's gang?" Shaw asked.

"They're a part of anybody's gang whose got some dirty deeds that need doing," said Neff. "But it's safe to say they spend most of their time with Talbert. I don't know that they were with him when your wife got killed."

"If I see them, Cray Dawson can tell me. He saw Talbert and his men leaving after they killed Rosa," Shaw said.

Sheriff Neff noted how Shaw's voice softened when it came to saying his dead wife's name. "I'd say that makes your friend Dawson a very dangerous man to Talbert and his bunch," the sheriff speculated. "Does he realize how bad Talbert and his boys will want to kill him, knowing he can identify them?"

"Cray Dawson doesn't care, Sheriff," said Shaw. "He just wants to see them pay for what they did." Changing the subject slightly, Shaw said, "How many days does

Sidlow Talbert have left to serve?"

"Only eighteen days left," said Sheriff Neff, "but he acts like it's killing him. You know how these wild boys are . . . can't stand a set of bars between them and anything they could destroy if they took a notion. He keeps thinking his brother Barton and Blue Snake and the rest is coming to bust him out — I thought it too the first few days. But they're not coming for him. They sent Willie the Devil to pay his way out, but that's all they're going to do. They must figure thirty days ain't going to hurt him none, and it ain't worth getting me and a posse down their shirts. I probably couldn't catch them, but I would sure cramp their style."

"They must have big plans of some kind," said Shaw, considering it.

"That kind of scoundrel always has some kind of big plans they're counting on," said Sheriff Neff. "But whatever it is, they ain't coming to bust Sidlow out, so there's no use in you waiting around here for them, hoping that will happen."

"I see," said Shaw, contemplating it further. The two grew quiet the rest of the way to the office. Then, before stepping through the door, Shaw said, "I still want to look this rat in the eyes . . . I'll know whether or not he was there when my Rosa died."

"I understand," said the sheriff, eyeing Shaw's tied-down holster, the big Colt close to his hand. Neff knew there was nothing he could do to stop Lawrence Shaw from drawing that gun and splattering Sidlow Talbert all over the wall of his cell if Shaw decided to. But Shaw had already given his word. Sheriff Neff couldn't question it now. "Just don't expect him to tell you much," Neff added, reaching out and opening the door.

Inside the door, Shaw stopped and looked over at the two cells along the wall. One cell sat empty, its door open wide and a mattress rolled up on a wooden-framed cot. In the other stood Sidlow Talbert, a thin young man with his hair disheveled and a week's growth of beard on his hard-edged face. He stood in his sock feet wearing dirty canvas trousers over his summer long johns, the buttons open down the front of his uppers. Before Sheriff Neff could say anything, Sidlow called out, grasping the bars with both hands, "Three more rats deserted this pus hole while you were gone, Sheriff. They said to tell you they wouldn't be back until you cleaned this up and started feeding better." His words ended in a short fit of harsh laughter.

"You're a real funny man, Sidlow," said the sheriff. "But if I was you I'd simmer it down and show some manners here. This is Lawrence Shaw. He came all the way from Somos Santos to see you. I expect you already know why."

"No, I expect I don't know why," said Sidlow Talbert, showing an expression of contempt even as he gave a wary look at the big Colt on Shaw's side. "If it's about killing that Mexican woman, he's wasting his time," he said to the sheriff as if ignoring Shaw. "I didn't have a damn thing to do with that." He cast another short glance at the big Colt, then looked away from it.

"Sidlow Talbert," Shaw commanded, "look at me when you talk."

"Yeah? Why?" said Sidlow, defiant, showing nothing but contempt.

"Because if I see in your eyes that you had anything to do with killing my wife, I'll be waiting for you when you get out. You have my word on that." Shaw's hand went to his pistol butt and rested there.

"Fast Larry gives me his word he'll be waiting for me." Sidlow chuckled, trying to sound unconcerned, but not doing a very good job of it. When he saw Shaw's hand go to the pistol butt, a sudden look of fear moved across Sidlow's face before he caught it and masked it behind his surly attitude. "Well, now, ain't I just scared to death thinking about that." He managed a nasty grin. "Looks like you've got a nice long wait. Meanwhile my brother might just sweep through here any minute and get me out of here. Now what do you think of that?"

Shaw fell silent, staring at him with a blank expression, his hand poised on the pistol butt.

Sidlow squirmed on the spot, but he held on to his bold front, saying, "Well, what about it, Shaw? Are you going to say anything else . . . or just stand there and eyeball me all day?"

Shaw stared, his face stonelike, his hand looking as if it were just a hairbreadth away from streaking the Colt up from the holster.

Unable to read what Shaw's intentions might be at any second, and knowing there was no escape if Shaw decided to snatch the big Colt up and kill him before he knew what had hit him, Sidlow felt his devil-may-care smile turn waxen and tight with concern. A nerve twitched in his jaw. Without taking his eyes off of Shaw's he said to the sheriff, "You can't let him do this, Neff! This is murder, is what this is! Brother Barton and the boys might have done a terrible thing, but this is even worse! You're supposed to be a lawman, for God's sake! You can't let him kill me like this!"

Sheriff Neff had also grown concerned, unable to discern the killing-cold look on Shaw's face. He whispered, "Shaw, you gave me your word."

Shaw didn't respond.

"What's that? What did you say, Sheriff?" Sidlow asked, a thin sheen of sweat having formed across his forehead. "He gave his word? His word on what? That he wouldn't kill me?"

Neither the sheriff nor Shaw answered him. Sidlow's fear seemed to subside a bit, his smile coming back a little. "That's it, ain't it, Sheriff?" he said. "Fast Larry gave you his word he wouldn't kill —"

Sidlow's words were cut short as Shaw's Colt appeared in his hand as if by magic and exploded. "Aiiieee!" Sidlow screamed, falling away from the bars with his right hand grasping his clipped ear. Blood spewed from between his fingers. He wallowed on the cot against the cell wall, throwing a terrified glance back and forth between Shaw and the sheriff, knowing Shaw could do whatever he pleased and there was nothing anyone could do to stop him. "Jesus, Sheriff!" Sidlow sobbed, losing control, his tough exterior diminished to that of a whimpering wretch. "Please don't let him kill me! Please don't! I never touched that Mexican woman! I wasn't there; I swear to God I wasn't!"

"Get on your feet, Sidlow," Shaw demanded. "I want another bite out of you."

"Shaw!" said Sheriff Neff, powerless to stop him but having to make a plea for the sake of his station as a lawman. "You gave me your word!"

"That's right, Sheriff," Shaw said coldly and evenly, "I gave you my word that I wouldn't kill him while he's behind bars." As he spoke, Shaw walked over and lifted the key ring from a peg on the wall and walked over to the cell door with it. He unlocked the door and threw it open. "Get out, Sidlow," he hissed, "so I can keep my word to you too."

"Huh?" Sidlow looked confused and shaken, blood flowing freely between his fingers from his clipped ear.

"I gave you my word I'd be waiting," said Shaw, snatching Sidlow by his hair, yanking him to his feet and shoving him

112

from the cell. Sidlow landed near the sheriff's feet, sobbing, pleading. "And you can bet I will be, you murdering coward son of a bitch," Shaw said.

Sheriff Neff stood helpless, staring, his hands chest-high, knowing better than to get between Shaw and Sidlow. "This ain't right, Shaw!" he said, making a plea rather than a command. "I don't know if he had anything to do with it or not, but this ain't the way the law is supposed to work!"

"The law?" Shaw had a distant look in his eyes, as if he had somehow detached himself from what was happening. "There was no law to keep these sons of bitches from killing my Rosa. I'll be damned if there's a law to keep me from killing them."

Shaw moved quickly, snatching Sidlow to his feet. At the same time he jerked the sheriff's pistol from his holster and shoved it into Sidlow's hand. Giving Sidlow a shove toward the door, Shaw holstered his big Colt and held his hand poised, ready to draw.

"Start shooting or start running, Sidlow Talbert," Shaw said with finality. "It makes no difference. Either way, I'm going to kill you."

"This ain't fair." Sidlow sobbed as he

backed away, shaking. "I ain't even wearing boots! I ain't got a chance against a gunman like you!"

"Boots?" said Shaw. "It's fairer than what you offered my Rosa. She wasn't even armed," Shaw whispered, taking a step toward him, "and there was all you big tough *hombres,* boots and all." His voice had turned low and chilling.

Sidlow saw the slightest twitch of Shaw's gun hand and became unnerved. He ran screaming out the door. "Help me! Somebody help me! He's going to kill me!"

Taking his time, Shaw said to the sheriff, "I kept my word, Sheriff, but there was deceit in it. I'm ashamed of doing that . . . but this is where life has taken me. Sidlow is carrying your gun . . . tell whatever story suits you. I'll understand."

"Get out of here, Shaw," said Sheriff Neff. "When this thing is over don't ever come back."

Shaw turned and walked out the door, paying no attention to the bullet that Sidlow had managed to turn and fire as he ran screaming and sobbing, blood running down his face from his half-moon-shaped ear. The shot hit the post no more than an inch from Shaw's head. Yet he didn't flinch even as splinters stung his cheek. His pistol came up, a shiny blur, and Sidlow screamed louder and longer as Shaw's bullet clipped the top half off of his other ear.

"Look, everybody, please! He's killing me! You're all witnesses!" Sidlow sobbed aloud, stumbling to his knees and catching himself, his blood-covered hand going from one clipped ear to the other. Feeling warm blood pour down both of his cheeks, and seeing it drip to the dirt, Sidlow cursed in his hysteria and fired two more shots at Shaw. One shot grazed Shaw's shirtsleeve; the other shattered a water pot hanging from a post beam along the boardwalk.

As Sidlow arose, Shaw effortlessly put a bullet through his left ankle, knocking his feet from under him and sending Sidlow to the ground, blood spewing from his dirty sock. "You cold-blooded son of a bitch!" Sidlow screamed, and fired again. "Everybody look what he's doing!" Sidlow shouted. But he didn't have to tell anybody. All heads had turned toward the shooting. The townspeople had gasped and watched in morbidly rapt fascination each time Lawrence Shaw put another bloody hole in Sidlow's body.

"Oh, God!" Sidlow screamed as Shaw's

next shot nailed him through his left arm at the elbow. His arm flopped back and forth, broken and loose at the joint. Blood spewed. Sidlow held on to the pistol and recovered from the terrible surge of pain.

"Somebody stop this!" a lady's voice pleaded from the boardwalk. But no one dared venture forward.

Sidlow yelled as he fired another round, "Why my left arm? Huh, Shaw? Why not my shooting arm? Why not in the head? Kill me if you're going to kill me!" His shot sliced past Shaw, dangerously close. Shaw ignored it, walking slowly forward.

"Here!" said Sidlow, "I'll make it easy for you!" He turned his face sideways to Shaw, saying, "Go ahead, get it over . . . right through the temple!"

Shaw's pistol exploded. Sidlow fell sidelong on the dirt, his nose missing from the bridge down. The ground beneath his face quickly became a thick red puddle. He sobbed, half-conscious, trying hard to raise the pistol for one last shot, his eyes blinded by blood.

"Damn you, Shaw!" he sobbed, his voice distorted now with his nasal passages lying open and exposed, bleeding in the hot Texas sun. "Damn you to everlasting hell!"

Shaw stopped and stood over him,

staring straight down, his pistol pointed and cocked. "That's already been done . . . the day you devils came to my house."

From down the street Cray Dawson and Jedson Caldwell came running, slowing as they neared, Dawson with his pistol out as he scanned back and forth, offering Shaw backup should he need it for any reason. But then, seeing Sidlow Talbert on the ground in a pool of dark blood, his ears and nose missing, his elbow shattered, Dawson whispered hoarsely, "Oh, my God, Shaw!" Then, seeing Shaw's hand tighten on the pistol butt, Dawson said, "No, don't kill him, Shaw, please!"

Shaw ignored him. Every onlooker winced as Shaw pulled the trigger and Sidlow Talbert's body bucked in the dirt, then relaxed in death. Shaw raised his eyes level to the boardwalk and looked all around slowly as he opened the hot chamber of the smoking Colt and dropped out his spent cartridges on Sidlow's body. Cray Dawson swept his Colt back and forth, providing Shaw cover while he popped fresh cartridges from his gun belt and began reloading, taking his time.

"Anybody here who rides with Barton Talbert," said Shaw, "go tell him how I killed his brother, Sidlow." As he shoved bullets into the chamber, he raised a boot and propped his foot callously on Sidlow's dead face. "Tell Barton Talbert that his brother Sidlow died squealing and screaming. Tell him I would have killed him slower; I just didn't have the time!" He studied face after face as his eyes searched for anyone who looked suspicious. "Take a good look, anybody riding with the Talbert gang. This is what I'm bringing to you sons of bitches. Let God bear witness here and now: I won't stop until every last one of you has died by my hand."

As Cray Dawson looked back and forth, backing Lawrence Shaw, he noticed the strange look of questioning curiosity on Jedson Caldwell's face. Caldwell asked secretively, gesturing at the body on the ground, "Is he one of the men you saw that day?"

Cray Dawson only looked at Sidlow Talbert for a second, then whispered to Caldwell without answering him, "Shaw's right in what he did. This is not the time for me to go second-guessing him."

Dawson looked doubtful and whispered persistently, "Was this or was this not one of the men you saw that day? If he wasn't then you better ask yourself what you've gotten into."

"Mind your own business, Caldwell," Dawson hissed, going back to scanning the street.

From near the boardwalk a portly man wearing a brown suit coat and a bowler hat stepped down from a dust-covered buggy and walked out into the street. He stopped a few cautious feet back from Shaw and Dawson, pointed a cane in Shaw's direction, and said "Sir, I'm Councilman Winston Burns, and I demand to know who you are and why you shot this poor fellow!" But his eyes widened and his face took on a ghostly white pallor when Shaw turned, facing him with his Colt half raised in his direction. Burns hadn't been in town earlier when Shaw and his party rode in. Recognizing Shaw, the frightened man took a step back and appeared to be on the verge of bolting away at any second. "M-Mr. Shaw!" he stammered.

"What's your complaint, Councilman?" Shaw said in a flat yet threatening voice.

"Easy, Shaw," said Sheriff Neff, walking into the street from his office. "I'll handle this." He stopped a few feet from Burns and hooked his right thumb into his gun belt, showing no fear in front of the townfolk but at the same time letting Shaw know that he had no intention of going for his gun. He stared into Shaw's eyes as he spoke to Councilman Burns. "Shaw just stopped a jailbreak." Without taking his eyes off of Shaw's he pointed down at Sidlow's body and said, "That's my gun in Sidlow's hand. I let him out of his cell to escort him to the jake. He snatched my gun and took off. Luckily, Mr. Shaw was there."

Burns swallowed a knot in his throat and said with a shaky smile, "Oh . . . well, then, my apologies, Mr. Shaw. It appears we all owe you a thanks." His eyes passed over the bloody, mutilated body of Sidlow Talbert, then went to Sheriff Neff, still looking frightened. "Sheriff, I also owe you an apology. I should have realized instantly that whatever is going on here, you have it under control."

"That's right, Councilman," said Sheriff Neff, looking back at Lawrence Shaw as he spoke. "Rest assured that whatever I'm doing, I'm doing with the town's best interest in mind."

Shaw slid his Colt into his holster and gave Cray Dawson a slight nod, prompting him to do the same.

Chapter 7

Inside the bat-wing doors of the saloon, Willie the Devil and Elton Minton had watched and listened to everything that happened in the street. Willie's pal Donald Hornetti had joined them, and the three stood off to the side away from the other drinkers who had crowded the doors, some of them having stepped out along the boardwalk.

"There's what our boy is up against," Willie whispered to Elton. "Think he'll have any problem taking Fast Larry down?"

Elton just stared dumbstruck at the grizzly scene in the street as four townsmen picked up Sidlow Talbert hand and foot and carried him away, his head bobbing with each step. After a moment Donald Hornetti gave Elton a rough nudge. "Hey, you, idiot! Didn't you hear what the Devil asked you?"

"Oh, uh, yeah, I heard," said Elton. But still he couldn't take his eyes off of Lawrence Shaw and the bloody corpse.

"Well?" said Hornetti, growing impatient with him.

"Well what?" Elton was rattled senseless by what he'd seen happen on the street.

Donald Hornetti snarled and grabbed him by his shirt collar. "Let me crack this fool's head like a ripe walnut, Willie," he said.

"No, not now, Donald," said Willie.

"Not *now?*" said Elton, getting alarmed. "What does that mean, *not now?*"

Donald Hornetti palmed Elton roughly on the side of his head and let out a dark, cruel chuckle. "It means not right now, but maybe real soon if you don't straighten up, idiot."

"Stop it, damn it," said Willie. "We've got to get word to Barton and Blue Snake. Barton is going to blow sky-high when he hears about Sidlow. The first thing he's going to ask is what did we do to protect him."

"Wasn't nothing we could have done," said Hornetti, turning Elton's collar loose with a gruff shove.

"I know that and you know that," said Willie the Devil, "but we better come up with some kind of story that Barton's going to believe, or else we're going to look worse than old Sidlow out there."

Listening to the two, Elton felt a nausea creep upward from deep in his belly. He'd no idea Barton Talbert was who these men rode with. He made a strange sound in his throat and Donald Hornetti snapped around facing him, saying, "What are you laughing at, idiot? You're in trouble too . . . you didn't try to help Sidlow either."

"Whoa," said Elton. "I'm not laughing, I swear! But I'm not a part of this in any way. I don't ride with nobody. I just have a pal who's going to call down Fast Larry and shoot him. This is strictly a onetime business deal for me."

"In a pig's eye you're not a part of it, idiot," said Hornetti, grabbing Elton's shirt collar again. "You're a part of it if I say you're a part of it!"

"Turn him loose, Donald," said Willie, "and stop grabbing him. We need to think this thing through."

"Yeah," said Elton as Hornetti turned loose and shoved him back again. "And stop calling me *idiot.*"

"I'll stop calling you an idiot when you quit being an idiot . . . *idiot!*" Hornetti snapped, once again palming the side of Elton's head. "What are you going to do about it?" He stepped real close to Elton, almost nose-to-nose, except Donald Hornetti stood a full head taller than Elton and his shoulders were twice the width.

"It just doesn't look right," said Elton. "Nobody wants to be called an idiot. What if I called you an idiot? Would you like it?"

"Try it," said Hornetti. "I dare you, idiot!"

"All right, that's enough," said Willie the Devil. "We've got to get this shooting going with Sammy and Shaw. At least if Sammy kills him, we've got some good news for Barton and Blue Snake. If Shaw kills Sammy, we can always say we did our best."

Elton just looked at Willie, wishing he'd never met these men. Now he was on the spot, and so was Sammy Boy.

"Sammy will have to call him out tonight right before dark," said Willie, looking at Elton. "Is that going to be all right? Can you get all our bets down by then?"

"Sure," said Elton, trying to muster up the courage he needed to get back into the scheme. "But I'll need to get moving on it. Give me the money and I'll start making the rounds."

"Not so fast," said Willie the Devil.

"Yeah, *idiot,* not so fast," said Hornetti, feinting a palm to Elton's head, then stopping himself at the last second, causing Elton to flinch nervously.

"I'm going along with you," said Willie,

pulling out a large roll of money.

"But these are my people; they don't know you from Adam," Elton protested.

Willie shook the money in Elton's face. "This is *my* money, it don't know *you* from Adam," he said, chuckling.

"Yeah, so shut up, and do like you're told, idiot," said Hornetti.

Elton gritted his teeth. He had to get the money down on the gunfight, half on Sammy Boy, and half on Shaw, making sure he and Willie the Devil won either way it went. For the time being he'd have to put up with Donald Hornetti's insults and bullying. He'd made the mistake of letting the big man get away with calling him an idiot the first time, an hour ago when Hornetti joined him and Willie in the saloon. Like any bully, Hornetti had gotten worse. Now it had gone too far for Elton to tell him to leave him alone and get any results other than a thump on his head for his effort. He'd have to find a way to straighten this big man out once and for all. He couldn't keep taking this kind of treatment from him.

"All right, Willie," said Elton, ignoring Hornetti, "let's get going."

The first person Elton led Willie the Devil to was Fat Man Hughes, who still sat on the high stool at the end of the bar. When Elton told Hughes that Sammy Boy was going to call Shaw out into the street, the big man's face lit up with anticipation and greed. "Sure, I'll take some of your wager," Hughes said, reaching for his thick roll as he eyed Willie the Devil, saying to Elton, "I see you found yourself a backer, huh?"

Willie the Devil offered a crafty smile and replied before Elton got a chance, "I believe we've met before, Mr. Hughes . . . I'm Willie Devlin, Willie the Devil, as you may recall? I'm somewhat of a sporting man myself."

"Yeah." Fat Man Hughes shrugged, unimpressed. "I remember you. Your roll never was as large as mine."

Willie the Devil didn't let Hughes's words bother him. "Perhaps after today it will be, though."

Hughes grinned. "I like a man who thinks positive!" Flipping out his thick roll of money, licking a thumb, and riffling through the bills, he asked, "Now, sir, what can I do you for?"

Elton said, "I've got one thousand and five hundred dollars that says Sammy Boy is going to beat Lawrence Shaw straight up . . . outdraw him and outshoot him, plain and simple. Since Shaw's the big gun and Sammy Boy's an unknown, what odds are you going to offer me?"

"Odds, huh?" Fat Man Hughes's belly bounced up and down as he laughed and shook his head. "Boy, Elton, you're so full of shit, if I stepped on your foot it would squirt out both ears." He quickly peeled off a stack of bills, saying, "Five to one, Elton; take it or leave it."

"I'll take it," said Elton, turning to Willie the Devil for the money.

Fat Man Hughes flagged the bartender over to hold the bets in the small tin lockbox he kept under the bar for wagers of this sort. "Porter," he said to the broad-shouldered bartender, "we have a gunfight in the making between Elton's friend Sammy Boy White and Lawrence Shaw. Hold this for safekeeping, if you please."

"Whoa," said Porter Chapin, looking excited at the prospect, "Sammy Boy is fast with a gun; I've got to give him that." He took the money from Willie the Devil and Fat Man Hughes, counted it quickly, folded it, then held it up and said, "Can I get some money down on this thing?"

Fat Man Hughes had lowered his big body from the stool, picked the seat of his trousers, and adjusted his wrinkled suit coat. "You'll have to talk to Elton here," he said to the bartender. "It's his endeavor . . . I've got to go to the jake. Keep my seat open, if you will, please."

Elton and Willie the Devil waited until Hughes was out the back door before Elton said, "How fast do you think Sammy is, Porter, just between you and me?"

"He's damn fast," said Porter, reaching behind his white apron into his trouser pocket. "I know Shaw is supposed to be the fastest gun alive . . . but everybody's got to fall someday. Give me twenty dollars on Sammy Boy."

"Done," said Elton. "Of course you know Sammy and me are pals; I'm not offering any odds."

"I don't care," said the bartender, "I can take even money any day on a gunfight. The main thing is just to be able to say I had an interest in it."

"Yes, that's the spirit." Willie the Devil beamed. "I bet there are many here who feel the same way." He looked around the saloon as he rubbed his hands together.

Cray Dawson and Lawrence Shaw had carried their saddlebags to their separate rooms at the Desert Flower Inn. As Dawson unpacked a clean shirt and socks,

Shaw stepped in from the hall, first rapping quietly on the wooden door. "I know you think I did the wrong thing killing Sidlow Talbert," Shaw said. "But you covered my back anyway. I'm obliged."

Cray Dawson looked at him with a flat expression. "I didn't come along to judge you, Shaw," he said, unfolding his clean socks, shaking them out, and pitching them on the bed. "Just to back you up. I want them dead too, don't forget."

"He was with them," said Shaw. "I know damn well he was. I could see it in his eyes when I talked to him."

"I'm not saying he wasn't with them," said Dawson, "but I've got to say he wasn't with them when I saw them riding away." He stared evenly at Shaw. "I wish I could say he was, but I'd be lying."

"It's water under the bridge now anyway," said Shaw. "He's dead either way. One thing's for sure: This is going to flush his brother and the gang out once word gets to them."

"Yeah," said Dawson, "I have to admit, if anything will bring Barton Talbert to us, that ought to do it."

Shaw knew Dawson had a problem with what he'd done, whether he admitted it or not. "Let me make myself understood,

Dawson," he said. "I'm not calling what I'm doing anything but what it is. I'm out for blood vengeance, and there's no way to clean it up or pretty it up. What you saw today was dark and ugly. But there's a good chance it's going to get darker and uglier before it ends. I'll kill anybody close to Barton Talbert just to get his attention, just to make him turn and fight. Think of it like a war. I'm out to win . . . damn the cost, and damn the casualties."

"I understand," said Dawson with a grave expression.

"Do you really?" Shaw asked, stepping closer to him. "Because if you don't understand, I won't hold it against you if you cut out now."

"What about what you said the other day?" Dawson asked. "You said there wouldn't be any giving out riding with you."

"After today there won't be," said Shaw. "Until today, maybe you didn't realize how far I will go, or how low I'll reach to drag these rats up out of the slime. Now that you see it, if you've got no stomach for it, go ahead and leave. Leaving might be the smartest thing you'll ever do."

Dawson studied Shaw's face as the gunman tried to avoid eye contact with him. It occurred to Dawson that Shaw was ashamed of what he'd done to Sidlow Talbert. Yet as he'd deliberately tortured Sidlow Talbert there had appeared to be no hesitancy, no show of remorse, no spark of mercy. "I'm in, Shaw," said Dawson. "No matter what, I'm on this trail until it ends."

"All right," said Shaw, "I won't mention leaving again." He let out a deep breath and wiped a hand across his forehead.

Dawson saw the torment he seemed to be in and offered a tired smile, saying, "You need a drink bad, don't you?"

"I need one something awful," Shaw said, shaking his head, "but I'm not giving in. From here on it's either cold water or buttermilk for me. I'm off the whiskey. . . ."

While the two settled into their rooms at the Desert Flower Inn, Jedson Caldwell and Dillard Frome had gone back to the livery barn to finish tending the animals. When the last mule and horse were rubbed down with a handful of fresh straw, the two sat aside the water bucket and grain sack and walked to the Big Spur Saloon still talking about the shooting. Inside the saloon they found the atmosphere to be crackling with excitement over the shooting; but they didn't realize what part of the commotion was until Willie the Devil slid in beside them and asked who they had picked to win the gunfight between Lawrence Shaw and Sammy Boy White.

Frome and Caldwell looked stunned. Caldwell started to answer, but before he could speak, Elton Minton said, "Hey, these two men rode in with Shaw!"

Willie squinted, studying Frome and Caldwell closer. "Say, Elton, I believe you're right." As he continued to speak he poked his finger into Caldwell's chest. But Caldwell never backed an inch as the Devil said, "This fight is supposed to come as a surprise to Fast Larry. Looks like you two boys aren't leaving here until Shaw shows up and we get this thing settled."

Caldwell looked back and forth as Sammy Boy White and Donald Hornetti closed in on either side of him, rendering him unable to make a run for it. He saw he had no chance to get out of the saloon and tell Shaw what awaited him, but he also could see that Frome had a clear run for the doors if he moved quickly. "Frome! Run! Tell Shaw!" Caldwell shouted suddenly. Frome needed no coaxing. He'd already seen what was at hand. He turned and bolted out the bat-wing doors.

"Damn it!" Willie the Devil shouted. "Hornetti, get him!"

The big gunman ran out the doors onto the boardwalk, drawing his pistol on his way. Frome ran straight down the rutted dirt street toward the Desert Flower. "I've got him," said Hornetti, raising his pistol, calmly taking aim as onlookers veered out of the way. The gun bucked once in his hand, the explosion resounding along the street, and Frome seemed to be thrust forward by a powerful blast of wind. "Got him dead center." Hornetti chuckled, raising his pistol and blowing smoke from the tip of his barrel. He turned and walked back into the Big Spur Saloon without giving Dillard Frome another glance.

"I didn't mean for you to shoot him, damn it!" said Willie. "I only meant for you to stop him."

"Then you should have made it more clear." Hornetti grinned. "He's laying out there deader than hell." He patted the pistol he'd slipped back into his holster. "The way I just shot, I don't know that we really need ol' Sammy Boy here." He gave Sammy Boy White a look that could be read different ways.

Noting it, Sammy Boy said flatly, "You're a bag of fish guts, Hornetti. If you think shooting a man in the back while he's running is anything like facing Fast Larry Shaw, then I'm tempted to stand down and let him shoot your eyes out."

Hornetti looked stunned. "Hey, wait a minute, ol' pard, I was only joking around with you!"

"Sure you were," said Sammy Boy, his hand poised close to his pistol butt, "now that you see I ain't taking a nickel's worth of your bullying horseshit. I've noticed that old 'I was only joking' is the ace every coward keeps up his sleeve. You'll push a man a little; then if that sticks you'll push him a little more." He jerked a thumb toward Elton Minton. "You started off calling my friend here an idiot . . . once you saw he wasn't going to call you down for it, you started pecking him on the head, like this." He took a step with his gun hand still poised and with his free hand palmed Hornetti on his forehead. "There, *idiot*, how does that feel? Dare me to do it again." Sammy Boy offered a flat, mirthless grin.

"Why you . . ." Hornetti bristled, his hand going instinctively toward his pistol butt, then stopping short as he felt the tip of Sammy Boy's pistol against the tip of his nose.

"You wasn't going to draw it anyway, idiot," said Sammy Boy. "I'm doing you a favor. Think how bad it would look if I'd waited for you to draw. We'd have been here all day."

"All right, stop it, Donald! We've got business to attend to!" said Willie the Devil, directing his attention to Hornetti and giving him a shove, deciding it wouldn't be wise to push Sammy Boy White. "Go get a drink and calm down," he said to Hornetti. "I'm going to be counting on you to back this man when the time comes."

Hearing Willie the Devil, Sammy Boy White looked at Elton and asked, "What's he talking about, *backing* me?" He cut a glance at Hornetti, making sure Hornetti heard him say, "I don't need that piece of rat bait backing me up, he'd soil his trousers."

Hornetti's face reddened. He bristled with anger and humiliation, but he made no offer of retaliation. Instead he turned and walked to the bar.

"Easy, Sammy Boy!" said Elton. "We just thought in case things went bad — which we know they won't, of course . . ." He looked around and lowered his voice. "Willie just thought it might be a good idea to have Hornetti near about with a shotgun. Sort of a secondary plan, you might call it."

"Secondary plan, like hell," said Sammy Boy. "This is not going to be some crooked scheme. I'm fast and I'm good. I'm younger than Shaw and I want his handle, 'fastest gun alive,' more than I think he wants it these days. That's what this is all about, Elton, nothing else."

As Sammy Boy and Elton spoke, a drunken old man wearing a miner's cap staggered in between them and shook a bag of coins in Elton's face. "Have I got time to get the rest of this down on Fast Larry Shaw?"

"Not now," Elton said quickly, giving the old man a shove, hoping Sammy Boy hadn't heard what he'd said. But Sammy Boy had heard. He caught the old man by his arm before he staggered away.

"What did you ask, old-timer?" Sammy Boy said.

The old miner said in a blast of sour whiskey breath, finally recognizing Sammy Boy White, "No offense, Mr. White, but I watched Shaw outgun D.C. Hanson on the street in Laredo. I just don't believe there's a man alive who'll beat him."

"Bet the way you feel, old-timer," said

Sammy Boy, letting the old man stagger away as he turned a cold gaze to Elton Minton.

"Let me explain, Sammy!" said Elton, looking worried.

"You bet against me," Sammy Boy said flatly.

"Listen to me, Sammy; it ain't like you're thinking it is," Elton pleaded.

"My pardner," said Sammy Boy in a hurt and disgusted tone. "You went behind my back and bet on Shaw."

"No, Sammy, I bet on both of you! See, I was looking out for you and me, just in case something went wrong! We'd still have something coming."

"You were looking out for me?" Sammy looked amazed. "Elton, this ain't no sporting event! If I lose, there ain't no 'looking out for me' — I'm dead!"

Elton looked down at the floor in silence and shook his head, as if he had just come to realize what a deadly situation Sammy Boy White was in. When he looked back up at Sammy Boy he said, "Sammy, I'm sorry. I just got so caught up in the money we was going to make, I plumb forgot what losing would cost." He cupped his forehead in his hand. "Jesus, what have I gotten us into?"

Sammy Boy took a deep breath and let it

out slowly, releasing his anger and his disappointment in Elton. "You didn't get me into it, Elton. I want this awfully bad. It just cut me deep, you betting against me."

Willie the Devil had overheard part of the conversation; then, seeing the two talking between themselves, he backed away and turned toward the bar.

Seeing him slip away, Elton said, "He caused it . . . he caused me to do it. I never should have listened to him."

"Don't blame him," said Sammy Boy. "If I hadn't been wanting this kind of gunfight, the rest wouldn't have happened anyway."

"What are we going to do, Sammy?" Elton asked in a shaky voice. "It's too late to stop it."

Sammy Boy raised his pistol and checked it, turning the cylinder slowly, listening closely to it click. "Have you got all the bets down the way you want them?"

"Well, yes, but —"

"Then just stay out of my way until this is over," said Sammy Boy, cutting him off. He turned and walked away to a lone table in the far corner, hooking a bottle of rye off the bar on his way. Standing at the crowded bar, Willie the Devil and Donald Hornetti watched Sammy Boy pull out a chair, sit down, and pull the cork from the bottle.

"What do you think, Willie?" Hornetti asked, the two of them seeing Sammy Boy turn up a long drink of whiskey. "Has this whole plan gone to hell on us or what?"

"Naw, we're still on track," said Willie the Devil. "They're both in too deep to pull out now." He chuckled. "What gets me is how easy it was for us to get somebody to do our killing for us."

"But don't forget, I'm still facing Shaw if things go bad," said Hornetti.

"Yes, you're facing him, all right," said Willie the Devil, filling a shot glass for himself and sliding the bottle to Hornetti. "But with Sammy Boy calling him down, you'll be facing Shaw's back . . . from behind cover." He raised his glass in a short salute. "I think that makes all the difference in the world, don't you?"

Hornetti grinned. "Yeah, it does at that. I almost hope Sammy Boy loses, just so I can put a bullet in a big-time gunslinger like Fast Larry Shaw." Having poured himself a drink, Hornetti raised it in a return salute, then tossed it back in a quick gulp and let out a whiskey hiss. "I like the idea of killing him without him ever seeing it coming."

Chapter 8

Had Donald Hornetti waited a moment longer out front of the Big Spur Saloon after shooting Dillard Frome, he would have seen that Frome was still alive. The shot had knocked him unconscious, but only for a few seconds. As soon as he came to, he lifted his face from the dirt and began crawling toward the Desert Flower Inn. In his addled state he waved away the few onlookers who offered to help him. In his wake Frome left a smear of dark blood across the dirt from the exit wound in his shattered chest. He had just managed to drag himself onto the boardwalk of the Desert Flower when Lawrence Shaw and Cray stepped out the door, having come down from their rooms to investigate the single gunshot they'd heard.

"Oh, no, Frome," said Cray Dawson, hurrying forward and kneeling down, cradling Frome in his arms, "who did this to you?"

The gaping wound in the man's chest bubbled with each breath. Frome struggled to speak, letting a long string of blood spill from his lips. "I came to warn . . . you . . . Shaw." Unable to continue, he pointed a weak, trembling hand toward the Big Spur Saloon.

Shaw had also stooped down at Frome's side, but he remained on guard, poised and watching the street. "There's somebody waiting for me?" he asked, as if he weren't at all surprised.

Frome nodded his head. "They're . . . holding Caldwell. They mean to kill you." At that Frome's words seemed to give out on him.

Shaw stood and stared long and hard at the Big Spur Saloon. Cray Dawson looked up at him and said, "Forget them! We've got to get Frome to a doctor!"

Still staring at the saloon, Shaw said down to Frome in a calm, solemn voice, "What say you, Dillard Frome? Do you need a doctor? Or would you rather I go kill the man who did this to you?"

Frome managed to look down at the gaping hole in his chest. He gave Dawson a look of hopelessness, then rasped to Shaw, "There's more than one of them . . . watch your back —" His words stopped short, followed by a long exhale of breath.

"You can bet I will," Shaw said under his breath, his right hand raising his Colt gently in its holster, then turning it loose. He stepped to the edge of the boardwalk, looking up at the evening sun standing low behind the Desert Flower and stretching long onto the dirt street.

"Frome?" said Cray Dawson, shaking him slightly as if to wake him. Then, seeing that no amount of shaking would wake him, Dawson reached down with a gloved hand and closed Frome's eyes.

"Your game, ol' pard," said Shaw without looking down. "I'll finish your hand for you."

"Shaw!" said Dawson, sounding ready to do some serious killing for the sake of the man who had just given his life to come and warn them. "What do you want me to do?"

Shaw said without turning to face him, "Go along the boardwalk across from the Big Spur — watch the rooflines. Then follow me inside the saloon and stay to my left. Give me room." He stepped down from the boardwalk and headed toward the Big Spur Saloon, the sun standing like a fiery red ball behind his left shoulder.

"You got it," said Cray Dawson, hurriedly taking off his right glove and shoving it into his belt. He veered off and hurried ahead of Shaw a few feet until he'd gotten onto the boardwalk across from the Big Spur. He moved along with caution, scanning the roofline on the other side of the street, his pistol drawn and ready.

Out front of the Big Spur Saloon, Shaw stopped in the middle of the street and stood with his feet planted shoulder-width apart. Back at the Desert Flower Inn, Sheriff Neff had arrived, hearing the onlookers tell him what had happened as he stared down at Dillard Frome's body. "You've got to do something, Sheriff," a woman said, wringing her hands. "What's happening to our good town?"

Before Sheriff Neff could reply, he turned toward the sound of Shaw's voice calling out to the doors of the saloon: "I want the craven coward who shot Dillard Frome in the back to step out here. We both know why you shot him, so there's nothing to talk about. You want killing? Come on out and let's commence."

"Damn it," Sheriff Neff whispered under his breath at the far end of the street. "Right *there* is what's happened to our good town." He hurried along the boardwalk out front of the Big Spur, his hands chest-high, offering no threat to Shaw. When he stopped, it was at Shaw's insistence.

"Stop right there, Sheriff," said Shaw,

his left hand raised, his eyes still on the Big Spur Saloon. "These cowards shot that man in the back because he was coming to warn me that they're waiting for me."

"Shaw, it's got to stop!" said Sheriff Neff. "I can't have no more of it."

"I never asked for none of this, Sheriff," said Shaw. "They keep coming at me, no matter where I go."

Cray Dawson kept scanning the roofline, the boardwalk, the streets and alleys, feeling his palms grow moist around his gun butt.

"I know you don't start trouble, Shaw," said Sheriff Neff. "You don't have to. It's your name that starts it! But I can't go no farther with it. Eagle Pass is a peaceable town right now. I want to keep it that way. Do you understand me, Shaw? I want you to leave . . . leave right now."

Shaw didn't seem to hear him. He called out to the Big Spur, "Are you coming out, or do I have to come drag you out?"

"Shaw, do you hear me?" the sheriff said.

"I hear you, Sheriff Neff," said Shaw, not taking his eyes off of the doors to the Big Spur. "I know you're just doing your job . . . but so am I." He took a step closer to the Big Spur Saloon. "Hear me in there? You wanted a gunfight. Come get it!"

Inside the Big Spur, Elton Minton looked scared. Sweat glistened on his brow as he turned from the sound of Shaw's voice and looked back into the corner where Sammy Boy sat nursing a glass of whiskey. The bottle in front of him was not nearly as full as it had been when he'd sat down only moments earlier. "Well, Sammy, here he is," said Elton. "What are you waiting for?"

Sammy Boy tossed Elton a sidelong glance, saying, "Go to hell, Elton." Then he stared down at his shot glass.

"Hey, what is this?" Willie the Devil raged at Elton, hearing Sammy Boy's response. He grabbed Elton's forearm. "Is he going to crawfish on us, after me putting up three thousand dollars?" Willie's hand rested on the butt of his pistol.

"No, Willie!" said Elton. "He'll be all right; just give me a minute with him." Elton hurried to the table where Sammy Boy White sat staring into his shot glass. "Sammy, what are you doing to me?" he pleaded. "I set this whole thing up for you . . . now you've got to get out there and face Shaw or Willie the Devil and the whole Talbert gang are going to be down our shirts!"

Sammy Boy said flatly, "You set this up

for yourself, Elton. All I am is a target you're hanging in front of Shaw. Whether I live or die doesn't matter to you." He picked up the bottle and swallowed a shot.

"Sammy, you can't do me this way . . . these men will kill me!" Elton pleaded.

Sammy Boy White stood up slowly, adjusting his tied-down holster and slipping his pistol up and down to keep it loose. "Don't worry, Elton; I ain't like you — I wouldn't double-cross a friend. I'll go face Shaw. Afterward, whatever money you make off this deal is mine . . . don't even try to talk about it later. I'm calling it quits with you."

"Well," Willie the Devil called out to Elton from the bar, "is Sammy Boy going out there or not?"

"Yes, he's going," said Elton. "I told you we've got nothing to worry about with Sammy Boy White. He's as game as a prize rooster! Right, Sammy?" Elton started to slap Sammy on his back, but then he thought better of it, seeing the look on the gunman's face.

As Sammy Boy started for the bat-wing doors, Willie gave Donald Hornetti a nod and Hornetti quietly slipped over to the stairs to the second floor with his rifle in his hand. Sammy Boy took note of what

Hornetti was doing but pretended not to see him. As Sammy Boy stopped and looked out over the bat-wing doors, Donald Hornetti hurried to the front of the building to a small room overlooking the street. Inside the room he stepped up to the window and opened it stealthily.

At the bat-wing doors, Sammy Boy White called out to Shaw standing in the middle of the street. "Fast Larry Shaw," he said, "I'm Sammy Boy White from Abilene. I expect you've heard of me lately."

Shaw had heard his name over the past year, but he made no reply. He stood silent, relaxed but poised, ready to move at the slightest provocation.

"Well," Sammy Boy said, seeing Shaw wasn't going to talk to him, "I want you to know I had nothing to do with killing that man. I'm a straight-up gunman, not a backshooter." As he spoke, he made an upward gesture with his eyes, warning Shaw of Donald Hornetti's position above them. "I'm coming at you with nothing in mind except to show the world that I'm the fastest gun." He pushed the doors open and stepped out on the boardwalk. "All I want is a fair fight," he said. Again he lifted his eyes, trying to warn Shaw.

But it wasn't necessary. Shaw had already

caught the slow movement of the window. So had Cray Dawson.

Shaw decided that the young gunman was worthy of some respect. He nodded slightly, letting Sammy Boy know that he had gotten his message. Then he said in low, calm voice, "Yep, I've heard of you, Sammy Boy White. You killed Deacon Hurley and Frank Topp. I guess that's what's got you thinking you're ready for me."

"I've been ready, Fast Larry," said Sammy Boy.

Shaw looked around at the people who had begun to gather along the boardwalks and in the doorways. He looked at the faces pressed close to the large, dusty windows of the saloon. "Sometimes I wish these bet makers would strap on a gun and walk out. I believe I'd enjoy shooting a few of them."

"They put the odds in your favor, Fast Larry," said Sammy Boy, as if that should matter to a man like Lawrence Shaw.

"Mr. White," said Shaw, "I haven't been interested in what odds they give me for a mighty long time." As he spoke he backed up a step and turned quarterwise, inviting Sammy Boy to come down and take a step into the dirt street.

But instead of stepping down from the boardwalk, Sammy Boy White walked along the storefronts until he reached a distance of twenty-five feet. Then he stepped down and moved slowly to the middle of the street, facing Shaw.

Across from the saloon Cray Dawson came forward into sight at the edge of the boardwalk and looked deliberately up into Donald Hornetti's face.

Hornetti ducked back out of the half-open window and pressed his back against the wall. "Damn it!" he said to himself. "They've seen me!" Sweat glistened on his forehead. He tried to force himself to turn back to the window and make his play, but the trembling in his stomach wouldn't permit it.

Cray Dawson felt that same trembling inside himself, but he forced himself to stand fast, facing the window, knowing that at any second the man could spring back into position and begin firing. He reminded himself that he was here to watch Shaw's back. Nothing would stop him from doing what he'd said he would do, even if it meant his life. Keeping a watch on Shaw and Sammy Boy White in his peripheral vision, he stared straight at the half-open window, keeping his gun hand poised an inch from the butt of his Colt.

"Speaking of odds," said Shaw, "what's the odds on you not going through with this? I already see that you're not the backshooting coward who killed that man a while ago."

"The odds on me not going through with this are *none*," said Sammy Boy. "It wasn't right what happened a while ago . . . but it doesn't change a thing as far as I'm concerned. It was meant for me and you to meet here. This is fate. The other is just the bad stuff that happens."

Shaw nodded slowly. "Then let's quit talking and get at it. This sun's too hot for a social gathering."

Without another word, and no sooner than Shaw's words had cleared his lips, Sammy Boy White's hand came up filled, the big Colt cocked. He was young and fast and hungry to make a name for himself. But before his gun leveled and fired at Lawrence Shaw, the bullet from Shaw's Colt struck him in the right side of his chest, the impact of it knocking him backward and spinning him so fast that one boot came off his foot and tumbled across the ground.

Shaw immediately turned his Colt toward the upstairs window above the saloon. Yet even as he did so, he heard Cray Dawson's Colt explode. With a short scream, Donald Hornetti came forward through the half-open window in a spray of broken glass, crashed onto the overhang above the boardwalk, and rolled off of it into the dirt street. As the man landed in a rise of dust, Shaw turned toward the bat-wing doors as if expecting more trouble. And he was right in his expectation: The bartender, Porter Chapin, came running out with a shotgun in one hand and a pistol in his other, his white apron still around his waist. He let out a loud yell, jumping down into the street, but he didn't manage to get either gun pointed at Lawrence Shaw before Shaw's Colt nailed him through the heart and sent him backward, dead on the ground.

"Jesus!" Cray Dawson whispered, his Colt still smoking in his hand. He wondered for a second if it would ever be safe to holster his gun. He stepped out into the middle of the street a few yards away from Shaw, turning back and forth, taking in every face, every hand, searching every doorway and alley.

Both men turned quickly toward the sound of two horses pounding away from the direction of the livery barn a block away. Shaw raised his Colt toward the riders, then stopped himself, seeing no guns pointed in his or Dawson's direction. Cray Dawson had also raised his Colt toward the two fleeing riders. But seeing him ready to fire, Shaw said, "Let them go."

Dawson replied even as he lowered his Colt slightly, "I'd bet anything they were in on this in some way."

"So would I," said Shaw. "But if they're part of Talbert's gang, letting them go will make sure he hears about what happened here." He lowered his Colt but kept it in his hand, replacing his spent cartridges, watching Willie the Devil and Elton Minton ride away in a rise of thick dust.

Sheriff Neff appeared from within the crowd of onlookers on the boardwalk and hurried over to where Sammy Boy White lay sprawled on the ground. "This one is still alive!" he shouted. "Somebody go get Doc Phelps; tell him to hurry it up!"

Cray Dawson saw Lawrence Shaw turn his attention to where Sammy Boy White lay in the dirt, the sheriff squatting down over him. The look in Shaw's eyes and the gun in his hand caused Dawson to say, "No, Shaw, don't do it."

But Shaw walked over to Sammy Boy White without acknowledging Dawson, his pistol still in his hand. Seeing Sammy Boy's gun lying close to his outstretched hand, Shaw nudged it away with his boot toe, then reached down and picked it up and shoved it down into his belt. "Mr. White," he said, "can you hear me?" His pistol pointed down at Sammy Boy, but without conviction.

Sammy Boy White strained his face and opened his eyes slightly. "I-I hear you," he said, putting forth much effort, blood welling up around his wound and running in a steady stream down to the dirt.

"Then listen to me close," said Shaw. "You showed honor, telling me about the man above the saloon. That's why you're still alive. I never leave a man breathing who might come back on me someday." Shaw's Colt tensed slightly as he asked in a firm tone, "You're not going to be something I'll live to regret, are you?"

Sheriff Neff cut in, saying to anyone listening, "Has anybody gone to get the doctor? This man is bleeding bad!"

"I can't . . . promise nothing," Sammy Boy said, straining for the words. "I ain't a liar. I want the name awfully bad."

"Yeah." Shaw shook his head. "At least you're honest about it."

"Shaw, don't!" shouted Cray Dawson,

seeing Shaw's grip tighten around the Colt's handle.

Sheriff Neff saw it too, and at the sound of Dawson shouting, he ducked back away from Sammy Boy White.

But Shaw didn't shoot. Instead he drew a deep breath, relaxed his gun hand, and took a step back. "You were fast, Mr. White, as fast as any I've seen. You'd be wise to satisfy yourself with that and leave things as they are between us. There's more to life than being fast with a gun."

"Dang it, where's that doctor?" Sheriff Neff said under his breath.

"I want what . . . you've got, Shaw," said Sammy Boy, struggling harder for his words as an old doctor and a young boy came running from the far end of the street, the doctor carrying a small black bag and holding a hand on his bowler to keep it from flying off his head.

"You only want the things you can see, Mr. White," said Shaw. "If that's all there is to you, you'd be better off if I killed you." Shaw turned and walked to the Big Spur Saloon. Cray Dawson fell into step behind him, still watching both sides of the street.

While the two stepped up onto the boardwalk out front of the Big Spur, the dust left behind by Willie the Devil and Elton Minton still hung in the air at the far end of town. Willie and Elton didn't even slow their horses until they reached a fork in the old Northern Trail five miles out of Eagle Pass. When Elton finally brought his horse to a halt, Willie the Devil looked back at him, then circled his horse and came riding back, drawing his pistol from his holster. "I told you we ain't stopping! Now get that horse in front of me where I can keep an eye on yas!"

"Willie," said Elton, "this horse is going to drop dead beneath me if I don't rest him for a while!"

Willie pointed the pistol at Elton. "You're going to be dropping dead if you don't come on and do like I tell you!"

Elton raised a hand toward Willie as if holding him back. "Please, Willie. This was a bad idea, me coming with you . . . I'm only going to slow you down. Why is this so important to you, anyway? We made our play in Eagle Pass. It didn't work out the way we wanted it to. So what? We still made some money! You took the whole cash box!"

With his free hand, Willie the Devil patted the tin cash box he held on his lap. "Oh, yeah, we made some money . . . we took it all, once I saw that loco bartender was more interested in being a big gun than he was in watching the betting money." Willie managed a slight laugh that soon disappeared, leaving him with a dark, solemn expression. "But the money was only part of it. I meant for Fast Larry Shaw to be laying dead in the street back there. Thanks to your slow-as-hell friend Sammy Boy White, I've got to go tell Barton Talbert how his brother Sidlow got shot up like a target board and I didn't kill the man who did it!" As he spoke Willie's voice grew louder until when he'd finished he seemed on the verge of losing his temper. "I've never seen anything get so messed up as this! I ought to kill you and be done with it!"

"Willie, please," Elton pleaded, "you've got all the money, yours and mine. Keep it; just let me go!"

"Huh-uh," said Willie, "you still owe me. You promised me that Sammy Boy was going to kill Shaw. When you make a promise to the Devil, you better be prepared to make good on it."

"Willie, I'm sorry," said Elton. "There's no way I can make it up to you. I thought Sammy Boy would kill him cold. Okay, I was wrong. We still made our money, just like you said we would betting both ways. What more do you want from me?"

"I want your soul, you sorry scarecrow son of a bitch," Willie hissed, gesturing Elton forward with his pistol barrel. "Now get yourself moving."

Chapter 9

Inside the Big Spur Saloon, Lawrence Shaw walked straight across the floor toward the bar with all eyes on him. Jedson Caldwell slipped in beside Cray Dawson and said, "I feel responsible for poor Dillard Frome. I couldn't get away, but I told him to run for it and go warn Shaw."

"It wasn't your fault, Caldwell," said Dawson. "You did the best you could at the time. Nobody is blaming you."

"Thanks," said Caldwell. "Does he feel the same way?" He nodded at Lawrence Shaw's back as Shaw stopped at the bar.

"He's not blaming you either," said Dawson, "so put it out of your mind."

When Porter Chapin had grabbed up the pistol and shotgun earlier and run out the front door to make a play for Shaw, the owner, Max Renner, had been left to tend bar for himself. He was taking off his suit coat and hanging it on a peg when Shaw and Cray Dawson came in. He wore a worried look as he ran a hand across his brow and rolled up his shirtsleeves as Shaw,

Dawson, and Caldwell stood at the bar. "What will it be, Mr. Shaw?" he asked.

Without answering, Shaw reached forward, took three clean shot glasses from along the inside edge of the bar top, and set one beside him and one in front of him. He reached sidelong, picked up a half-full bottle of rye, and poured both glasses full.

Seeing Shaw raise the glass to his lips, Cray Dawson said, "But Shaw, I thought you said you weren't going to drink —" He cut his words short, seeing the look Shaw gave him above the rim of the shot glass.

"Drink up," Shaw said gruffly, nodding at the glassful of rye he'd poured for Cray Dawson.

"By the way, those drinks are on the house," Max Renner said nervously. Getting no response from Shaw other than a flat stare, he went on to say, "As a matter of fact, so are the rest of your drinks, Mr. Shaw." He cleared his throat, then added as an afterthought, "for both you and your friend here, that is." He picked up the bottle in front of Shaw and refilled the shot glass. "In fact, anything we have here is on the house."

"Much obliged," Shaw said grudgingly, giving him the same flat stare.

Max Renner summoned two barroom

girls from among the onlookers. "Suzette, you and Lizzy get over here . . . I want you to meet Mr. Shaw and his friend!" He ignored Jedson Caldwell.

Feeling out of place and unwelcome, Caldwell said to Dawson standing beside him, "I think I'll go see if my services are needed with the dead." He slipped away and out the front door, avoiding the eyes that followed him through the bat-wing doors.

"Pour me a beer," said Shaw to the bar owner, paying no attention to the two young women who approached him and Dawson warily.

"Yes, sir!" said Max Renner, hurriedly hooking a clean mug and sticking it under the long tap handle. "I suppose you want to know who was behind all the betting going on? Well, it was Willie Devlin and Sammy Boy's friend, Elton Minton. Them two got it going. Everybody else just followed their lead. There was no offense intended. In fact, I don't mind telling you, I had my money on you."

"I'm used to it," Shaw said flatly.

"Not that it matters," said the bar owner, "since those two took the cash box from under the bar and left with all of it anyway."

As the bar owner finished filling the

mug, Shaw asked, "What got into that bartender of yours?"

"Beats me, Mr. Shaw," said Max Renner. "I hope you don't hold that against my establishment. Porter was one of those proud, restless kinds . . . never got the kind of respect he thought he deserved. He was pretty good with a gun." He shrugged, then added, "Well, until today anyway. I reckon he must have seen you as a chance to get ahead, and he couldn't stand to let the opportunity pass him by." He slid the fresh, foamy mug of beer over in front of Shaw.

"Then here's to him," said Shaw. He raised the mug, took a long, deep gulp, then set it down, shoved it away from him, and wiped a hand across his lips. He reached into his pocket, took out a bill without checking it, and shoved it down into the bodice of the bar girl standing nearest him. "See to it that my friend here gets whatever suits him," he said. Then he turned and headed for the doors.

The two girls giggled and moved over beside Cray Dawson, one on either side, pressing themselves against him. "Well, Lizzy," said Suzette, "it looks like we're going to have to share this big, handsome man."

"Excuse me, ladies," said Dawson,

watching Shaw leave. He squeezed from between the two and walked outside to the boardwalk. "Shaw, wait up," he said, catching up to him. "What I started to say back there about you drinking . . . I had no right to mention it."

"It's all right," said Shaw, still walking toward the Desert Flower. "I had no intention of standing there drinking . . . I told you I've quit. I suppose I just needed one to calm my belly."

"Calm your belly?" said Dawson. "It looked to me like you were the only person in town who *was* calm through the whole thing. You mean to tell me you were rattled, facing Sammy Boy White?"

"No," said Shaw, "I wasn't rattled. But I'd be lying to say that killing doesn't leave me sick inside. Whiskey settles it, most times." He looked at Dawson. "What about you? Didn't it bother you, shooting that man in the window?"

Cray Dawson considered it for a moment, then said, "Yes, it did bother me. I didn't realize it at the time. But now that I think about it, something felt out of place inside me. The shot of whiskey got rid of it — sort of, anyway."

"Whiskey and gunfighting go together," said Shaw.

"I've noticed that," said Dawson.

"Be careful you don't get caught up in either one," said Shaw. "One seems to lead to the other."

"I've noticed that too," said Dawson, seeing three men carrying Porter Chapin and three others carrying Donald Hornetti from the street toward the barbershop. Jedson Caldwell tagged along carrying Donald Hornetti's hat. "I don't think I'll ever have to worry about getting caught up in this."

They walked back to the Desert Flower Inn and stood on the porch for a moment, looking back along the street toward the Big Spur Saloon. Foot traffic had started back along the boardwalks. Buggies and horseback riders began to move back and forth across the spot where Donald Hornetti and Porter Chapin had died, and where Sammy Boy had lain bleeding into the dirt until townsmen had helped carry him back to the doctor's office. "It's like nothing ever happened out there," said Cray Dawson.

"That's how long it lasts," said Shaw, nodding. "Some folks might talk about it for a while, long enough to help the news spread and make a man feel important. But it's over that quick; the rest is just waiting for the next time, being ready for it. Some people think you're special for being able to kill a man quicker than a rattlesnake. Hell, it takes nothing more than a willingness to do it."

"You let Sammy Boy live," said Cray Dawson. "I thought you were going to kill him. You could have and nobody would have tried to stop you. I don't think you're as heartless and cold-blooded as you make out to be."

"How do you know I didn't mean to let him live in the first place?" Shaw asked quietly. "How do you know I wasn't saying the rest just to make him understand something?"

"I don't know," said Cray Dawson. "I only know that this is the first time I've seen you shoot a man and him still be breathing afterward. If you were only *acting* like you wanted to finish him off, you sure convinced me."

Shaw offered a tired smile. "Well, he's alive. I just hope I don't have to kill him down the road somewhere."

Cray Dawson shook his head slightly. "Kill him now . . . or kill him down the road." Dawson seemed overwhelmed by the narrow alternatives in Lawrence Shaw's way of life. "You're a better man than to live like this," he said. "How do you stand it?"

"I got caught up in it early, and I got used to it. You remember how it was when we were kids, don't you?" Shaw said.

"Yeah, I remember," said Dawson. "You always was the one wanting to be recognized. The one who broke up the fight and beat up the bully if he happened to be picking on somebody smaller than himself. Most of us thought that someday you might become a lawman. You had the makings for it."

"Yeah," said Shaw, still looking back along the street. "I might still be someday, who knows? The thing is, there's little difference between being a gunman and wearing a badge. Wearing the badge just makes it more respectable. If a sheriff would ever admit it to you, he always wanted to be the fastest gun." He smiled thinly. "If a gunman ever admitted it, he'd tell you he always thought of wearing one of them tin badges." He turned and looked at Cray Dawson more closely. "But there's always a shade of difference between the two . . . that small thing that always keeps one from being the other. Some gunmen try being a lawman. Most times it gets them killed. I don't fool myself much anymore. I've lived a gunman . . . I expect I'll die a gunman."

"You can change it if you want to, Lawrence," said Dawson.

"Yeah, I can change it," said Shaw. "That's what I was thinking about the day I got the telegraph about Rosa. That's also the day I put any such notion out of my mind." He looked back along the street. "We'll head out come morning. See where these two are going. Their dust says they're headed north. They won't be hard to follow. As soon as they make contact with Barton Talbert he'll be back looking for me, if there's any sand in him at all. With any luck maybe we can end this thing soon."

"Maybe," said Cray Dawson, "but I'm not counting on it."

Della Starks had made herself scarce during the trouble in the street. Nor did she appear when Shaw and Dawson had come down from their rooms for dinner. In a cool dining room that spent most of the day in the shade of a large ancient oak, Dawson and Shaw joined two men and a young woman who were also guests at the Desert Flower. Albert and Fannie Jenkins were busily laying the meal out on a long wooden table. The five diners stood behind their ladder-backed chairs for a moment until a tall man wearing a neatly groomed hairpiece and a fashionable plaid suit said with a note of excitement in his voice, "Allow me to begin the introductions. I am Otto Watts from Pennsylvania. This is my dear daughter, Ladelphia, who accompanies me on my travels west."

Shaw, Dawson, and the other guest nodded politely at the man and his daughter. Otto Watts swept a hand toward his daughter as if presenting her as a figure of royalty. She was a finely sculpted young woman with long blond hair. She smiled warmly and gave a curt nod of acknowledgment. Otto Watts turned a gaze to the other guest, a lean, hard-boned elderly man with what looked like the heat of a century's worth of high plains burned deep into his furrowed, weathered skin. "I'm Thomas Ledham. I'm a cattle broker from up Colorado way," the old man said with a trace of a toothless lisp. He wore a no-nonsense suit coat, but one that plainly had taken a good beating to get the trail dust out of it. A pearl-white mustache mantled his sunken upper lip. The bone handle of a Walker-style Colt stood in his belt in the center of his concave stomach.

Cray Dawson introduced himself, then looked toward Lawrence Shaw, standing to his left. Shaw started to introduce himself, but Otto Watts interrupted him, saying, "Of course we all know who you are, Mr. Shaw. And might I say that it is indeed an honor meeting you."

"Thank you, Mr. Watts," Shaw said humbly. "Now let's all take a seat and enjoy our dinner."

They sat down, Shaw and Dawson both noticing the empty place settings and chairs around the large dinner table. When Shaw asked about Della, all the Jenkinses said was that she was busy going over the legal documents and account ledger of the Desert Flower and did not wish to be disturbed. "She sends her regards," said Albert as he laid down a wide wooden bowl filled with chilled fruits and vegetables.

Shaw and Dawson just looked at each other, neither one commenting on Della's behavior as they watched Fannie Jenkins make two trips in from the kitchen out back, bringing in first of all a wide platter full of mesquite-charred steaks, followed by a large platter filled with racks of blackened beef ribs. "Well, then," said Shaw, sipping cold water from a long-stemmed glass, "we're disappointed, but we'll just have to do the best we can without her."

Albert carried the platter of ribs from one guest to the next. When he made his way around to Shaw, Dawson said as Shaw used a two-pronged meat fork to pick up a section of ribs and lay it across his plate, "We seem to be missing a few guests here tonight, Albert."

As Dawson spoke, Shaw stopped for only a second, then continued to carve his section of ribs into strips easier to handle. Albert stood silent for an uncomfortable second. Then Ledham said in a blunt tone of voice, "Why not tell him why there's so many guests missing tonight?"

"Please, Mr. Ledham," said Otto Watts discreetly.

"Please nothing," said Ledham, his ancient voice sounding raspy but strong. "I didn't get to be eighty-seven by beating around the mulberry bush." He gave Shaw a cold, hard gaze. "The other guests didn't want to dine with you, Mr. Shaw. It appears that the thing about you that *attracts* them to the street is the very same thing that *repels* them from the food trough."

An awkward silence loomed for a moment as the rest of the diners waited to see how Shaw would take such a remark. Shaw stared at the old man for a moment with a flat, indiscernible expression. Then he raised a water glass in salute and said to the other three guests, "Then let them find themselves a trough to eat from. I'm grateful that you three have honored me here in these fine surroundings." He narrowed a gaze at Ledham and said with a slight chuckle in his voice, "And were you as sharp with your aim as you are with your words, Mr. Ledham, I'm grateful our paths never crossed when you had your bark on."

"You done well saying it." Ledham grinned, raising his water glass in a return salute, the group feeling any sign of tension dissipate. "And I say if they don't like eating with us it's their own loss."

"Hear, hear," said Otto Watts, raising his glass. Dawson joined the toast, as did the young woman.

They ate amid an atmosphere of pleasant conversation that included nothing about gunfights or reputations. When the dinner was over, Cray Dawson noted how at peace Lawrence Shaw seemed to be for the first time since the two had left Somos Santos. What Dawson found particularly pleasing was the fact that the young woman did not spend the entire meal ignoring everyone but Shaw. It appeared to Dawson that Shaw even seemed to enjoy that fact himself. But then, at the end of the meal when Ledham arose stiffly, excused himself, and, with the aid of a walking cane, made his way out of the dining room, Cray Dawson was surprised to see Lawrence Shaw turn his attention to Otto Watts and in a businesslike manner say, "All right, Watts, lay it out for me."

"Sir?" said Watts, as if not knowing what Shaw meant.

Cray Dawson was genuinely bewildered. But studying the two, he began to see that something was in the works. He chastised himself silently for not having seen it before, the way Shaw had.

Shaw said to Watts, "I can understand Mr. Ledham wanting to dine with a real live gunman. He likes going back to his home and telling everybody he knows. I might understand you wanting to do the same, except I doubt very seriously if you would have brought your daughter along if that was the case." He turned a slight smile to Ladelphia, looking her up and down, then said to Watts, "If Miss Ladelphia really *is* your daughter."

"You have keen senses, Mr. Shaw," said Otto Watts. "My compliments to you, sir." He cut a glance toward Dawson, seeing whether it was all right to discuss business before him.

"Mr. Dawson can hear anything you've got to say to me," Shaw said, encouraging Watts to continue. "What is it? Do you want me to run some squatters off some land you own? A business partner who cut out with your part of the profit?"

"No, nothing of the sort," said Watts, dismissing the idea with the toss of a thick hand. "What I do have is a very lucrative proposition for you." He started to reach inside his coat pocket, but, reminding himself of his present company, he slowed his hand as if to show there was no intent to draw a gun. Shaw nodded his approval and Watts slowly produced a business card and handed it to him. "I think you'll be interested in what my business can do for you, Mr. Shaw." He turned a short glance to Cray Dawson. "Mr. Dawson too, if he is anywhere near as good a shootist as you are . . . and I expect he must be, since he's traveling with you."

"I'm no shootist," said Cray Dawson flatly, already sorry Otto Watts and the young lady had joined them for dinner. Ladelphia sat watching with a pleasant smile.

As Shaw picked up the card, Watts said,

"I traveled all the way from St. Louis up to Arizona Territory to make this same offer to Mr. Clayton Mumpe. But as you know, Mr. Mumpe died suddenly." He offered a proud smile. "I might say he died the second you put a bullet in him."

Shaw ignored Watts's words. He read the card and turned it over as if to see if there was anything more on the back. He offered a tired but curious expression, saying almost to himself, "You're a bearbaiter, Watts?"

"No, indeed," said Watts. "The Otto Watts Troupe is much more than a bearbaiting spectacle! Although I do have a bear who will take on all comers, be they man or beast." As he continued he raised a finger to accompany each item he mentioned. "I presently have a fire-eater who also swallows swords, a lady contortionist who has performed both here and in Europe, a bareback rider, and a spiritualist who communicates with those who have crossed over into the great beyond."

"But you started as a bearbaiter?" Shaw said, laying the card on the tabletop and keeping his finger on it.

"Well, I admit, the bear fights were sort of a stepping-stone for me," said Watts, his face reddening a bit. "But I have expanded into a complete carnival-type entertainment

173

enterprise!" He spread his hands. "We are sweeping the Eastern towns and might very well be heading for jolly old England come next spring!"

"I suppose the bear fights still draw a sizable audience?" Shaw said.

"Yes, that's true, but —"

"No, thank you, Watts," said Shaw. He slid the card back in front of Otto Watts, then stood up, letting him know the conversation was over.

Dawson started to stand up too, but Shaw placed a hand on his shoulder. "Finish your coffee, Dawson," he said quietly. "I'm going to step upstairs to my room." He looked at Otto Watts and Ladelphia. "If you will both excuse me."

Dawson could tell by the look on Watts's face that he was bursting to say more, to try to pitch Shaw the idea of traveling with his troupe. But Shaw's stern expression discouraged him.

When Shaw was out of the dining room, Watts picked up a white napkin and wiped it across his forehead, saying to Dawson, "I wish you would relay my offer to Mr. Shaw, sir . . . perhaps at a time when he is more receptive?" He slid the card across the table to Cray Dawson, who only stared down at it.

"He meant what he said." Dawson looked back and forth between Watts and the woman and raised his coffee cup to his lips. "I reckon he feels the same way I do about bearbaiting. I have no use for it."

"Mr. Dawson," said Ladelphia, her voice dropping to a seductive tone, "is there anything I can do tonight that would make you change your mind?"

Dawson set his cup down and just stared at her.

Outside the dining room Lawrence Shaw had lingered for a moment, hearing what Otto Watts and the woman had to say. At the sound of Dawson's reply to Watts, and Ladelphia's alluring question, Shaw shook his head as he walked to the stairs and climbed them with a trace of a smile. He wondered for a moment what Cray Dawson's response would be. He liked the way Dawson had handled Watts. The more he saw of Cray Dawson the better he felt about riding with him. Dawson struck him as a good man to have by his side. He knew there were more things that had to be talked about between them, but they would come when they were supposed to, when the time was right. Shaw was certain there was still some rough road ahead before he settled accounts with Barton

Talbert and his gang.

At the top of the stairs Lawrence Shaw turned toward his room, but then stopped with his hand on the doorknob when he heard Della Starks whisper his name. Turning, he saw her standing in her doorway, wearing a French evening gown. She cut a glance back and forth to make sure no one was around, then gave him a welcoming nod. "I've been waiting for you," she whispered, watching him step quietly to her door, then past her into the candlelit room. Closing the door softly, she leaned back against it and said in a hushed, breathless tone, "I thought you'd never get here!" Behind her Shaw heard her lock the door. Then she stepped forward and he wrapped his arms around her.

They kissed long and deep, and when it ended he still held her, lingering cheek-to-cheek. Shaw whispered, "You missed a good dinner. You should have been there."

"I know," she said, her voice trembling in anticipation. "But I was too hungry for other things to bother with eating." The two pulled away from each other enough to walk to the bedroom.

She fell back onto the big feather bed and threw open her gown wantonly. "Come here, you big gunman . . . I'm on fire."

Shaw stared into her eyes, but took his time, taking off his gun belt and pitching it past her, up by the pillows. He unbuttoned his shirt, took it off, and dropped it on a small stuffed footstool.

"For God's sake, Lawrence!" she said, cupping her breasts toward him, sucking air between her lips as if she were in pain. "Come on down here this instant!"

He did.

Chapter 10

In the night, Shaw awakened with a start at the sound of a pistol shot resounding from somewhere deep in his unconsciousness. He sat up on the side of the bed in the silent darkness, running his hands back through his sweat-dampened hair.

"Lawrence," Della whispered, her hand coming around his waist, lying on his thigh, "what's wrong?"

"Nothing, Rosa — I mean, Della. Go . . . go on back to sleep," he said haltingly. But she only scooted over closer to him, her arm going farther around him, encircling him as she slid upright behind him, her hand rubbing the center of his chest.

"Hey, it's all right. I'm Della, remember?" she whispered, her lips caressing his ear as she spoke. "You're safe here."

"Sorry," Shaw said, still shaken slightly by a dream that had already vanished except for its terrible lingering intensity. "I must have slept too soundly."

"I know," she said, "you had a bad dream. But it's gone now." She soothed him with her lips, her hands, her body warm against his back. "Look at you; you're shivering like it's cold." She coaxed him back into the bed and down beside her, drawing a blanket across them both.

"I'll be all right," he said, relaxing against her, feeling her breasts hot against him, her body warm against the length of him.

"Yes, you will," she whispered. "Here, let me hold you. I want to hold you and take care of you." She pressed his face to her bosom and they lay in silence for a moment, Shaw feeling her hands upon him like warm velvet gloves. Then she whispered, "I want you to stay here with me, and I want to take care of you."

"Della," Shaw said softly, "you know that I'm on the trail. I can't stop until this thing is settled."

"I know," she said. "I won't try to stop you. I know what you have to do. But when it's over, Lawrence, I want you to come back to me. Will you come back to me?"

Shaw didn't answer, yet somehow his silence gave her reason to create an image of the two of them together. "Just think," she whispered, "you and me, with all the time in the world, all the money we'll ever need. We can go to Europe. We can live in

New York. You won't have to do anything . . . but accompany me, of course." She drew delicate circles on his warm back with her finger as she spoke. "We'll have everything two people could possibly want."

"It sounds wonderful," Shaw whispered.

"Then you'll do it?" she said, sounding hopeful. "You'll come back here to me?"

A silence passed; then Shaw said, "Yes, I'll come back to you. We'll travel; we'll do all those things."

"Oh, Lawrence." She held him tighter. "It *will* be wonderful! You'll see." She began making plans aloud. "Of course, I'll maintain the pretense of being the Widow Starks. We'll say you are my personal assistant . . . a gentleman bodyguard, so to speak. We'll have a room for you, a whole suite of rooms. But that will just be for show, just until we can manage to get you a title of some sort."

"A title?" Shaw asked.

"Yes, a title," she replied. "Or at least a legitimate calling, say cattle rancher, or land investor."

"I see," said Shaw.

Catching a different note to his voice, Della said, "Well, I know you don't want to be thought of as a gunman for the rest of your life, do you?"

"No," said Shaw, "I sure don't." He considered it, lying warm against her firm, ample breasts. "A title, huh? How about, Lawrence Shaw, principal of Shaw Enterprises? That sounds important, but really doesn't say much of anything."

"We'll think about it," Della said, kissing his face, his neck.

"And this suite of rooms," Shaw said, "I suppose it will be close to yours but not so much so that anyone will know we're sleeping together?"

"Right," she said. "At first, anyway. Later, who knows . . . we might go ahead and let everybody know. We can be daring and progressive, scandalous even." She giggled playfully. "I think the public enjoys a certain element of lusty wickedness now and then."

"I like it," said Shaw, nuzzling her, kissing her as he spoke. "I can keep a suite of rooms and be a kept man . . . property of Della Starks."

"Wait," said Della, nudging him away an inch. "You're not angry, are you? I didn't mean to offend you."

Shaw chuckled. "No, I'm not angry, Della, not in the least. Hell, that's the best offer I've had in a *long*, long time." He drew her back against him and held her tightly, staring across her naked shoulder into the deep, endless darkness of the room.

Early in the morning, Shaw slipped out of bed without awakening her and dressed in the silver morning light through the window. He and Cray Dawson had breakfast by themselves in the large dining room. Dawson didn't ask why Della Starks hadn't joined them for breakfast. He'd already gotten the idea that while the woman wanted Shaw to share her bed, she was a bit hesitant about being seen with him. When the Jenkinses had served breakfast and left the dining room, Dawson said to Shaw, "When you asked me to stay here last night and finish my coffee . . . did you know Ladelphia was going to make a play for me, to try and get me to influence you?"

Buttering a biscuit, Shaw offered a trace of a smile. "She did that? She made a play for you?" he asked instead of answering Dawson's question.

Dawson studied him for a second. "Yes, she did," he said.

"And you think I might have known she was going to?" said Shaw. He laid his butter knife down, took a bite of the biscuit, and gave Dawson a flat expression, his eyes revealing nothing.

"It crossed my mind," said Dawson, already seeing that Shaw wasn't going to give him an answer. Shaw was good at letting things hang, making a person come to his own conclusion, be it right or wrong.

"We'll be on the trail by daylight," said Shaw, distancing himself from the subject.

"Can I say something?" said Cray Dawson.

Shaw just stared at him.

"I don't need anybody setting things up for me when it comes to a woman," Dawson said firmly. "So if you did that . . . I'd appreciate it kindly if you didn't do it again. All right?"

"All right," said Shaw, sipping his coffee, still giving no indication whether he'd done it or not. "Do you have Watts's card?" he asked, taking another bite of biscuit.

Dawson lowered his eyes. "Yeah, I've got it somewhere . . . just in case you ever happened to want it." He sipped his coffee again, then said, "For what it's worth, I'm glad you didn't let Watts's proposition spoil the evening. I thought we were just having a good ol' dinner among sociable folks. I never saw it coming, him waiting to shanghai you into working for a . . . whatever it is."

"A circus," said Shaw, "a bearbaiting show full of exhibitionists and oddities."

He shrugged. "It was just another job offer. I can spot them coming a mile away. Most times it's gun work of a different type . . . somebody they want taken down a notch, or in some cases even killed. There was a time when I took on jobs like that, and I made a good living at it. But not anymore." Shaw seemed to consider it for a moment, then said, "It's not the first time I've been propositioned to join a circus." He seemed to consider something. "Hell, it's not even the *last* time, come to think of it."

"What do you mean by that?" Dawson asked.

"Nothing," said Shaw, "just thinking out loud. Everybody wants a watchdog, but nobody wants his fleas."

Dawson gave him a curious look, getting the idea that something had happened between Shaw and Della Starks during the night. "Can I say something?" he asked again, seeing the sullen look on Shaw's face.

"That's twice you've asked me." Shaw stared at him.

"You could do something else," said Dawson. "Something besides being a gunman, that is."

"Yeah? What?" Shaw asked.

"I don't know . . . something, though," Dawson said.

"It's all I know. It's all I was ever any good at," said Shaw.

"You could *learn* something else," said Dawson. "I remember in school you weren't thickheaded. And working the ranches around town, and breaking horses alongside me. You did a good day's work same as the next. You weren't lazy . . . you just never seemed interested in anything besides drawing a gun and shooting it."

"I know it," Shaw said, this time with a trace of a tired smile. "See, that's what I mean. Gun handling is all that ever came to me naturally . . . it's all that ever held my interest." As he spoke he shoved his empty plate away from him and turned up the last drink from his coffee cup. Dismissing the subject, he said, "I'll go tell Della good-bye and meet you at the barn." He stood up. "It might take a few minutes." Seeing the look on Dawson's face, Shaw added, "It's expected of me."

Dawson shook his head, saying, "Um-hm," under his breath.

"What's that supposed to mean?" Shaw asked.

"Nothing," said Dawson, standing up himself. "If it's *expected* of you, I reckon you best go get it done. I'll go get the horses ready."

Dawson left the Desert Flower Inn and took his time preparing the horses for the trail. A half hour had passed when he'd arrived back at the hitch rail out front of the inn, leading Shaw's buckskin by its reins. Another five minutes passed before Shaw stepped out onto the boardwalk carrying his hat in his left hand. The sun had begun to break over the eastern edge of the earth. As Shaw placed his hat atop his head and stepped down from the boardwalk, Sheriff Neff called out, "Shaw! I want to talk to you."

Shaw and Dawson both turned at the sound of the sheriff's voice and saw him walking slowly across the street toward them, a rifle cocked and held in a fire-from-the-hip position. Behind the sheriff two of the town councilmen stood watching. "What's this all about?" Dawson asked Shaw under his breath, his hand poised near his pistol butt.

"Easy does it," Shaw replied to Dawson. "It looks like he's just needing to make a show before we leave . . . let everybody know he's worth his keep."

"Shaw, you're not welcome here anymore," said Neff, stopping fifteen feet away, appearing to take a stand. "I want you and your friend to get out of my town."

"Yep," Shaw whispered sidelong to Dawson, "this is just a formality. I'll give him what he needs." He raised his voice. "I don't want no trouble, Sheriff," Shaw said, making it a point to lift his gun hand away from his holster. "We're not breaking any law."

Even as Shaw played along with the sheriff's farce, he kept his senses tuned warily toward the roofline, the alleyways, and the councilmen themselves.

"I know you're not, Shaw," said Neff. "But there's already been killing and there's apt to be more if I don't make you clear out of here." Without making any menacing move with the rifle, the sheriff said, "Now get in your saddle and ride."

Shaw nodded toward a restaurant up the street and said, "Sheriff, can't we at least go have breakfast first?"

"No," said Neff. "You can stop and eat alongside the trail. Now get going. This is my town and I run it free of gunfighters."

"All right, Sheriff, you win," said Shaw. "We're leaving." Without making any sudden moves he stepped around the buckskin and up into his saddle. "Sorry for the trouble," he said, touching his hat brim as the two turned their horses toward the end of town.

The sheriff nodded and stood stonelike in the middle of the street until Shaw and Dawson rode past the town-limits sign.

"Well," said Dawson, glancing back over his shoulder as they rode away, "that beats all I ever seen. He had to know we were already on our way out of town."

"Sure he knew it," said Shaw matter-of-factly. "The councilmen had to see it too. But it made everybody look good . . . and it didn't cost us a thing." He gave his buckskin a nudge with his boot heels and quickened its pace. Dawson shook his head and stayed a step back from him.

They rode to the fork in the trail and had started to head north when Shaw looked back and said, "Somebody's following us from town."

Dawson looked back at the rise of dust along the flatland, but he wouldn't have had to see the dust; a hundred yards away a lone rider had come up out of a dip in the land and rode toward them, waving a bowler hat back and forth in the air. "It's Caldwell," said Dawson.

"I might have known," said Lawrence Shaw, turning his mount a bit, ready to ride away. "It looks like everywhere we go we're going to have that undertaker hanging around behind us."

"I swear I'd almost forgotten all about him," said Dawson.

"I can see why. He's not an easy man to remember," Shaw said, gazing toward Caldwell with no interest.

"Shouldn't we hold up to see what he wants?" Dawson asked, seeing Shaw was ready to ride on.

"Why?" said Shaw. "It's not likely he'll miss us." But he stayed the animal anyway, and lifted his canteen from his saddle horn and drank from it while Jedson Caldwell raced his horse along the trail.

Reaching them, Caldwell slid his horse to a halt and turned it sideways on the trail facing them. "Whew!" he said, "for a while there I thought I'd lost you fellows." He fanned himself with his bowler hat and caught his breath. "Do either of you mind if I tag along a ways farther? I'm not ashamed to tell you that I'm afraid to travel alone out here."

Dawson and Shaw looked at him, noting that both his eyes were black and his nose was swollen and bruised. Neither of them said it was all right for him to ride with them, but neither of them turned him away. "What in the world happened to your face, Caldwell?" Dawson asked.

"Oh, this," said Caldwell, playing his injury down. "It's nothing, really. The barber I helped prepare the dead did this to me." He offered a painful smile. "Apparently he considered my offer of services to be competitive to his business. He was friendly as could be while there was folks around . . . and not too hard to get along with while I washed the bodies and covered their wounds. But once I'd done most of the work, he grew belligerent . . . then abusive, as you can see." He gestured a hand at his bruised and battered face.

Showing no interest in Caldwell, Shaw gave Dawson a flat expression, capped his canteen, and turned his buckskin back to the trail. But Dawson stayed beside Caldwell, the two following Shaw a few feet behind. "Is it all right with him, me coming along?" asked Jedson Caldwell.

"It's all right," said Dawson. "Just stay out of his way."

"Where are we headed?" Caldwell asked.

Dawson checked his expression as he said, "We're heading after Willie the Devil and Elton Minton, the two who left town in such a hurry yesterday."

"Oh," said Caldwell, seeming concerned. "So there could be shooting if you catch up to them?"

"I believe that's a possibility," said Dawson. "Are you game for that when it comes down to it?"

"Well, I would be," said Caldwell with hesitancy, "except that barber took away the gun you gave me. Do either of you have another one?"

"No, that was the only spare I could come up with," said Dawson.

Listening, Shaw slowed his buckskin, reached inside his saddlebags, and took out the Colt he'd taken off of Sammy Boy White. He held it out at arm's length and gave it to Jedson Caldwell. "Whatever you do, Caldwell," Shaw said, "you better not lose that gun."

Caldwell looked frightened, saying, "Wait a minute, Mr. Shaw! Perhaps I'd better not take it then!"

"Take it," said Shaw forcefully, riding on without looking back at him. "Just don't lose it." Then he said to Cray Dawson, "Why don't you teach him how to shoot that gun first chance you get? It might make the world safer for all of us."

"What did he say?" Caldwell asked Dawson, sounding jittery.

"Never mind," said Dawson, gigging his horse forward. "We've got a long, hot ride ahead of us. Just relax and take it easy."

191

PART
Two

Chapter 11

Barton Talbert stood on the abandoned gallows at Brakett Flats and looked south toward the Anacacho mountain line. It had been almost an hour since he'd first spotted the two thin, wavering figures riding toward town in the scalding midday heat. The first thing he'd said to Blue Snake Terril, who sat beside him, one haunch perched sidelong on the gallows rail, was, "Where's Bo Kregger?"

"He was out behind the old cemetery a while ago," Blue Snake said, squinting toward the two distant riders.

"What's he doing back there?" Talbert asked.

"Shooting cans," said Blue Snake. "Didn't you hear him?"

"Oh, yeah, that's right," said Talbert. "I wasn't thinking there for a second." He tossed a glance toward the cemetery, from where three shots rang out in rapid succession.

Blue Snake looked him up and down, realizing how nervous and preoccupied he'd been lately. Then he looked back out toward the riders, saying sarcastically, almost to himself, "Kregger must figure if Fast Larry Shaw shows up and throws some cans at him, he wants to be prepared."

"I know you've got no use for him, Snake," said Talbert, "but the plain, simple fact is, we need Bo Kregger."

"Like hell," said Blue Snake. "I can handle Shaw."

"I'm not saying you can't," said Barton Talbert, "and like as not you'll get a chance to prove it before this is over. But I'm saying we need somebody like Bo Kregger just in case you *can't* handle him. Fast Larry Shaw is still the fastest gun alive."

Blue Snake spit and shook his head. "This whole thing is such a stupid mess, anyway. None of it should have happened. You go out of your way to stop by a man's house to pay him your respect; damned if you don't wind up killing his wife. What are the odds of something like that happening? You idolized the man! Now he's out to kill you."

"You know I idolized him, and I know I idolized him," said Talbert. "The problem is, Shaw ain't going to hear of this all being a terrible situation that got out of control." He also shook his head slightly, recalling the event in his mind. "How do you tell a man you killed his wife but didn't mean to?"

"Just like that," said Blue Snake, giving a slight shrug. "You say, 'Shaw we killed your wife but we didn't mean to.' If that won't stick, then you settle with him, man-to-man. You don't go hire some other gunman to take care of your business for you. It's my belief that all these fast guns are a little *loco* to begin with. The less you get tangled up in their world, the better off you are. I might be nothing but a damn half-breed outlaw and cattle rustler, but I'm smart enough to stay away from those crazy jackrabbit gunfighters."

"Well, she's dead, and I can't call it back and change it," said Talbert with a sigh of finality. "We got to deal with Shaw and get it done." He stared harder at the riders through the shimmering heat. "I almost wish that *was* him coming."

"So do I," said Blue Snake, studying the figures closely as they neared, "but it ain't; it's the Devil."

"That's what I thought too," said Barton Talbert. They watched in silence for a moment; then Talbert reaffirmed, saying, "Yep, it's the Devil, all right. But that's not Brother Sidlow with him." There was a sound of concern in his voice.

"No sign of Donald Hornetti either," said Blue Snake, the long tails of his bright Mexican neck scarf fluttering on a hot Texas breeze. Around Blue Snake's neck a strip of rawhide held a Colt .45 hanging down his chest like some religious object. He wore black leather gloves with the fingers and thumbs cut off. His own fingers were ingrained with dirt and black gun oil. His thumbnails were painted bright blue but badly flaking. "Who's this peckerwood beside him?"

"I'm wondering that myself," said Talbert. He slapped a sand flea that had worked its way up through the wiry beard stubble on his cheek. Then he picked the dead flea off and flipped it away. Watching Willie the Devil and Elton Minton ride onto the main street, Talbert said, "I told the Devil not to bring me anything but good news about my brother. . . . Let's go see what's he got."

"It ain't good, I'm already thinking," said Blue Snake, rising from the gallows rail.

Turning and walking down the gallows steps, they looked at two small boys who swung back and forth, playing on the hangman's rope, each supported by one bare foot in the noose. The rope creaked eerily with each pass. On the bottom step a dark bloodstain marked a time long past when someone had killed the hangman, dragged him from his gallows into an alley, and stuffed him headfirst down into a rain barrel.

"You kids get the hell out of here," said Talbert to the two boys. Then he called out to the empty storefronts and closed doors and windows, "Somebody better get these knothead kids out of here! I bet I end up pistol-whipping some mommies and daddies in a minute!" He looked menacingly along the deserted boardwalks, where the only sign of life was an occasional gunman who leaned against a pole with a rifle in his arm and a bottle of whiskey hanging in his hand. The buildings were silent as stone except for the small saloon, where both large windows had been busted from the inside and shards of glass littered the street. Beyond the broken windows a banjo played feverishly, its rhythm speeded up and goaded on by random gunshots and loud laughter.

On their way toward the two approaching riders, Talbert and Blue Snake saw a dark-haired woman run out from a building with a worried look on her face. She chastised the two boys loudly in Spanish and shooed them away from the gallows with both hands. *"Gracias, Mamacita,"* Talbert sneered at her. "Now keep them the hell out of my hair! If I wanted to be aggravated by kids, I've got a dozen of my own scattered out some-damn-where!"

The widely flared legs of Blue Snake's Mexican vaquero trousers stirred a low swirl of dust at his boot heels. His big Mexican spurs rang out like small bells with each step. By the time they had gone fifteen yards, a couple of the gunmen had stepped down from the boardwalk and joined them. "What's the deal coming here?" one gunman asked, nodding toward Willie the Devil and Elton Minton as they slowed their tired horses to a walk.

"Beats, me, Curley," said Blue Snake, his hand around the bone handle of the pistol hanging around his neck. "You've seen as much as I have."

Curley Tomes noted Blue Snake's hand, flaking painted nail and all, and he tightened his grip on the rifle cradled in his arm. Another gunman drifted in beside Curley Tomes and asked in a lowered voice, "What's the hash, Curley?"

Curley gave him a barbed sidelong glance. "Do I look like I know every damn thing, Stanley?"

"Pardon the hell out of me then," said Stanley Little.

As Willie the Devil and Elton Minton halted their horses and started to step down into the middle of the street, Barton Talbert said, "Don't even get out of the saddle unless you've got some good news for me, Devil."

Willie the Devil stopped midmotion, swung his leg back over the saddle, and sat down. "It's all bad, Bart," Willie said, letting out a breath of dread.

Barton Talbert gave Blue Snake a look, then said, "Get on down, Willie. Tell me everything."

This time Willie and Elton both stepped down. Elton looked around nervously at the gunmen staring at him. "Who is this scarecrow?" Blue Snake asked, sizing Elton up with a sneer of contempt.

"This is Elton Minton, Bart," said Willie the Devil, addressing Barton Talbert directly instead of answering Blue Snake.

"Where's my brother?" Talbert asked, barely giving Elton a glance.

Taking his hat off, Willie the Devil shook his lowered head. "Bart, ol' pard, I hate to say it, but poor Sidlow is dead . . . there was nothing we could do about it. Not one damn thing."

"What? You lying son of a bitch!" Barton Talbert shoved him hard, causing him to lift his lowered head and hold both hands out to keep Talbert back away from him.

"Please, Bart! Listen to me!" Willie pleaded, seeing Talbert's hand snap tight around his gun butt. "It's the truth; we couldn't help him!"

"Who killed him?" Talbert hissed. "That damned Sheriff Neff? I'm going right now to that little pig rut of a town and shoot his eyes out!"

"Uh, no," said Willie, "it wasn't Neff. It was Fast Larry Shaw."

A sick look came over Barton Talbert's face, but he tried to hide it. "Oh . . ." His word trailed off as he considered it. Then he said, "Fast Larry Shaw be damned! I'm still going to Eagle Pass. Shaw's going to pay!" He spoke loudly enough for all the gathering gunmen to hear him, yet there seemed to be less iron in his tone than there had been only a moment earlier. "How did it happen? Face-to-face? One-on-one? Everything on the up-and-up?"

Willie shook his head. "I swear I can't say, the way it all happened so fast. Me and Hornetti had already set up a way to kill Fast Larry," he continued, not giving the details in the exact sequence in which they happened. "Neff was escorting Sidlow to the jake, if you can believe the sheriff's version. But then ol' Sidlow, God love him, he tried to make a break for it, like any free-thinking man would do! And that damned Fast Larry saw him and shot him over and over in the worst sort of way!" Willie seemed to be on the verge of weeping. "It was terrible! And there was me and Hornetti, couldn't do a thing about it. I was sickened by it!"

"Where is Hornetti?" asked Blue Snake, looking around as if the man might suddenly appear.

"He's dead too," said Willie the Devil. "Fast Larry's pard shot him dead. Poor Donald fell all the way from a window atop the saloon."

"Shaw's pard?" said Talbert. "You mean Shaw's got somebody riding with him? Another slick gunfighter, I reckon?"

"Oh, yes, no doubt about it," said Willie, "this man is just as cold-blooded and lightning-fast as Shaw! It would have been nothing short of suicide for me to try to take them both. Shaw called out to everybody around that if they rode with you they were fair game. Said he wanted you to know what happened to Sidlow. Sounded like he's out for a showdown, just like we figured. I ran into Mace Renfield and some pards of his in Turkey Wells on our way here. I know Mace has been aching to kill Shaw for a long time. Maybe he'll just up and do it, save us some trouble."

"Yeah," said Barton Talbert, "*maybe . . .* but I can't chance hanging my hat on a maybe."

"I know," said Willie, "and it's a damn shame what Shaw done to those two good men . . . both Donald and Sidlow shot down in their prime! I tell you again I was sickened by the whole thing!"

"You seem to sicken pretty easy for a man who doesn't do much," said a deep voice from off to the right of the other gunmen.

"Who the hell said that?" Willie asked, incensed by such an insult.

"Bo Kregger," the voice said bluntly. Now Willie saw the broad shoulders and the long-hanging riding duster step forward, the other gunmen giving this man plenty of room. "If you didn't understand it, I'll say it again."

Willie looked at Barton Talbert, then at Blue Snake. "I asked him to ride with us, Willie, just because of Fast Larry Shaw," said Barton Talbert.

"Yeah, he asked," said Bo Kregger to

Willie the Devil, "but I haven't gave an answer yet. I was doubting this is the kind of men I want my name associated with." He looked Willie up and down. "Listening to you, I doubt it even more."

"I've heard a lot about you, Bo Kregger," said Willie, making sure his hands came up a good distance from his gun butt. "I'm not a big gunslinger . . . I don't want no trouble."

"I've heard a lot about you too, Willie the Devil," said Kregger with contempt. "But nothing yet that makes me think you're anything but a bummer and a low backshooting coward."

Willie glowed red, but wasn't about to backtalk the gunman. He looked at Talbert and said, "I don't deserve to be treated this way, Bart . . . as far as we go back together? Huh-uh. It just ain't right."

"We've only known one another a year or so, Willie," Barton Talbert said with a shrug. "I don't call that going far back together, do you, Bo?"

"No," said the fierce-looking gunman. "I call that a short spell. Not long enough for him to want to save your brother from Fast Larry Shaw, anyway." He stared coldly at Willie the Devil until Willie grew so rattled he began to sweat and shake all over.

"All right," said Willie, "maybe I could have done more. But the fact is, I had a deal going with this peckerwood and a friend of his named Sammy Boy White. Sammy was supposed to kill Fast Larry, but that plan went plumb out the window and Shaw nailed him too. And that was with Donald Hornetti ambushing him! I tell you, that Shaw ain't human, he's so fast! So all right, maybe I was a little afraid I might get killed too. Does anybody blame me?" His eyes searched the unyielding faces of the gunmen, who offered him no sign of support.

"Everybody here thought the world of Sidlow, Willie," said Curley Tomes. Beside him Stanley Little nodded in agreement. Next to Stanley stood Denver Jack Fish, Jesse Turnbaugh, Bobby Fitt, and the Furlin brothers, Harper and Gladso. The group nodded solemnly as one.

Bo Kregger took on a more serious look. "Did you say Sammy Boy White?" he asked Willie.

"Yep, that was his name," said Willie. "Do you know him?" he asked Kregger, feeling the heat lessen on him a bit.

"Yeah, I know him," said Kregger. "Sammy Boy White was damn good with a gun. That's a known fact."

"Better than you?" asked Talbert.

"I wouldn't go so far as to say that," said Bo Kregger. "But if Fast Larry killed Sammy Boy White, I have to respect the man a little bit more."

"I don't know if Sammy Boy was dead or alive when we hightailed it," said Willie the Devil. "But he came in second place against Fast Larry . . . so did a crazy bartender named Porter something or other."

"It wasn't Porter Chapin, was it?" Bo Kregger asked.

Barton Talbert looked disgusted with Willie, knowing that every time he mentioned somebody fast whom Shaw had killed, Bo Kregger's price as a hired gun was going to get higher.

"Yep, that's his name," said Willie. He looked at Elton Minton for confirmation, and Elton nodded his head vigorously.

"Damn . . ." Bo Kregger rubbed his chin in contemplation. "Sammy Boy White, Porter Chapin. What the hell is Shaw so worked up about?"

"Never mind," said Barton Talbert. Then, with a snap of sarcasm, he said to Willie the Devil, "Tell me something, Willie: Is there anybody left in Eagle Pass that Fast Larry didn't kill . . . or is the whole damn town dead?"

"Hold it!" said Bo Kregger to Talbert, before Willie had time to reply. "Did you just tell me *never mind?*" He took a menacing step forward. "Maybe you forgot who you're talking to. Nobody tells me *never mind.*"

Talbert stood fast, but said apologetically, "No offense, Bo; I've just got a lot on my mind lately. I suppose you never heard all the way up in Silver Wreath. There was a terrible thing that happened to Fast Larry's wife, and he blames all of us for it."

"Oh?" Bo Kregger gave a dubious look. "What kind of terrible thing?"

"Well, the fact is, we killed her," said Talbert.

"Whew," said Kregger, "I bet he is angry over that." He gave Talbert a strange look, then said, "Were you going to tell me about it at some point or other?"

"I just did," said Talbert.

"You know what I mean," said Kregger. He pushed up his hat brim and backed away from amid the gunmen. "I want nothing to do with this. As far as I'm concerned, if you men killed Shaw's wife, he's got every right in the world to hunt you down, skin you, and salt you." He looked around at his horse standing free-rein at a hitch rail. He let out a short, sharp whistle and the big, fancy paint horse came trotting to his side.

"Wait a minute, Kregger," said Talbert. "I need your gun hand. I'm talking about good money!"

"How good?" said Kregger, reaching up and taking the horse's reins from around the silver-trimmed saddle horn.

"One thousand dollars!" said Talbert. "Paid upon delivery."

"Bull," said Kregger, raising his boot to the stirrup, "a thousand is what we agreed to in the first place."

"That's right," said Talbert, "one thousand dollars is what we agreed to. That's what you said you always get, and I accept it."

"That was before you told me what this was all about," said Kregger, stepping up into the saddle. "If I was to take this job on at all, it would have to be for twice that amount."

"Two thousand dollars?" said Talbert, sounding outraged. "Just to back us up so we can get the drop on the man?"

Without answering, Kregger turned his big paint and started to put his heels to its sides.

"All right then, hold it, damn it!" said Talbert. "Two thousand it is."

Kregger smiled to himself, then backed the horse and looked down at Talbert, saying firmly, "That's one thousand dollars now . . . another thousand when I nail his shirt to his chest."

"All right," said Talbert, looking embarrassed in front of his men. "We've got a deal then?"

"Absolutely," said Bo Kregger. He stepped down from his saddle, wrapped the horse's reins loosely around the saddle horn, and gave the animal a short slap on its rump. The paint horse trotted over and stopped at the hitch rail. "Let's go have a drink to it, while you count out my first thousand."

"All right," said Talbert. "After that we head out of here."

"Why?" asked Bo Kregger as they started walking to the saloon. "What's your hurry? If Shaw is on his way here, what better chance will we ever have to kill him?" He grinned. "I find it is always better to have a person come to me than it is to ride all over hell looking for him."

"I can go along with that," said Talbert, thinking it over. "Yeah," he concluded, "who the hell is Shaw that I should have to go looking for him? If he wants me let him come and get me."

"Who knows," said Kregger, "the way everybody is always looking to kill a big gun like Shaw, it could take him a long time to get here. He might not even get here at all. Every place he stops there'll be somebody wanting to put him down in the street. Somebody could be standing over him right now, putting that next bullet straight down into his eyeball."

"Damn right," said Talbert, getting more and more confident as they crossed the dirt street toward the saloon. "He could already be dead, for all I know!"

Following Talbert and Bo Kregger to the saloon, leading their tired horses behind them, Elton sidled up close to Willie the Devil and said, "Now that it looks like everything is all right for you here, can I go?"

"Sit tight, Elton; what's your hurry?" said Willie without facing him.

"I've got no business here," said Elton. "You fellows have your own way of doing things. I'd just as soon not get involved, no offense."

"You ain't going nowhere until I say you can go," said Willie. "Since your boy Sammy was such a letdown, who knows, I might have you fighting Fast Larry before it's over."

"Please, Mr. Devlin," said Elton, "I can't take this kind of living. I'm no gunman, no outlaw!"

"Don't wet yourself, Elton." Willie chuckled. "I was only funning you." He stared at Bo Kregger's back as Kregger walked along with Barton Talbert and the others in front of them. "But seriously, let me ask you this, Elton. You saw Shaw shoot those boys in Eagle Pass." He nodded with contempt at Bo Kregger. "Do you think this bag of wet crackers would stand a chance against him?"

Elton considered the question for a second, then said, "That's hard to call . . . but if I was going to bet on Kregger, you'd have to give me some strong odds, make it worth my risk."

"Yeah," said the Devil, tweaking his thin mustache with a crafty grin, "that's sort of what I thought." He hooked an arm up around Elton's shoulder and gave him a slap on his back. In a lowered voice he said, "You did good keeping your mouth shut about the money. Far as I'm concerned there's nothing in this world that means as much as having a good fat roll of cash in your pocket."

"To be honest, Willie," said Elton, "I've always sort of felt that way myself."

"No kidding!" The Devil seemed genuinely moved. "My *amigo*, stick with me. It looks like we might just have ourselves a match in the making."

Chapter 12

"Let the shot come as a surprise to your ears," said Cray Dawson, cocking the Colt in his hand. "That way your nerves don't have time to flinch at the sound of it."

The pistol bucked, the explosion sending a streak of smoke and blue-orange fire from the tip of the barrel. Ten yards away where a line of rocks lay on the sun-bleached carcass of a downed pinyon tree, a rock shattered as it jumped into the air. Before the pieces of it landed another shot exploded, another rock shattered and jumped, then another. Jedson Caldwell held his fingers in his ears until Cray Dawson lowered the pistol and looked over at him. "I-I see," Caldwell said haltingly. "Maybe if I stuck some cotton in my ears? Think that would help?"

Dawson just stared at him. Then he opened the Colt, took out the spent cartridges, replaced them, and closed the cylinder. He held it out on the flat of his hand toward Caldwell, the barrel pointed in the direction of the rock targets. "Come over and give it a try."

"Uh, all right," said the young under-taker hesitantly, taking a look around as if to make sure no one was watching. A few feet above them on a slope down from the trail stood Lawrence Shaw, holding the reins to his big buckskin, watching with an air of detachment. "You fellows won't laugh, will you?" He slid a quick glance to Shaw, then looked away.

Dawson gave Shaw a look, then said to Caldwell, "No, we won't laugh. There's nothing funny about it. It's a *gun* . . . you're learning to shoot it. Everybody has to start somewhere."

"Well, that's true," said Jedson Caldwell, stepping over and taking the Colt in his right hand. He held it out at arm's length. Unprepared for the weight of the big Colt, his wrist let it droop until Dawson reached out and raised it.

"Now do what you need to do to take your shot," said Dawson, taking a step back from him and giving Shaw a glance, seeing his flat expression.

"Here goes," said Caldwell. He squeezed the trigger back steadily, but still flinched a bit. When it didn't fire, he let out a breath, looking embarrassed, and said to Cray Dawson, "I forgot to cock it."

"I see you did," said Dawson, being patient with him. "Don't get rattled; take your time . . . this is practice. Aim it like I showed you . . . keep both eyes open."

Caldwell tried to cock the big Colt, but he'd already been holding it out too long. The weight of it caused his arm to tremble. He lowered the pistol, switched it to his left hand, shook out his right hand, and wiped his moist palm on his trouser leg. "It got too heavy for me!" He offered a weak grin, then took the gun into his right hand again, cocked it, and raised it. "Here goes."

It took him a long time to get the Colt aimed; then he squeezed the trigger slowly, far too slowly. But when it fired, Dawson was watching his eyes. He didn't flinch until after the shot was made. The bullet fell short by three inches, but when it struck the pinyon log, the impact caused the rock above it to fall to the ground. "Hey!" Caldwell beamed. "At least I moved it! Does that count?"

Dawson smiled thinly. "No, but if that had been a man you would have hit him. That counts."

"Oh . . ." Caldwell stared at the log as if imagining it had been a man. "My goodness! Somebody would be lying there dead . . . just because of me."

"Maybe not dead," said Dawson, "but hit in an awfully painful bad place, provided you'd been aiming at their belly."

It took Caldwell a second to put it together. When he did, he winced at the thought of it and said, "I hope I never really have to do anything like this."

"We all hope that," said Dawson. "But it's a dangerous world we live in. Take a few more shots."

While Caldwell aimed the pistol again slowly, then fired it, Dawson walked up the slope and stood beside Lawrence Shaw. "There are some people who shouldn't be allowed to even stand near a loaded gun," Shaw said just between them. "It looks like your pard Caldwell is one of them."

"I wouldn't call him my pard," said Dawson. "You asked me to teach him to shoot. That's all I'm doing."

"We might want to leave him behind, next town we come to," said Shaw. "If we don't we'll likely get him killed once we catch up to Talbert and his bunch."

"He seems to really want to ride with us," said Dawson. "I could give him a shotgun."

"He'll shoot one of us," said Shaw. "Or himself, one."

"Let me work with him until we get to

Clearly," said Dawson. "If he's not showing us something by then, we'll cut him loose. At least he'll know enough, maybe he won't have to tolerate a black eye from a town barber."

"That sounds fair enough," said Shaw. "But there are some folks who are going to wear a black eye their whole life. This undertaker might be one of them."

"We'll see," said Dawson, seeing another shot hit the pinyon log. They watched in silence for a second; then Dawson said, "Can I ask something?"

Shaw just looked at him.

"How did you shoot the first time you ever held a gun?" Dawson asked.

"I don't remember any *first time*," said Shaw.

"You weren't born firing a gun, Lawrence," said Dawson. "I remember a time when we were kids and neither one of us had a gun to even shoot a rabbit with."

"I remember that short period of time," said Shaw, "but it didn't last long. As soon as I saw what a powerful influence a gun had on a man's life, I knew I had to have one if I never had anything else." He stared at Caldwell, watching him take aim. "Sometimes it seems like once I got one I never really had anything else."

They stood feeling a hot breeze blow down off the trail above them. "I saw her in town the day before," said Dawson out of the blue.

But Shaw knew he was talking about Rosa, as if the whole of the conversation had been about her all along. "You did, huh?" Shaw said flatly, watching Caldwell closer now, seeming to take a sudden interest.

"Yes," said Dawson, "I saw her out front of the telegraph office. She smiled and spoke to me like she didn't have a care in the world." He turned silent for a moment while a shot rang out from the Colt in Caldwell's hand. This time a rock exploded up into the air and Caldwell let out a short cry of joy.

"There, I got one!" Caldwell called out. "Did you see it? I hit it!"

"Good shot," said Dawson. Then he said to Shaw, "I can't get over how happy she seemed. Do you suppose she might have just gotten a telegraph from you?"

Shaw's jaw tightened, but he didn't answer. Instead he walked a few steps closer to Caldwell, stooped down, picked up a rock, hefted it in his hand, and called out, "Here, Undertaker, hit this."

"Wait up!" said Caldwell. "I'm not ready!" But as the rock sailed upward in a high, slow arc, he adjusted the pistol quickly in his hand, cocked it, and fired, trying to take aim on the rock long after it had passed the high point of its arc and started speeding toward the ground. "Missed it!" he shouted. But the sound of Shaw's Colt roared and shattered the rock as it dropped to shoulder height. Caldwell felt sharp particles sting him from twenty feet away. "Good Lord!" Caldwell shouted. "What a shot!"

Dawson had walked down beside Shaw, and upon seeing the shot he said, "If that was meant to make a powerful impression on him, I think you succeeded."

Shaw stared at the open space in the air where the bullet had struck the rock and blown it into a thousand tiny bits. "You never know if the man you're teaching might be the next one who tries to kill you."

"It ain't been but a few minutes ago you said he shouldn't be allowed to stand near a loaded gun."

"That was before he hit something," said Shaw. He walked back to where he'd dropped his horse's reins on the ground.

"Shaw," said Dawson, "I'm sorry I brought it up, what I said about seeing her in town. I shouldn't have mentioned it."

Shaw only nodded, picked up the reins, and said, "When you two get finished busting rocks we'll ride on into the Turkey Wells station, spend the night, and see which way Willie the Devil went from there." He turned and began to lead the big buckskin up toward the trail.

Caldwell listened, then asked Dawson as Lawrence Shaw led the stallion back up to the trail, "What is the Turkey Wells station, and how do we know those two men went through there?"

"It's a cattle-shack, town near Turkey Mountain," said Dawson. "Turkey Wells gets its water from the west fork of Turkey Creek. The station is the best place around there to swap out tired horses and pick up some snakehead whiskey. They went through there; you can count on it."

"Snakehead whiskey?" Caldwell gave him a dubious look. "I'm almost afraid to ask you why they call it that."

Dawson gave a thin smile, watching Shaw as he walked a few yards ahead of them. "They used to claim the whiskey drummers put rattlesnake heads in the whiskey barrels to give it a little bite. But that was mostly just some hot air blowing." He watched Caldwell reload the Colt, noting that his small, delicate hands had already become

220

more adept at handling the pistol mechanism. "So how does it feel Caldwell, getting the hang of gun-handling?"

"I don't know if I'd say I'm getting the hang of it yet," Caldwell replied, "but I must say, I feel like I've already learned a lot." As he spoke, he closed the cylinder on the Colt and hefted the gun in his hand as if getting a better feel for the weight of it. "I think if I stick with it I could become self-sufficient."

"That's the spirit," said Dawson, watching the young undertaker try to twirl the big Colt on his trigger finger.

The gun made only a half turn before the weight of it caused Caldwell's finger to bend sideways and lose its hold. The pistol fell to the ground, landed on its hammer, and sent a shot whistling wildly toward Lawrence Shaw's back. Before Caldwell even realized what had happened, Shaw had spun with his Colt out and cocked, pointed at him. "No! Please!" Caldwell shouted in terror, looking up at the open bore of Shaw's big Colt, seeing the dead, expressionless look on Shaw's face.

"Shaw, it went off!" Dawson called out in Caldwell's defense. But Shaw had already seen what had happened, and had already lowered the tip of his barrel. His expression was still flat and indiscernible. "Dang it, Caldwell," said Dawson. "Don't try things like that until you get to where you know what you're doing!" He stooped and snatched up the Colt from the rocky ground. "Never keep a full six load . . . always leave one empty, for safety, unless you're in the middle of a shooting situation!"

"I-I'm sorry," said Caldwell, visibly shaken, staring wide-eyed at Lawrence Shaw, seeing the unyielding look on Shaw's face. "Mr. Shaw! Please! This was an accident! I had no idea —"

Shaw cut him off, saying, "Dawson, you better set up to boil some water. Strip up some clean cloth."

"What?" Dawson asked, a puzzled look coming to his face.

"He's put a bullet in me, sure as hell," said Shaw. It took him two tries to slip his Colt into his holster. Only then did Cray Dawson and Jedson Caldwell see the trickle of blood running down the palm of his right hand and dripping to the ground. Shaw raised his left hand around under his right arm and winced in pain.

"Oh, my God! Oh, my God!" Caldwell clasped his hands to his mouth, on the verge of tears. "I'm so sorry! I'm so sorr—"

"Shut up, Caldwell!" Dawson snapped,

hoping to settle him down. "Get a canteen off the horses! Hurry up!"

As Caldwell hurried to the horses, Dawson rushed forward and helped Shaw seat himself on a flat rock. "See what I meant a while ago?" said Shaw with a trace of a wry smile. "The fool's already shot one of us."

"All right, but it was an accident," said Dawson. "I saw it happen."

"I know it was," said Shaw, having difficulty raising his right arm so Dawson could help him get out of his riding coat. "But this is the worst time for it to happen. Of all the luck. I just get over a bullet graze in my *left* shoulder. Now he shoots me in my *right*. That'll be the last I draw my Colt until this thing heals."

Helping Shaw out of his shirt, Dawson remarked, "That was a pretty fast response for a man with a bullet in him."

"Nothing quickens the blood like somebody shooting at you from behind," Shaw said with a slight grunt, lifting his arm again, this time noticing how much his upper arm had already started to swell. "I just wish I knew who to ask. Why the right arm?" He rolled a skeptical glance upward at the wide Texas sky. "Why not the left?"

Caldwell came sliding down beside

Dawson with two canteens, hastily uncapping one and handing it to Shaw. "So help me God, Mr. Shaw," he said, his voice still trembling, "I wouldn't have had this happen for anything in the world!"

Lawrence Shaw gave him his flat stare. "There's hardened gunmen who would give anything they own to say they shot Fast Larry Shaw," he said with a twist of irony in his voice. "You shot me before you even learned not to pack a sixth load."

"Mr. Dawson told me the first thing not to load six unless I knew I was in trouble and needed it . . . I just forgot for a second."

"A second is all it takes with a gun, Caldwell," said Shaw, wincing as Dawson pulled him slightly forward and leaned around, taking a look at the bullet hole just above his right shoulder blade. He also took a glance at the healed but still tender-looking graze on Shaw's left shoulder. Shaking his head, he went back to the fresh wound.

"Did it come out anywhere?" Dawson asked.

"Not that I've seen," said Shaw, feeling around on his chest with his left hand as if making sure he hadn't missed seeing an exit wound.

"Then it looks like you've got some cutting in store soon as we get you to the Turkey Wells station," said Dawson.

"Huh-uh," said Shaw. "I'm not going into that cowhand-shack town letting everybody know I'm not up to myself. I might as well hang a target board around my neck. That's why I said get some water boiling."

"I hate cutting a bullet out," said Dawson. As he spoke he uncapped the other canteen.

"But you have done it?" Shaw asked.

"If I said no would it keep me from having to?" Dawson asked, raising the other canteen and pouring a trickle of water on the bandanna he'd loosened from around Shaw's neck. He touched it carefully to the bleeding bullet hole and held it for a second.

"No, you've got the job," said Shaw, "like it or not."

"That's what I figured," said Dawson, already focusing his attention on the task at hand. He pressed firmly on the bandanna, soaking up the blood from the wound. Then he removed the bandanna and judged how long it took for the wound to well back up with blood. "Looks like it's in there pretty deep," he said. "Probably lodged up against a bone good and tight."

"Whatever it takes," said Shaw, "just get it done. The longer it lays in there, the better my chance at getting blood poisoning."

Dawson turned to Caldwell. "Start us a fire and get some water boiling. Then unsaddle the horses and let them graze awhile. When I get the knife ready, you'll have to help hold him down while I cut in there and get the bullet out."

"No, he won't," said Shaw. "This ain't the first bullet I've had in me. I don't require holding."

"Suit yourself," said Dawson.

Caldwell built a small fire out of mesquite and scraps of downed oak branch kindling. When the flames stood steady in a bed of glowing coals, Dawson poured some water from a canteen into a tin pot and set it on the fire. Shaw watched, appearing uninterested until Dawson swished the long knife blade around in the boiling water. "Bring me a saddle over here, Caldwell," said Shaw, watching Caldwell tear a clean shirt into long strips for bandages.

Caldwell stopped what he was doing, fetched a saddle, and brought it back to where Shaw sat a few feet from the fire, his bare back bowed forward, blood oozing from beneath the bandanna Dawson had wadded and laid over the wound temporarily. "Lay it across my lap," Shaw said to Caldwell.

"Across your lap?" said Caldwell.

"You heard me," said Shaw. "I need something to hold on to when he commences to cutting."

Caldwell shuddered at the thought, but eased the saddle down in a way that Shaw could bow over it and wrap his arms under the far edge.

"This ought to do," Shaw said to Dawson. "Are you about ready?"

"Just about," said Dawson, his sleeves rolled up, his hat off. He raised the knife blade and dried it on a clean strip of cloth from the pile Caldwell had torn. He began whistling steadily under his breath as he prepared the knife.

"I don't need the entertainment," said Shaw a bit gruffly.

"It helps settle me," Dawson replied, going back to the whistling but keeping it even lower. Caldwell watched in rapt fascination, a pained look on his face.

"Caldwell," said Shaw, "you want to get good at gun handling . . . I'm about to tell you something that will make you better than you ever believed you could be with a pistol."

"What's that, Mr. Shaw?" Caldwell asked hesitantly.

"It's going to take me a week or more before my shoulder heals," said Shaw. "After me taking a bullet from you, if you're not handling that Colt to my satisfaction by the time my wound mends, you have my word that I'll take that gun you're wearing and bend the barrel over your head."

Cray Dawson stifled a laugh and busied himself testing the temperature of the knife blade by holding it close to his forearm.

But Caldwell saw no humor in it. He looked terrified. "Mr. Shaw, please!" he pleaded. "I'll never get proficient with a pistol in that short a period of time!"

Shaw ignored him and said to Cray Dawson as he bowed forward over the saddle in his lap, "I don't mind if it's a little too hot, Dawson. Let's get it done."

"I wish we had some whiskey first," Dawson said, taking a deep breath, getting ready.

"I don't require whiskey either," said Shaw, getting a grip around the saddle with both arms, the pain radiating in his wounded shoulder.

"I wasn't talking about *you*," said Dawson on his knees, leaning forward over

Shaw's bowed back. He lifted the bloody bandanna, handed it to Caldwell, then said, "Here goes."

"Oh, my, Mr. Shaw!" said Caldwell, growing faint as he watched the sharp point of the knife sink down into Shaw's flesh.

"Caldwell," said Dawson, annoyed by the man's squeamishness, "you handle dead bodies; how can this bother you so bad?"

"It's just different handling the dead," said Caldwell. "I'm aware that they feel nothing. This is too painful! Oh, *mercy!*" he said, watching Dawson go back to the wound with the knife point.

Gripping the saddle until his whole body trembled violently, Shaw said in a strained and rasping voice, "No mercy for me, Caldwell . . . this is just a part of my game."

Chapter 13

At the bunkhouse of the Turkey Track Ranch, Rafter One spread, Buddy Edwards stepped inside out of the noonday heat and looked around, his eyes taking a second to adjust from the stabbing sunlight to the darkened shade. At the far end of the long plank building he saw a slim young cowboy pulling a clean bib-front shirt over his head. "Hey, Vince! What're you doing? Sully and us have been looking all over for you!"

"So now you've found me," Vincent Mills replied in a not-so-pleasant voice. Before raising the shirt bib and buttoning it, he stuffed the tails down into his denim trousers and buttoned his fly. "Now what?"

Buddy had walked forward, but stopped and watched Vincent pick up his special Mexican hand-tooled holster from his bunk and swing it around his waist. Buddy shrugged. "I'm supposed to tell you to get back to work! Sully says you and me gotta round up stray calves from the basin and bring 'em back before dark. There's a bitch wolf prowled in from the Llano plain. She'll go through them calves like a kid eating rock candy."

"Let her," said Vincent Mills. He took his range Colt from his worn work holster hanging from a peg beside his bunk. Buddy watched him check it and shove it down into the hand-tooled holster. "I'm through carrying calves in my lap for the day." He raised a boot to the edge of his bunk frame and tied the holster to his thigh. "Watch this," he said, swinging his hands back and forth, clapping them in front of his chest. "Start counting," he said with a grin.

"All right!" said Buddy, always eager to see his pal put on this little exhibition. Each time Vincent's hands clapped, Buddy counted, "One . . . two . . . three." But as he said "three," Buddy saw Vincent's Colt pointed straight out, its hammer cocked back, ready for action. "*Gol-ly!* Vincent, I *swear*, I never do see you draw the pistol! One second it's in the holster; the next it's in your hand! How do you do that?"

"Practice, *mi amigo*," said Vincent, uncocking the Colt, and looking at it admiringly as he turned it back and forth in his hand; then he slipped it down into the holster. "While you and this bunch of steer jockeys are playing checkers or swapping each other tall tales, I'm out there drawing this pistol against the wind — shooting heads off rattlesnakes and prairie dogs." As he spoke his hand effortlessly began drawing the pistol on a smooth forward swing of his arm, then slipping it back into the holster on the back swing.

Buddy Edwards stood staring, mesmerized, his expression that of a child watching a magician conjure miracles out of thin air. But then he caught himself and batted his eyes and said, "Vincent, we got to go. Will you show me that again tonight?"

"You go, Buddy," Vincent said flatly. "I got plans."

"Sully said we still got work to be done before we can go to town, Vincent," Buddy persisted. "He said Mr. McNalty is talking about cutting some hands out of here anyhow, the way beef has dropped."

Vincent Mills gave a sarcastic toss of his head. "McNalty is the owner; he can cut who he wants to cut, I reckon. Far as I'm concerned him and Sully can both kiss the broad side of my ass. I'm going to town and that's that."

"Why so early?" Buddy asked. "Turkey Wells station ain't going nowhere." He spread his hands with an uncertain grin.

"Heck, I'll go with you just as soon as I finish with them calves."

"I'm already finished with them calves, Buddy," said Vincent. "And you're right, the station will still be there . . . but the person I'm going to see might not be."

"You mean Lori Harmon?" said Buddy. "I don't reckon she'll be gone either by this evening."

"No, I don't mean Lori," said Vincent. His expression grew more serious and excitement glittered in his eyes. "I got word from Tugs Albin that Mace Renfield is waiting in Turkey Wells for Fast Larry Shaw. Renfield means to face him off in the street and kill him!" As he'd spoken, Vincent had stepped closer to Buddy Edwards until he began tapping his finger on Buddy's chest for emphasis.

Buddy's eyes widened. "You mean there's going to be a gunfight? Right there at the station?" But then Buddy cut a dubious glance at him and said, "Vincent, you ain't funnin' me, are you?"

"No, this is on the square and by the level," said Vincent, the very thought of it causing him to also get excited. "A fellow who goes by the name Willie the Devil came through and tipped off Renfield that Fast Larry is on his way. The way I got it figured is, Shaw should be riding in sometime today. I wouldn't miss being there for every wet-assed calf twix here and the Red!"

"Dang," said Buddy, growing more interested, "the fastest gun alive coming right here . . . right here where we live!"

"That's just a figure of speech," said Vincent, "the thing about the fastest gun alive. There ain't no such thing as the fastest gun alive."

"Why ain't there?" Buddy asked.

"Because, pard," said Vincent, "there is always somebody faster." He tapped himself on his temple. "Use your head, Buddy. The world is too big for any one person to be the best at any one thing. You can understand that, can't you?"

Buddy struggled with it for a second, then said, "No, not really . . . but I admit that I don't know a whole lot. Not like you do, anyway."

"Well, take my word for it. There is no such thing as the fastest gun alive." As he spoke he once again began drawing and holstering his pistol. "Anybody who is mighty damn good with a gun has the same chance as the next against a man like Fast Larry Shaw. Given the right timing, the right situation, I might beat him."

"You're not thinking about trying something like that, are you, Vincent?" Buddy asked warily.

"Me? Naw, don't worry about that," said Vincent, tossing the idea aside. "I'm going just to watch. But I ain't so sure I couldn't take Shaw or Renfield either one, if it ever came right down to it."

"Whew, good," said Buddy, letting out a breath of relief. "I'm glad to hear you say that."

"Hey!" said Vincent, refocusing on his plans. "Do you want to go with me or not? I'm all ready to go!"

"Heck-fire, yes! I'm going!" said Buddy Edwards, snapping into motion, jerking his shirttail up out of his trousers. "Just let me put on my St. Louis shirt and wash my face! I'm ready!"

Lawrence Shaw, Cray Dawson, and Jedson Caldwell rode into the Turkey Wells station during the busiest part of the day. Out front of a long line of plank buildings with tin roofs, wagons creaked back and forth across sun-hardened ruts in the wide dirt street. Cow ponies stood at hitch rails out front of crude shacks and makeshift tent saloons, where the sound of banjos and mouth harps gave way to occasional shouts and fits of laughter. Behind the shacks and across a short rise of land Turkey Mountain stood five hundred feet in the air, looking down on its namesake with blank indifference.

Riding single-file with Shaw in the lead, the three maneuvered their animals toward a building that had a physician's sign hanging out front — the only building there having a front porch with a roof over it. Shaw rode straight in his saddle, knowing that there would be those who would recognize him. Behind him Caldwell rode a bit slumped, and behind Caldwell, Dawson rode, keeping a watchful eye on building fronts and rooflines. When Shaw stopped and stepped down from his big buckskin, he did so with no regard for the pain in his wounded shoulder. But he turned to Caldwell as the other two stopped; and when Dawson had also stepped down from his saddle, he and Shaw assisted Caldwell down from his saddle and up onto the doctor's porch. "I feel funny doing this," Caldwell said in a lowered voice.

"It was your bullet that caused the problem," Shaw reminded him.

"Oh, I'm not complaining," Caldwell said quickly as Dawson reached for the doorknob and opened the door. "It just seems odd, I mean. Like when a young boy plays sick to take off from school, you know?"

"No, I don't," said Shaw without interest. He allowed Caldwell to enter first; then he and Dawson followed.

A white-haired doctor stood up from a threadbare divan and walked stiffly forward to greet them.

Seeing that Caldwell had walked in a bit stooped, he centered his attention on him, saying, "Well, now, what have we here?"

But as soon as Caldwell heard Dawson close the door behind them, he straightened up and stepped to one side as Shaw came forward. "It's not him, Doctor; it's me," Shaw said. "I took a bullet in the shoulder from behind." As Shaw spoke, he raised his right arm slightly, as if the doctor could see the soreness. "This man cut the bullet out, but I'm obliged if you'll check it and dress it clean for me."

"Oh . . ." The old doctor's word trailed off in concern. "Well, come on in here and let's take a look at it." He adjusted his wire-rimmed spectacles up on the bridge of his nose, giving Shaw a closer look as the three filed past him toward the wooden chair and a sheet-covered gurney in the far corner. "I'm Dr. Isenhower," he said, "and you look familiar. I believe I myself once removed a bullet from your torso."

Shaw stopped and turned to him before sitting down in the chair. "That you have, Doctor." He slipped his left arm from his coatsleeve and eased the right sleeve down carefully. "It has been a long time, but your memory serves you well. I'm Lawrence Shaw."

"Ah, yes, Lawrence Shaw, the gunfighter." The old doctor nodded, rolling up his shirtsleeves with thick, clean fingers. "Now I understand why you have your friend here walking in like he's got a bellyache. You can't afford to have anybody see that you're not up to your game, eh?"

"That's right, Doctor," said Shaw. "So I'm trusting you to keep quiet about my being here with a gunshot wound. This *is* my gun hand."

"Of course," said the doctor. He shook his head as he sat down on a three-legged wooden stool and scooted it over and around beside Shaw, giving himself a good view of Shaw's back. "We wouldn't want folks to know that you're temporarily incapable of killing a person, now, would we?"

Shaw cocked his head toward the doctor and said, "I didn't come here to be talked down to, Doctor. But what you just said is true . . . there's men who'd come at me like vultures if they thought I was down in my arm. That's not by my choosing. They're the ones smelling blood, not me. You think this is something I want? I'd have to be a fool to want it."

"My apologies, Mr. Shaw," said the doctor. "Sometimes my sense of humanity gets the better of me." He gave Shaw a slight nudge with his left hand beneath the bandaged wound, saying, "Lean forward for me."

While the doctor examined Shaw's wound and changed the bandage, Cray Dawson and Jedson Caldwell stood at the window, looking out onto the busy dirt street.

Across the street and to the right, a man wearing a tall Stetson with a Montana crown stood out front of a ragged saloon tent, holding a mug of beer in his gloved hand. As Dawson and Caldwell watched, three more men walked out of the tent, one carrying a bottle of whiskey, one twirling a long knife by a ring on its handle. "This must be Saturday night coming up," Dawson said absently.

"Yes, it must," Caldwell said, looking back and forth along the street, seeing two more riders arriving in town, coming in from the northwest. "It looks like every cowhand for fifty miles is riding in and liquoring up."

Out front of the Ragged Tent Saloon, the men passed the bottle around while the one with the beer mug nodded toward the doctor's office and said something to the others, causing them to also look in the same direction.

"They already know you're here, Shaw," Dawson called out over his shoulder. "I suppose Caldwell and me could take the horses around back. When you're ready to go we can slip out of town."

"That's a bad idea, Dawson," said Shaw from the back corner. "No gunman leaves town without a meal or a drink or two. That's a sure way to get a bad rumor started."

"What do you propose then?" Cray Dawson asked.

"We'll go have a beer, ask if anybody's seen Willie the Devil and Elton Minton. Then we'll leave here in our own time."

"I understand," said Dawson, "but what if one of these drunken cowhands decides he wants to hang your name on his belt? Then what?"

"I'll just have to be extra careful not to let that happen," said Shaw.

"But if it does anyway, then?" Dawson asked.

"Then I just have to play it the best I can," said Shaw. He turned to the doctor, asking, "Doc, can you paint that wound with laudanum once you're finished, get it good and numb up there, so's I can move without the pain stopping me?"

"That's a foolish idea, Lawrence," said the old doctor. "You can't make something work when it's in need of healing. That's the law of nature."

"So is staying alive," said Shaw. "Paint it good for me . . . we'll see which law is the strongest."

"I'd tell you you're crazy, Mr. Shaw," said the doctor in a sharp but respectful tone, "but I've got a feeling you already know that."

"It has crossed my mind some," said Shaw, returning the old doctor's wry sense of humor.

As the doctor continued to attend to Shaw's wound, the two arriving riders turned their horses to a hitch rail and stepped down out front of another saloon farther down the street, this one a plank shack with a wide rack of white-tailed deer antlers fastened above the door. "Goodness gracious, Vincent!" said Buddy Edwards, looking along the street as if in amazement. "You can just feel something in the air today! I reckon everybody must know that Fast Larry is on his way!"

"Yeah," said Vincent Mills, "that's the feel of tension and excitement that always comes when a couple of big guns is on the prod." He grinned. "I truly love that feeling." Taking off his worn range gloves and shoving them into his belt, he walked ahead of Buddy into the Buck Horn Saloon.

At the crowded makeshift bar, a set of rough oak planks lying across the tops of a row on wooden whiskey barrels, Vincent called out above the steady roar of conversation, "Frenchy, pour us a couple of shots of rye and leave the bottle. Some beer too."

As the bartender nodded and reached for two shot glasses, a bearded face at the bar turned toward Vincent and Buddy. "Hey, Vincent! I thought I heard your voice." Scooting sideways, forcing an opening at the bar, the man said, "Here, y'all step right in."

"Much obliged, Parker," said Vincent. He and Buddy Edwards squeezed in beside the man. "Guess what I heard was true," he said, fishing a coin from his trouser pocket and laying it on the bar for the drinks.

"If you mean about Renfield having a gunfight in the making, you're right," said Parker Phelps. Then he looked surprised and said, "Say, what are you Turkey Track boys doing in here so early? I thought McNalty and Sully kept everybody busy till dark, even on Saturdays."

"Did you think I wouldn't show up with Fast Larry Shaw, the fastest gun alive, coming to town? I'd have to be nailed to the floor with guns held on me," said Vincent, grinning, lifting his shot glass in a salute while beside him Buddy Edwards did the same.

Parker Phelps laughed, returning the salute with his shot glass. The three tossed back their drinks in a gulp. Then Phelps licked his lips and said, "You don't have any notions about taking on Fast Larry Shaw, do you?"

"Naw, not me," said Vincent, liking the idea that someone might even consider him worthy to face a man like Shaw. "Where'd you get such an idea as that?"

"Hell, it's no secret you're mighty handy with that pistol of yours. There's some already saying you'd give Mace Renfield a run for his money."

"Not interested," said Vincent. He refilled their glasses as he said, "Besides,

Mace has too many pards always around. The man who outguns him would be lucky to make it out of town alive."

"That might be true," said Parker Phelps, accepting the full shot glass. "Want to hear what the smart money is saying?"

"Sure, tell me," said Vincent. Beside him Buddy sipped his glass of whiskey a little slower now that the other two weren't noticing him. He wasn't about to admit it, but he had no real taste for whiskey, or beer either, for that matter. He drank when he came to town rather than hear the rest of the Turkey Track hands tease him over it. The truth was, Buddy liked the world to move slowly and steadily. He didn't like the way alcohol made everything spin out of control.

"Smart money has Shaw able to beat Mace Renfield ten to one," said Phelps with a smile. "I bet Mace is madder than a pissed-on hornet over it."

Vincent considered it, then said, "I can't see Mace Renfield beating Fast Larry Shaw either, come to think of it. I know Renfield is fast . . . but he ain't in Shaw's class. Few men are, I reckon."

"Well, that's what the smart money is saying too," said Phelps, "but to be honest I had to put a few dollars on Renfield. Just think what it will pay if he'd happen to win!" He winked. "Of course, it doesn't hurt nothing either for a man like Renfield to see that I've got faith in him, eh?" He gave Vincent a friendly nudge.

Vincent grinned. "I suppose it never hurts to get on Renfield's good side."

Before either one could say any more on the matter a young cowboy burst in through the front door and cried aloud, "Boy! Fast Larry Shaw just rode in! He's over at the doctor's right now!"

"Holy Moses!" said Vincent. He stared at Parker Phelps, his eyes wide, his face ashen. "This thing is *really* going to happen!"

"Damn right," said Phelps, "it looks like it is, sure enough!" Drinkers turned away from the bar with their shot glasses and beer mugs in hand and crowded the open doorway, some spilling out onto the street for a better look.

"Until this very second," said Vincent, "I reckon I didn't completely believe it! But hot damn!" He turned to Buddy Edwards in his excitement and pulled his hat down on his forehead. "What do you think, Buddy? Is this the huckleberrys or what?"

Buddy quickly righted his hat brim and said, "I'll say it is! Look at my hands,

Vincent . . . they're shaking so, I can barely control them."

"Let's get out there where we can see," said Vincent.

But Parker Phelps cautioned him with a hand on his forearm. "Careful, now, Vincent," he said. "This is the time a man like you, wearing a Colt, ought to walk slow and watch where his boots lead him."

Vincent just stared at him for a moment, then said in a serious tone, "Much obliged, Parker . . . you bet I will."

Chapter 14

In a long tent hostel filled with row upon row of cots and blanket pallets, Mace Renfield thanked the whiskey-sodden mule skinner who had staggered in and told him that Lawrence Shaw was in town. Renfield flipped the man a coin, then said gruffly, "Now get on out of here; the air ain't supporting you worth a damn."

As the mule skinner snatched the coin in his palm and staggered out of the tent, Renfield turned to the two men standing beside him and said as he straightened his wide-brimmed hat on his head, "Well, gentlemen, let's let the games begin."

The two men fell in behind him and followed him as he left the tent and walked toward the crowd of drinkers gathered out front of the Buck Horn Saloon. One of the men said, "Mace, want me and Harvey here to set something up, make sure Shaw don't walk away from this alive no matter how the chips fall?"

Mace Renfield stopped dead still and turned to face the man. "Let me tell you something, Red . . . you too, Harvey." He pointed his gloved finger for emphasis. "There'd better not be any interference in this thing in any way!"

"Take it easy, Mace!" said Red Logan, noticing how eyes were turning toward them all along the busy dirt street. "I just figured it would be like other times! You know, me and Harvey on hand to tip the odds if they need tipping?"

"I understand," said Renfield, calming down, smoothing the front of his black brocade vest, "but this isn't going to be like the times before. This is a straight-up man-to-man gunfight . . . winner takes all."

Red and Harvey gave each other a look. "Whatever you say, Mace," said Harvey Tuell.

Mace stared at them. "I know what you're both thinking . . . I know Shaw is supposed to be the fastest gun alive. But I've got him cold! I can feel it in my bones!" He made a fist as he continued. "This is *my* time! I want nothing to tarnish how I bring this big gunman down. I know we've had to cut a few corners to get here . . . you boys have done your share of tipping the odds for me, and I'm obliged. But this is the big one . . . and I'm ready for it.

Just watch me take him." He turned and started walking again. Red and Harvey shrugged and followed.

Some of the onlookers out front of the Buck Horn Saloon hurried back inside when they saw Mace Renfield coming their way. Inside, they quickly crowded themselves along the bar, leaving a three-foot space in the center for Mace and his two followers.

Across the makeshift bar top from that open space stood a bartender with his sleeves rolled up and a short black cigar stub sticking out of his teeth. He set up a newly opened bottle of rye whiskey and stood three shot glasses in a line. Then he nervously tweaked his handlebar mustache and said to Mace Renfield when he walked through the front door, "Welcome, Mace! It is always a pleasure having you join us here at the Buck Horn —"

"Stick your thumb in it, Winston," Mace said to the bartender, cutting his words short. "I've been here every damn day for the past three weeks. Don't start acting like I just now arrived."

"Certainly, Mace," said Winston, the bartender, already lifting the bottle for Mace to see. "And will the three of you be having a drink . . . on the house, of course?"

Mace Renfield looked back and forth along the crowded bar and smiled proudly, saying for all three of them, "Well, we don't mind if we do." His eyes found Vincent Mills and Buddy Edwards standing away from the bar over against a wall. "Vincent, will you join me in a drink?"

Vincent Mills's mouth almost dropped open when he heard Mace call out his name. For a moment he stood, stunned.

"Go on, Vincent," Buddy Edwards whispered, coaxing him forward.

"Well, uh, yes . . . I don't mind if I do," said Vincent, feeling a headiness engulf him. All faces had turned to him, all eyes looked upon him with envy, he thought as he walked over to the bar, seeing men scoot sidelong, making room for him. Buddy followed only inches behind.

Mace held out a shot glass of rye to Vincent. "Here you are, *mi amigo;* drink and enjoy." He smiled. Seeing Buddy, Mace said over his shoulder to the waiting bartender, "Winston, pour one for Vincent's friend as well."

Mi amigo! Vincent repeated to himself, hardly believing his ears. He had no idea that Mace Renfield even knew his name. Now the man was calling him his friend! This was too good to be true. Vincent needed the drink Mace had just placed in his hand, just to keep himself steady.

"Much obliged, Mr. Renfield," Vincent managed to say.

"No, no," said Renfield, wagging a finger, "not *Mr.* Renfield . . . not to you, not today anyway. Just call me Mace, Vincent. Now drink up!" He raised his shot glass in a high toast to everyone along the bar. Then he set down the empty glass and pushed it away. "That will be enough for me today. As all of you know, I've got business to attend to."

A murmur arose along the drinkers. But in a moment they turned to one another in quiet conversation, as if to give Mace Renfield and Vincent Mills some privacy. "You know, Vincent, I've heard a lot about you since I got to the Turkey Wells station. You work for McNalty's Rafter spread, you mind your own business, and you're good with a gun." His gaze turned flat and cool. "Does that about size you up, boy?"

Vincent didn't know quite how to take this slight shift of attitude. "Well, yes. I'm just a cowhand, like all the others out there on the —"

"That's good to hear," said Renfield, interrupting him. "Just a cowhand . . . I like that. Because once I hear a man is real

251

handy with a gun, the first thing I wonder is whether or not he might be overly ambitious . . . you know, wanting to make a name for himself. Get himself some quick fame by facing me off in a street somewhere." His flat stare narrowed even farther. "But your being just a cowhand, I reckon I have no reason to consider that you might be that way, do I?"

Vincent Mills had listened and began weighing Renfield's words. Now he wasn't too stunned or impressed to speak up. "You're asking if I'm going to want to take you on after your showdown with Fast Larry Shaw, ain't you?"

Renfield said with a smug grin and a trace of sarcasm, "Say, you catch on pretty quick, don't you?" He leaned back against the makeshift bar, laying his arms along the edge. "Yes, that's what I'm asking . . . are you going to be looking for me tomorrow, after this gunfight today?"

Vincent Mills considered his answer for a moment, then said, "With all respect, Mr. Renfield . . . let's wait and see if you're still *around* tomorrow, after this gunfight today."

Mace Renfield stared at him blankly for a moment, a strange look on his face. Vincent wondered if he should have handled it differently. But it was too late to change it now. He returned Renfield's stare until at length the seasoned gunfighter chuckled under his breath. "Have another drink, Vincent. We'll let tomorrow take care of itself."

Before Vincent could respond, a man hurried through the front door and said in a breathless tone of voice, "Fast Larry's coming out! He's on the street!" Drinks spilled; glasses and bottles fell to the floor. The makeshift bar top trembled with the vibration of heavy boots scuffling and pounding across the plank floor.

"I've got ten dollars on this fight!" an excited voice called out. Vincent and Buddy stood firm; so did Mace Renfield and his two men. The five of them watched the drinkers crowd and shove one another through the narrow door.

Mace Renfield had kept an eye on Vincent Mills, checking his calm reaction, his expression. "What about you, Vincent? Do you have any money on this fight? Did you bet it on me, or Fast Larry Shaw?"

"I've got no money to spare," said Vincent, not revealing an answer.

Renfield nodded. "I see." He took his time, lifted a long cigar from his breast pocket, bit the tip off of it, and ran it in and out of his mouth, all the while keeping a steady gaze on Vincent Mills. "You remind me of myself . . . about fifteen years ago," he said, striking a match along the bar top and letting it flare against the tip of the cigar. "Will you at least be wishing me luck out there?" he asked quietly.

"Yep . . . good luck," said Vincent flatly.

Leaving the doctor's office, Shaw felt numbness engulf the back of his right shoulder. His whole right arm was stiff, his hand swollen slightly. Yet he knew if he had to he could pull a gun. The question was, how fast could he pull it? What could he hit with it? Dawson and Caldwell flanked him right and left, a foot back, leaving him room. As soon as their boots touched the dirt street, Shaw noted that the street traffic had died down some. A crowd of drinkers stood out front of the Ragged Tent Saloon across from the doctor's office, and down the street at the Buck Horn Saloon as well. All eyes were upon Shaw as he said over his shoulder to Dawson, "We'll go straight across the street, get a drink, and ask about Willie the Devil . . . then we're gone."

"However you want to play it, Shaw," said Dawson, his eyes scanning the street warily.

"Gentlemen, I don't mind telling you," said Caldwell in a shaky voice, "I'm just about to come un-strung here. I hope I'm not going to be sick!"

"Do the best you can," said Shaw. "You're the one they're going to think just came from seeing the doctor."

"So that was good thinking," said Dawson.

"We'll see," said Shaw.

The crowd out front of the Ragged Tent Saloon parted, giving first Shaw then the other two plenty of room. Inside, Shaw stopped long enough to look around, seeing a long plank bar lined with bottles, glasses, and beer mugs. A cigar burned in a large copper ashtray. Flies circled puddles of beer. The short, one-eyed bartender's mouth dropped open at the sight of Lawrence Shaw standing less than twenty feet from him. Behind Shaw and beyond the tent flap the crowd swelled, wanting to push forward into the saloon but unable to until he stepped aside and gave them room.

"Lord God. Fast Larry Shaw," the owner rasped. "It's you, ain't it!" He began wringing his hands together. "Welcome, welcome, *welcome* to my saloon, Mr. Shaw. And you two fellows too! My name's Leo Crumb. I can't tell you what an honor it is to have you."

Shaw nodded and touched his fingers to his hat brim, walking across the dirt floor to the bar. "Mr. Crumb, set us up three shots of rye and three mugs of beer."

"Yes, sir, at your service!" said Crumb, already snatching glasses, mugs, and a bottle of rye. Seeing Shaw reach for his money, Crumb said, "No, sir! Mr. Shaw, your money is no good here! Not now! Not ever!" As he spoke to Shaw he watched the drinkers crowd back in through the open tent flap and line up along the bar. Even as they shoved and poked one another for their own space, they left a wide, clear space for Shaw and his party.

"Much obliged," said Shaw to the bar owner. Cray Dawson noticed the uncommitted manner in which Shaw had reached for his money. Dawson realized that Shaw was just going through the motion and already knew that he wasn't going to pay for anything.

"How long since Willie the Devil was through here?" Shaw asked, implying that he knew Willie the Devil had been there; it was just a question of when. He looked along the bar, letting the drinkers know that he was talking to them as well as the bar owner.

A silence ensued. But then the whiskey-sodden mule skinner stepped away from the bar, staggered in place, and asked boldly and drunkenly, "What is it worth to you to know?"

"Shut up, Greasy!" said Crumb. "You don't know nothing no way!" He turned to Shaw and said, "To tell you the truth, Mr. Shaw, Willie the Devil ain't the kind of man I'd want thinking that I jackpotted him —"

"Nonsense," Mace Renfield called out from just inside the tent flap. "Tell Fast Larry Shaw what he wants to know."

A dead silence set in like a heavy cloud above the drinkers. Renfield walked across the dirt floor slowly, Red and Harvey stepping through the tent flap and following him closely. Shaw turned from the bar and gave him his flat stare.

"Look, Mr. Renfield," said Crumb nervously, "Mr. Shaw came to the Wells — this is the first place he came to, right here at my saloon!" He looked past Renfield and at the crowd that had gathered inside the tent flap. Even the bartender from the Buck Horn Saloon had left his post. He stood staring, his stained white apron still on. "What does that tell you about whose saloon is the best?" said Crumb.

Nobody answered.

"Good day to you, Fast Larry," Renfield said to Shaw in an almost mocking manner, without raising a hand to his hat brim.

"Renfield," was all Shaw said in acknowledgment, also without raising a hand to his hat brim.

Noting the silence among the drinkers, Renfield said, "Oh? What's this? Nobody wants to speak up?" He turned quickly toward Shaw, seeing how Shaw might react. But Shaw made no response. "Well, then, I'll tell you, Fast Larry Shaw, Willie the Devil was through here . . . oh" — he considered it — "about a week ago?" He looked at Red and Harvey for help.

"Yeah," said Red Logan, staring straight at Cray Dawson as if sizing him up. "A week ago sounds about right." Dawson didn't give an inch. He leveled his gaze into Red's eyes and seemed to lock on them until Red finally blinked and looked away.

Caldwell saw Harvey Tuell staring at him, but he couldn't bring himself to look the man in the eyes.

"Now that I think of it," said Renfield to Shaw, "the Devil told me that you might be looking for him . . . I believe he said there's some dirt between you and his

258

boss, Barton Talbert."

Shaw only stared silently.

Renfield shook his head and chuckled. "Barton Talbert . . . now there's a man who just seems to draw trouble at every turn in the road." He took on a serious expression, then said almost between the two of them, "I heard what he and his boys did. You have my sympathy."

Shaw continued to stare at him.

"But the Devil did ask me if I would do him a favor, and I told him I would."

"Why are you doing this, Renfield?" Shaw asked bluntly, cutting him off.

Renfield looked surprised. "I beg your pardon?"

Shaw said, "It's not because you need the reputation . . . you're almost as famous as I am."

"Almost?" said Renfield. "There's reason enough right there!" He spread a grin. Tossing a glance to Red Logan and Harvey Tuell. "Hear that? I'm *almost* as famous as Fast Larry Shaw."

Red and Harvey both responded with tight smiles. "Yeah," said Red, "ain't that the berries?"

"It's not for reputation, Renfield," said Shaw, raising his full shot glass, sniffing the aroma of the rye whiskey, then setting it down without drinking it. "Huh-uh, I can't buy that. You've done your share of killing. You're not out to prove anything to anybody. What is it?"

"Can I be perfectly honest with you, Shaw?" said Renfield, after a second of contemplation.

"Sure, why not?" said Shaw.

"The fact is, you offend me, sir," said Renfield. "You always have. I can't say why, but there it is. So with no further to-do over the matter, let's step outside, walk it off, and get it done. What say you, Shaw?"

Cray Dawson watched closely, seeing Shaw take his time, seeing Renfield grow impatient. For a man who had no idea whether or not his gun hand was going to fail him, Lawrence Shaw seemed to have all the confidence in the world. Shaw raised the shot glass again, sniffed the rye, and this time swirled it slightly in the glass, looking at the amber whiskey as if within it lay the secrets to life. Renfield stared in rapt anticipation. Shaw started to touch the glass to his lips, but then stopped and set it down again.

"Damn it to hell, drink it!" Renfield shouted. "I'm calling you out, Shaw! Quit fooling around! Let's go!"

Shaw took a deep breath, let it out in a

sigh, then said, "No, I'm not going to kill you, Renfield . . . not today, anyway." He shrugged. "I've got too much to do. Now if you had given me a good reason, like some of those others did . . . like I killed your cousin, your brother, something like that, I might oblige you. But I'm not going to kill you just because you don't like me . . . just because something about me *offends* you."

"There, you see?" said Renfield, pointing his finger. "That's the very thing right there. That attitude of yours, you arrogant, self-centered son of a bitch!"

The drinkers held their breath.

But Shaw chuckled slightly and said, "Nice try, Renfield." Then he turned to Caldwell and said, "Are you feeling better yet? Did the doctor fix you up?"

"I'm all right," said Caldwell, amazed at how his voice didn't crack with fear the way he thought it would if he had to speak.

"Then let's get back on the trail," Shaw said to both him and Dawson. "We've got a long ride ahead of us."

"No, Shaw!" Renfield shouted. "You're not going to put me off! You either draw or I'll kill you where you stan—"

Renfield never finished his words. His hand never touched his gun butt. He flew backward, his head snapping back at an odd angle as Shaw's bullet hit him between the eyes. Dawson saw Shaw's Colt streak up from his holster, not as fast as the last time, he thought. But Shaw had rattled Renfield, then caught him completely off guard. In the split second it took for Renfield to hit the dirt floor, both Red Logan and Harvey Tuell went for their guns. From the corner of his eye Dawson saw Shaw's gun hand slump and knew that the one shot he'd made was all he was going to get.

Cray Dawson sprang forward, his Colt coming up toward Red Logan. He saw Logan's Colt explode straight toward him, he thought. But he had no time to duck, or even to flinch. His hammer fell and Red Logan flipped backward and landed atop Mace Renfield even as Red's shot whistled past his head. Seeing Red Logan go down, Harvey Tuell dropped his gun and bolted from the tent so fast his hat flew off his head.

At the open tent flap, Buddy Edwards yelled, *"Nooo!"* seeing his pal Vincent Mills sink to his knees with a gout of blood spewing from his chest. Dawson's shot had gone through Red Logan and hit Vincent by a sheer turn of fate. But Vincent, feeling himself shot, responded instinctively, drawing his gun with his right hand while his left hand pressed against the flow of blood.

Cray Dawson also responded instinctively. Seeing Vincent Mills's gun come up pointing at him, he fired again, his shot knocking Vincent backward against Buddy Edwards, who had knelt beside his fallen friend. Blood splattered on Buddy's face.

Dawson saw that a terrible thing had just happened; but as he lowered his Colt, he saw Buddy Edwards reach for his range pistol with tears in his eyes. "You killed Vincent!" Buddy shrieked hysterically, firing repeatedly at Dawson. "You killed my friend!"

"Don't!" cried Dawson. But Buddy kept firing, one bullet slicing through Dawson's shirtsleeve. Then Dawson fired once with deliberation and the shot silenced both the slow-witted cowboy and his rusty range pistol.

In the fury of gunfire, in order to protect himself and his saloon, Crumb grabbed a small pistol from his trouser pocket and started to aim it at Cray Dawson, but Caldwell, who appeared to have been frozen in place, suddenly drew his pistol and cocked it toward the bartender.

"Don't shoot!" Crumb shouted, letting

the small pistol fall from his hand as if it had turned red-hot. Caldwell stood visibly shaking, yet he kept himself under control.

Cray Dawson shot a glance around the saloon, then at Shaw, seeing the way his gun hand hung limp at his side. Shaw managed to raise his pistol enough to drop it into his holster, but Dawson could tell the move had taken everything out of him. "Everybody stand real still," Dawson said, fanning his Colt back and forth, making sure the fight was over.

"Mister," said the drunken mule skinner, "you just killed two cowboys who never done anybody any wrong in their lives!" He pointed at Buddy Edwards. "That one was simpleminded to boot!"

"I didn't mean to shoot them," said Cray Dawson.

"Shut up, Dawson," said Shaw. "We all saw how it happened."

"If he just hadn't drawn that pistol!" said Dawson.

"I said shut up, damn it!" Shaw snapped. "You don't have to justify saving your own life to anybody."

Dawson swallowed a tight knot in his throat and lowered his pistol. He knew Shaw was right . . . but somehow being right didn't help at all.

Chapter 15

Shaw led Dawson and Caldwell out of town quickly, keeping a close watch on the trail behind them. When the three stepped down from their saddles inside a strip of oak and juniper woodlands along the banks of Turkey Creek, Shaw took a bottle of rye from his saddlebags with his good hand and pitched it to Cray Dawson. "What's this for?" Dawson asked, giving Shaw a look that bordered on hostile.

Shaw pulled a sawed-off shotgun from his bedroll, clamped it under his arm, and said to Dawson, "What do you think it's for?" Then he turned without expecting an answer and gathered the horses' reins. "If you don't want it, throw it in the creek." He handed the three sets of reins to Caldwell and nodded toward a stretch of sandy soil filled with scrub brush, wild grass, and mesquite. "Better stake them instead of hobbling them, Undertaker," he said. "We might be getting some visitors from the Turkey Track Ranch tonight."

"But won't the folks tell them it wasn't

our fault?" said Jedson Caldwell, taking the reins.

"Yeah, the folks will tell them," said Shaw. "But my experience is that folks see and hear things the way they want to see and hear them. Sometimes the only thing that'll settle what happened in a gunfight is another gunfight." As he spoke to Caldwell he gave Cray Dawson a concerned gaze, seeing he had opened the bottle and raised it to his lips in a long, guzzling drink. "Go easy, Dawson," he said. "If we do get company, I don't want you walking sideways."

Dawson lowered the bottle and wiped a hand across his mouth. "Maybe we should have explained how it all happened to a lawman or somebody."

"There's no kind of law in Turkey Wells except the law hanging on a man's hip," said Shaw, "and that's the law that was played out the second Mace Renfield said he would kill me where I stood."

"How do you know he meant it?" Caldwell asked meekly.

Giving him a bemused look, Shaw said, "I took his word for it. To me, when a man wearing a gun says he's there to kill me . . . it's the same as him reaching for iron. It might be questionable if he meant it or not. It might be questionable whether or not I could have talked him out of it. The one thing that ain't questionable is who's alive and who's dead. A man who doesn't value his life above another's is apt to have a short career as a gunman." Seeing Dawson get ready to raise the bottle to his lips again so soon after his first drink, Shaw reached out and took the bottle, saying, "Are you going to share any of that yellow moon?"

But upon taking the bottle, instead of taking a drink, Shaw passed it to Caldwell, saying, "Here, you might need a couple swigs of this to smooth out a few wrinkles over what happened."

"I'm all right, just nervous still," said Caldwell. But looking at Shaw and Dawson he took the bottle and took a sip. When he handed it back to Lawrence Shaw, he turned and walked away, leading the horses.

Looking back at Dawson, Shaw said quietly, "All right, spit it out."

"Spit what out?" Dawson asked, reaching out for the bottle in Shaw's hand.

But Shaw held on to the bottle even with Dawson's hand on it. "You know what I mean, Dawson. Spit out whatever it is bothering you. Get it off your chest now, before it ends up causing bad trouble between us." Now he turned the bottle loose.

Dawson started to take a drink, but he stopped and stared at the bottle for a moment as if gathering his thoughts, then said to Shaw, "All right, I'll tell you. I thought you could have done different today. You didn't try very hard to talk the man down. You didn't take it out to the street where it should have been . . . where there was less chance of some bystander getting hurt."

"I see." Shaw nodded as Dawson spoke. Then he said, "I suppose I should have given you some sort of sign, let you know what I was about to do?"

"That would have helped," said Dawson.

"It would have helped Renfield too," said Shaw.

"Renfield never even got his hand on his gun, let alone tried to draw it!" Dawson said, raising his voice.

"That's called a surprise, Dawson," said Shaw, raising his voice with him. "Do you think I took unfair advantage? Hell, when I reached for my gun I didn't know if my arm was going to work or not! I gave him that much of an edge, whether he knew it or not! As far as taking it to the street, he picked the spot, not me. When he made his threat . . . he said, 'where you stand.' It doesn't get much plainer than that."

Dawson stared at him as he raised the bottle and took a drink, this one not as long as the first. When he lowered the bottle, he said, "All right, forget it."

"Are you sure?" asked Shaw. "Because it looks to me like you've still got things to talk about."

"Well, I don't," said Dawson. His voice lowered to normal. "I feel bad about those two cowboys I shot. It's just something I reckon I have to work out and get settled inside myself."

"You do that, Dawson," said Shaw, lowering his voice as well.

"I maybe could have done something different," Dawson added, still running the fight over and over in his mind.

"Like what?" Shaw asked bluntly.

"I don't know, maybe jumped out of the way when that one started shooting at me."

"Which way does a man jump when bullets are flying all around?" Shaw asked, seeing that Dawson was still having trouble turning it loose.

"I don't know, Shaw," said Dawson. "I suppose that's why I shot him . . . I just wanted those bullets to stop. I stopped them the only way I could." He took another drink, this one a short sip; then he handed the bottle back to Shaw.

"I expect I could say that about any gun-fight I've ever had," said Shaw. He put the cork in the bottle and popped it tight with the palm of his hand. "If you need any more of this, let me know."

"The whiskey or the talk?" Dawson asked.

Shaw didn't answer.

"Can I say something?" Dawson called out as Shaw walked away toward the edge of the creek.

Shaw stopped and just looked at him, taking the sawed-off from under his arm and holding it loosely.

"What Renfield said . . ." Dawson's words trailed away. "You do have some un-likable ways about you. I hate saying it, but you ain't at all like the Lawrence Shaw I grew up with."

"Ain't that the truth," said Shaw, almost to himself.

"Sometimes it looks to me like Lawrence Shaw and Fast Larry are two men in a fist-fight with each other," said Dawson.

"Most times, they are," said Shaw, turning away.

At dark, when they had finished a meal of jerked beef and coffee, Shaw put out the campfire and they moved four hundred yards farther along the creekbank. Staying inside the narrow strip of woodlands, they made a dark camp for the night and took turns sitting watch. Without a fire's light they couldn't be spotted from a distance, and while their tracks could be found along the creekbank, following them was not something a group of riders could do quietly through the mesquite, scrub brush, and juniper.

In the middle of the night, Jedson Caldwell awakened Lawrence Shaw by poking a stick against his sock foot. "Mr. Shaw, wake up, please. I think I hear something," Caldwell whispered. He poked Shaw's foot again.

"All right, Undertaker," Shaw growled under his breath. "I'm awake."

"I'm sorry, Mr. Shaw, but listen out there, upstream," he said. Then he fell silent for a moment. "There, did you hear it?" he whispered, his voice sounding excited.

"Yep, it's horses, moving slow," said Shaw, rolling up from his blanket, bringing the shotgun with him. "You did good, Undertaker."

"Thank you, Mr. Shaw," said Caldwell.

"Listen, Undertaker," said Shaw, pulling his boots on, "you can drop the 'mister.'

We've been in a gunfight together. I think that affords us a certain lack of formality, don't you?"

"Yes, you're right, Mi— I mean, Mist— I mean, Mr. —"

"Never mind," said Shaw. He stepped over to where Cray Dawson lay sleeping beneath what smelled like a vapor of rye whiskey. Kicking Dawson's leg gently, Shaw said, "Dawson, wake up. Somebody's coming."

Dawson groaned and sat up, cupping his face in both hands. "I feel like hell," he said in a pained voice.

"You better pull yourself together pretty quick," said Shaw. "If this is some of the boys from the Rafter One spread, the best thing we can do is keep you out of sight for the time being. Get up and make yourself scarce. But keep your ears open."

"I will," said Dawson, struggling to get to his feet, then searching around in the moonlight for his hat that had fallen somewhere on the ground.

Shaw picked up Dawson's blanket and pitched it over on his own, to make it look like there were only him and Caldwell there. Then he said to Caldwell, "Come on, Undertaker; let's see if we can convince these boys that we're by ourselves."

"What if they don't believe us?" Caldwell asked, sounding a bit frightened.

"I don't care if they believe us or not, so long as they take our word for it and go away," said Shaw, smiling thinly to himself. "Don't forget, my name is worth something. There's times when it doesn't hurt to be Fast Larry Shaw."

Caldwell noted that there was a tone of irony and contempt in Shaw's voice. He decided to keep quiet and calm down, realizing that he was into this with Shaw and Dawson up to his neck. He had to survive, and his best chance was to learn to handle matters the way these two did, he thought, with a lot more boldness and a lot less fear of the consequences.

He followed Shaw to the edge of the clearing along the creekbank where the two of them squatted down out of the moonlight in the dark shadow of a live oak along a thin, winding trail. After a moment of listening to the sound of horses moving quietly through mesquite brush, Shaw whispered, "They're on our trail, but they don't know how far away we are. You sit tight here; I'll be right across the trail. Don't shoot unless you have to. Like as not I can talk them down."

"What if there's too many of them?"

Caldwell asked, regretting his words as soon as he said them.

"There's always too many of them, Undertaker," said Shaw. He slipped away across the trail in the moonlight, then dropped out of sight. Caldwell felt his fear well up again now that he was alone in the dark, the sound of men with guns moving forward toward him in the night. A cold sheen of sweat formed on his forehead. He tried to prepare himself for a long, agonizing wait, yet it seemed like only a few seconds had passed when he heard Shaw's voice call out to the sound of the horses moving closer.

"Hello, the trail," said Shaw when he judged the riders to be within less than twenty feet away. "You've come close enough."

A short silence passed; then a voice replied, "I'm Martin Sullivan, the foreman of the Turkey Track Ranch. We're looking for the man who shot two of my drovers back at the Turkey Wells station."

"He's not here," said Shaw with finality. "What else can we do for you?"

"We've got to take a look all the same," the foreman said.

"I'm sorry you feel that way," said Shaw. "It tells me you're going to be hardheaded, and make me empty this double-barrel on you."

A worried voice among the riders said, "Damn it, Sully! If that's Fast Larry he'll do it too!"

"Pipe down, Ollie," said Martin Sullivan. "Let's all keep our heads here."

"Now there's a good idea," Shaw called out, overhearing them.

"Are you Fast Larry Shaw?" Sullivan called out.

"I am," said Shaw.

"Then you know it ain't you we're looking for. It's the other fellow, the one who killed our boys."

"That was an honest mistake, cowboy," said Shaw. "Your man took a secondhand bullet. Nobody meant for it to happen."

"I've heard a half dozen different accounts of it," said the foreman.

"But now you've heard the truth," said Shaw.

"What about our other boy?" the foreman asked. "Buddy Edwards didn't even have good sense. All's he ever could do was stick a horse or pitch a calf."

"He knew one other thing," said Shaw. "He knew how to point a pistol and commence pulling the trigger."

"Still, he didn't deserve dying like

this," said the foreman.

"Take it up with God, cowboy," said Shaw. "I don't aim to lose any more sleep over it. Turn and ride."

"We're staying on this trail," said the foreman. "I want to hear how it happened from the man who done it."

"I'm telling you straight up, nobody was out to kill them boys," said Shaw, cocking the shotgun hammers slowly, letting them be heard and considered. "They were in the wrong place at the wrong time . . . end of song. Now turn and ride."

"I can't do that, Shaw," said Martin Sullivan stubbornly. "I know you're a big gun out of Somos Santos, but I'm afraid I'm going to have to —"

"Hold it," said Dawson, appearing in the moonlight in the middle of the thin trail, facing the riders. "Here I am. If you want to hear it from me, you're hearing it."

Shaw whispered to himself, "Damn it, Dawson, this is not the place to clear your conscience."

"I killed them both," said Dawson. "God knows I didn't mean to, but I did it just the same."

"No matter whether you meant to or not, you killed them. As foreman of the Turkey Track Ranch, Rafter One spread, it's up to me to set things right," said Sullivan. He stepped down from his saddle.

"Let's get to it," he said, giving his horse a slight shove to the side. "Mr. Shaw, since this has nothing to do with you, I'm hoping you won't have any grudge agin' me once it's over."

"A grudge against you?" Shaw chuckled openly. "Don't worry about me, mister. Once this is over, the only thing left of you is what your boys there carve on a plank head marker."

"I reckon there's a fifty-fifty chance the same thing is going to happen to him," said Sullivan, giving a nod toward Cray Dawson.

"Then you're a damned fool," Shaw said bluntly. "Don't forget, besides your two cowhands, he also left one of Renfield's top gunmen lying dead and sent the other running."

"I realize that," said Sullivan, swallowing a tight knot that suddenly came to his throat.

Seeing the man begin to weaken, Shaw continued. "Here's something else you'd best realize. This man is Crayton Dawson, the fastest gun to ever come out of Somos Santos. But I reckon that means nothing to you." He backed his horse as if giving up in disgust, saying to Cray Dawson, "All right, Crayton, go on and shoot him. He's not smart enough to live."

"Stay out of this, Shaw," said Dawson. "I see what you're trying to do. But you're not going to stop it. I killed those two drovers and I'll face up to it."

"Wait a minute here," said Sullivan, getting anxious and a bit confused by the talk between Shaw and Dawson. He reached up and scratched his head under his hat brim, keeping his gun hand away from his pistol butt. Then he said warily to Lawrence Shaw, "*You're* from Somos Santos, ain't you?"

"We're both from Somos Santos," said Shaw. "We grew up there together. Broke horses together, swam the creeks together . . . shot jackrabbits together." His eyes narrowed on the man in the moonlight. "We learned to draw and shoot together."

"I said stay out of it, Shaw!" said Cray Dawson.

But Shaw continued, saying to Sullivan, "When I tell you this man is going to kill you deader than hell . . . don't think I haven't given it close consideration." He looked at the other drovers, then said to Sullivan, "You must have thought an awful lot of those two cowhands to be willing to die for them. I reckon that's admirable." He touched his fingertips to his hat brim. *"Adios."*

Having lost some of the heated urge to avenge his fallen cowhands, Sullivan looked troubled and bit his lip. "Shaw, if you're saying this was all a mistake —"

"I've said all I'm going to say." Shaw shrugged. "If you want to die this way, it's not my place to stop you." He turned to Dawson, saying, "Hurry up and shoot him, Crayton. Maybe the rest of these boys will drag him out of here, let me get back to sleep. Won't you, boys?" he asked the drovers.

The men nodded as one. Sullivan turned and saw them; then he said quickly to Cray Dawson, "Mister, I've never heard of you. But if Fast Larry Shaw says you're the fastest gun out of Somos Santos, I don't reckon anybody can blame me for not wanting to face off with you . . . 'specially with them two boys' deaths being an unfortunate accident, so to speak."

Not knowing what to say, Cray Dawson stood staring silently, his hand relaxed but still close to his gun handle.

Looking at the drovers behind him, then at Lawrence Shaw, then back to Dawson, Sullivan said, "I believe I'm going to ride away from here and call this thing square, if it's all the same with everybody?"

"You'd be wise to do so," Shaw said quietly.

Jedson Caldwell watched as if in awe as the foreman stepped back atop his horse in silence, backed it, turned it, and led his men away, one of them lifting a coiled rope from his saddle horn and flinging it to the ground. When the riders had vanished from the moonlight back into the night, Caldwell slipped over, picked up the rope, and brought it to Shaw and Dawson. "Look," he said in a hushed tone, "they'd already tied a hangman's knot in it!"

"There you have it, *Crayton*," said Shaw, taking the rope and shoving it to Cray Dawson. "It looks like one way or another, your newfound reputation as a gunman just saved your life."

Instead of taking the rope, Dawson took a step backward, letting it fall to the ground. "I've got no reputation, Shaw! I'm not a gunman! You had no right interfering!"

"I had *every* right interfering," said Shaw. "You're riding with me, watching my back. I've got to do the same for you. You've let killing those cowhands get to you so bad that you're ready to get yourself killed as some sort of punishment for it.

I'm not about to let that happen."

"How do you know I was going to get killed?" Dawson said defiantly. "How do you know that I haven't developed a taste for killing, just like you have?"

"I'm going to overlook that remark," said Shaw, "because I know you're not thinking straight right now." He took a deep breath and let it out slowly, as if letting it settle his patience. Then he said, "I'll tell you how I know . . . I know because I've seen too many men die in front of me *not* to know. Do you think staying alive in this life of mine has been all about who's the fastest to draw and fire a gun?" He gave Dawson a questioning look. "If it was, I'd have been dead years ago. This is about staying alive! This is about learning something more every time a man's face hits the dirt. I can tell how many gunfights a man has been in by the amount of sweat that runs down his face."

Cray Dawson also settled down, realizing that everything Shaw had said was true whether he'd realized it or not at the time. "All right," he said, "I do blame myself for those two cowhands being dead; there's no way around it."

"This place I live in somebody dies every day," said Shaw. "Get used to it, before it gets you killed."

"I *can't* get used to it, Shaw, at least not the way you have," said Dawson. "I'm not a part of it like you are. I'm here to take vengeance the same as you. But when it's finished, I go home and hang up my gun. What will you do?"

Shaw's demeanor seemed to soften in reflection. "I don't know . . . I wish to God I did." Then he seemed to snap out of such a line of thought and said, "But don't kid yourself thinking it'll be easy to stop, Dawson. You've got yourself a reputation to live up to whether you like it or not."

"Or live *down*," said Dawson, "the way I see it."

"Up or down is your call," said Shaw, reining his horse toward the trail. "But either way you'll have to live *with* it. That foreman and his men ain't about to tell anybody that you're an ordinary cowhand like themselves. How would that make them look, not bringing your body back facedown over a saddle? No, sir, they're going to see to it that your reputation grows, for a while, anyway. By then somebody else will add something to it, if you don't yourself." He tipped his hat brim down onto his forehead and added in a lowered tone of voice, "Welcome to the circus, Crayton Dawson. Hope you enjoy the show."

Chapter 16

In the spare room behind the doctor's office, Lizzy Carnes turned her nose away and picked up the bloody discarded gauze bandage from the nightstand beside Sammy Boy's bed. She dropped the soiled bandage into an empty washpan to be thrown away. "I think you're going to kill yourself if you don't take more time to let this wound heal," she said to Sammy Boy White, who sat on the side of the bed looking woozy and drained.

"This wound will heal just as well on horseback as it will on a feather bed," Sammy Boy said, stifling a groan as he stretched his right arm and tried to loosen the tight pain in his badly bruised chest. "I'm breathing all right now. The doctor says as young as I am, I'll heal up quick. I can't afford to let this opportunity slip past me."

Lizzy shook her head. "I swear it makes no sense to me, all this killing just to see who kills the other the quickest."

"You're a whor— I mean, a *woman,*

283

Lizzy," said Sammy Boy. "If you don't understand it, maybe it's because you ain't meant to understand it." He gestured toward a chair and said, "Hand me my shirt; help me get into it. Time is slipping away from us."

"You were going to say 'whore,' Sammy," said Lizzy. "But being a whore doesn't make me stupid!" She snatched up the shirt and tossed it to him.

"It doesn't make you real *smart* either, does it?" Sammy replied, grinning, catching the shirt and shaking it out with one hand. "The thing is, I've got a chance here to make something out of surviving that gunfight with Fast Larry Shaw. Whether he knew it or not, Shaw just opened a big door for ol' Sammy Boy. I'm going to take advantage of it. I'm going after him."

Lizzy looked puzzled. "That's what I can't understand, Sammy. The man could have killed you but he spared your life . . . why on earth would you want to kill him after him doing something like that? It looks to me like you would *thank* him for it."

"See?" said Sammy Boy. "That's how little you know about gunslinging. I've got Fast Larry Shaw all figured out, up here."

He tapped his finger against his forehead. "This is all about who makes the first mistake, and he made a *bad* one, not killing me when he had the chance. He showed me that he's tired of being who he is. He's getting old and worn out, and it won't be long before somebody has to put him to sleep, the way you do any old dog. I plan on being the person who does it."

"Well, all's I know is, me and Suzette met him and his friend, . . . I thought they were both real nice," she said, reaching out and helping him into his shirt, then beginning to button it for him.

"Wait a minute," said Sammy Boy, taking her by her wrist, stopping her. "You didn't, you know . . . with Fast Larry?"

"What?" Lizzy didn't catch on to his question.

"Damn it, Lizzy," said Sammy Boy, "don't make me come out and say it! You and Fast Larry, you didn't do anything, did you?"

Lizzy shrugged. "No, we just met at the bar, and then he left." She paused for a second, then added, "His friend left too, come to think of it."

"Then you can't really say he was *nice* or nothing else, can you?" said Sammy Boy.

"He seemed nice though," said Lizzy.

"Yeah, I bet," said Sammy Boy, letting her go back to buttoning his shirt. "Anybody can afford to be nice when they're on top of their game." As she finished up with his shirt, he ran his good hand along her back, up along her neck beneath her curly blond hair. "You stick with me, honey, nurse me along, help me get back to health while I find him. As soon as I kill him, we'll both be living it up somewhere, having food and drinks brought to our private railcar."

"Do gunmen live that well?" Lizzy asked, seeming to give the matter some close consideration. "The ones I've known haven't had private railcars, that I ever knew about."

"Why would they tell you what they had or didn't have, Lizzy?" said Sammy Boy, not liking the way she questioned his knowledge of gunmen. "All they ever wanted from you was one thing. They weren't about to tell you they had their own private railcar. Gunmen don't like telling too much about themselves."

Lizzy didn't seem to hear him. Instead she seemed to be concentrating on something else. "Sammy, how do gunmen make that kind of money?"

"By shooting people, how do you think?" Sammy said, sounding a bit put out by her question. "By hiring their gun to the highest bidders. To railroads, detective agencies, wealthy businessmen needing their services. If somebody squats on your land and refuses to leave, you hire a gunman. Somebody deals you dirt, takes a herd of cattle or a shipment of goods and doesn't pay you for them when the time comes, you hire a gunman. Hell, a gunman gets paid for all kinds of gun work. Sometimes they make money just in wagering themselves against some other gunman, the way me and Elton was doing. Hell, there's all sorts of ways a gunman makes money! Some that I don't even know about yet!"

"I don't think people who do that kind of work make much money, Sammy," Lizzy said. "The ones I've known are always living hand to mouth, sleeping wherever they can, eating whenever they get a chance to." She shook her head. "I think somebody has misinformed you about gunmen."

"There's some who make big money," said Sammy Boy, undaunted. "And that's the way it's going to be for me. I'll have folks bowing and scraping when I walk into a room. They'll be doing the same for you if they know you're with me. Stick with me Lizzy; you'll see. We'll both be living a whole new life before long. You can count on it."

"I'll stick with you, Sammy," said Lizzy, "even though Suzette says I'm making a big mistake. . . . I'll stick with you as long as you're honest with me and don't mistreat me."

"That's my girl," said Sammy Boy. He pointed at his gun belt hanging from a chair back, the butt of a new Colt sticking up from the holster. "Hand me that shooting rig. We best get on our way."

As Sammy Boy stood up on weak legs and Lizzy helped him strap his gun belt around his waist, Sheriff Neff stepped into the open doorway. Seeing Sammy buckle his belt and lift the Colt to check it, Neff said, "I see you've managed to get your hands on another gun before your wound barely dried over." He stepped into the room, shaking his head in wonder. "I reckon I shouldn't be surprised you're going after Shaw. You never struck me as a man with much sense."

Sammy Boy gave him a hard stare. "Sheriff, if you think I lived through that shoot-out in the street just to hear your law-dog mouth, you're badly mistaken." He spun the cylinder of the new Colt, then twirled the gun on his finger, getting a feel for the balance of it. Then he slid it expertly into his holster. "From now on I'll expect you to treat me the same as you treat Fast Larry Shaw. I might not have won that fight, but I damn sure stepped up and faced the man . . . that's something nobody else in this horse's-ass town would ever have the guts to do."

"I didn't treat Fast Larry Shaw any different than I treat any other man," said Sheriff Neff. "For your information I ran him out of Eagle Pass while you was still coughing up chunks of your dirty shirt."

"Yeah," said Sammy Boy knowingly, "I heard about how hard you ran him out of town. And I heard about how easy he gave in. You and Shaw ain't fooling me with a little stage show like that."

"I told him to leave and he left," said the sheriff, leveling his shoulders, but looking a bit rumpled by Sammy Boy's implication. "That's the way I've done it with his kind for years."

"Bull!" said Sammy Boy, also leveling his shoulders, feeling the pain and stiffness across his back and chest. "Everybody goes out of their way to treat Fast Larry Shaw like he's something special. From now on anybody don't treat me the same way, I'll

289

put a hole in them. I've proved myself. By God, I want some respect!"

"Respect?" said Neff. "Sammy Boy, you might have got pumped up on yourself enough to face Shaw, but except for a new hole in your chest, you're the same ragged-assed saddle bum you was the day you came to town. Don't look for any more respect than you've got coming. You're lucky Shaw didn't finish you off . . . and he might have if I hadn't been there. You might want to give some thought to thanking me for saving your worthless life."

Sammy Boy's new Colt streaked from his holster too fast for the old sheriff to respond. By the time Neff's hand wrapped around his pistol butt to draw it, Sammy's Colt was cocked and pointed squarely at his forehead.

"I don't pretend to know what makes you gunslingers tick," said Sheriff Neff, not backing down an inch, "but I do know that you ain't going to kill me, not here, not like this, because there ain't no gain in it for you. You need to show people how fast you are, not how stupid. Pull that trigger and I can promise you that whatever future you might have had shooting men down in the street is going to stop with one hard jerk on a hangman's rope."

Sammy Boy White calmed himself down and managed a thin smile, uncocking the pistol and twirling it into his holster. "Lucky for you I'm in a hurry today, old man," he said, "else I'd kill you just to prove you wrong."

"Sammy, I'm telling you the same thing I told Shaw. I want you to get yourself out of my town, and stay out," said Neff, carefully keeping his gun hand away from his pistol butt.

Sammy's smile widened but became no friendlier. "Since I was just getting ready to leave anyway, the same as Fast Larry Shaw was when you *ran him out,* all I can say is 'yes, sir, Sheriff! I'm on my way!' " He chuckled, looking at Lizzy, saying to her, "You run on over to the livery stable and bring us horses. I'll be waiting when you get back."

"All right, Sammy," said Lizzy, avoiding Sheriff Neff's eyes as she slipped past them and out through the open door.

"For God's sake, Sammy Boy," said Neff in disgust once Lizzy was out of hearing range, "it's bad enough you're in such a hurry to get yourself killed . . . why on earth are you dragging that poor soul along with you? Lizzy's dumber than a stump.

She'll never make it out there in the kind of life you're dragging her into!"

"Don't worry about Lizzy, Sheriff," said Sammy. "She'll be all right, long as she does as she's told. I'll take care of her, Sheriff."

"I hope you do," said the sheriff.

"Oh, I will." Sammy grinned. "I've always thought it might be nice having a partner who'll snuggle up to me at night. See? If it hadn't been for Shaw shooting me and me needing taking care of, I never would have hooked up with Lizzy. She was just looking for a man with promise, and all I need is some nursing along."

"You ought to be ashamed of yourself if you mistreat her," said the sheriff. "Any fool can see the poor girl has had a bad enough life already. Why in the world would you want to make it worse for her by putting yourself in her life?"

"You just can't stand the thought of me getting what she's got for free when everybody else in this town has had to pay for it," said Sammy Boy. "If you cared so much for this poor girl, why was she having to be a whore to every cowhand and tramp passing through this town?"

"Get on out of here, Sammy Boy," said Neff, losing his patience. Stepping aside and gesturing the young gunman toward the door, he added, "The less I see of *trash* like you, the better I like it."

"I'm gone, Sheriff," Sammy replied. "If you see the doctor, tell him I'll take care of the bill with him real soon." He started to turn away, but then stopped and said as if in afterthought, "And by the way, if our paths cross again and you ever make the mistake of calling me a name like that in public, you've got my word I'll kill you quicker than a cat can scratch its ass." He smiled, picked up his hat from a chair, and examined it before putting it atop his head. "Lizzy did a good job brushing my Stet. See, she's already worth her weight in beans and salt pork."

Sheriff Neff stood watching with a scowl on his face as Sammy Boy White left the room, Sammy making sure he walked straight and tall in spite of the pain in his chest and back. "*Trash* is one of the best names I could have called you," the sheriff whispered to himself.

On the street out front of the doctor's office, Sammy Boy met Lizzy as she came from the livery stable leading two horses by their reins. Sammy chuckled to himself, seeing her struggle with the big animals and at the same time try to keep her hemline hiked up off the dirt street. "Why didn't you ride one and lead the other, Lizzy?" he asked, taking the reins to the better-looking horse from her.

"I will next time," Lizzy replied sincerely, shoving a loose strand of hair back from her face.

Raising his foot to the stirrup, Sammy Boy stopped at the sound of Fat Man Hughes calling out, "Not so fast, Sammy Boy!"

Judging the tone of Hughes's voice, Sammy lowered his foot from the stirrup and turned to Lizzy, saying quietly, "Take the horses back a few feet."

"What?" Lizzy asked, unsuspecting. "Why?"

"Damn it, just do it," Sammy Boy hissed.

Lizzy took the reins from him and pulled the two horses to the side, but not as far away as Sammy would have liked.

Sammy turned and faced Fat Man Hughes and two of his bet collectors, C. W. Oates and Calvin Meadows, the three of them stopping in the street fifteen feet away. Oates and Meadows wore flat, nasty grins on their faces, but Fat Man Hughes was solemn, strictly business.

"What can I do for you, Fat Man?"

Sammy asked, already seeing that this was a standoff of some sort.

Hughes laughed under his breath, saying to his two gunmen, "Hear that? Asks me what he do for me? That's damned considerate of you, Sammy." C. W. Oates and Meadows also laughed slightly, both keeping their eyes on Sammy Boy, their thumbs hooked in their gun belts.

"That's me, all right, always aiming to please," said Sammy. Then his mood seemed to change instantly, along with the expression on his face. "Now what the hell do you want?"

"Money," Hughes roared, rubbing his thumb and finger together in the universal sign for greed. "Part of that cash your weasel friends Elton and Willie the Devil took off with was mine! I want it back!"

"Then you best tell them when you see them," said Sammy. "I'm sure they'll work something out with you."

Fat Man Hughes pointed a stubby finger at Sammy Boy. "Huh-uh . . . you're going to pay it to me, and right now!"

"Believe me, Fat Man," said Sammy with mock sincerity, "if I had any money at all, there's nothing I'd like better than to hand it over to a fat, greedy bastard like you. But the truth is, I'm broke to my boot heels. Ain't that right, little darling?" he said, hoping to direct some of the attention to Lizzy long enough to get an edge on the draw. With the pain in his chest and the stiffness in his shoulder, he knew he'd better take any advantage he could find.

"I've got a couple of dollars, if it will help," Lizzy said, not seeming to understand what was going on.

"Forget it, Lizzy," said Sammy. "This ain't about money. This fat turd has wanted to take me down a notch since the day I got here. Right, Fat Man?"

Hughes only smiled flatly and knowingly.

"The problem is," Sammy continued, as if explaining it all to Lizzy, "all he could come up with is C. W. and Calvin here." He looked the two gunmen up and down, then went on, saying, "And they both know that they can't either one cut it against me man-to-man . . . so they have to double up, the way a coward will do."

The two gunmen bristled; their thumbs came out of their belts and their hands were poised near their gun butts. "I'd face you any damned day, Sammy Boy," said Oates. "This just happens to be the way the boss wants it done."

"Yeah?" said Sammy. "And what about you, Calvin? Would you face me alone, if you had the opportunity, that is?"

"I was never afraid of you, Sammy Boy," said Meadows, jutting his chin. "It's like C. W. says. Hughes is the boss . . . we do it the way he says do it."

"Then let's *do* it," said Sammy. "We don't want to keep your boss man waiting, do we?"

"Everybody hold it!" shouted Sheriff Neff, stepping onto the street from the doctor's office. "There ain't going to be no more gunfighting here in my town! Sammy Boy, if you reach for that Colt, win or lose, you're going to jail!"

Without taking his eyes from the two gunmen, Sammy said, "To hell with you, Sheriff; if I lose, going to jail ain't in the cards. If they reach for their guns I'm killing them both. Hear that, C. W.? Hear that, Calvin? Just me, all by myself . . . that's the way I play *my* hand. Don't you both wish you had that kind of guts?"

"You son of a bitch!" Calvin Meadows shouted, losing his temper and making the first move.

"No!" shouted the sheriff, seeing Meadows's hand snatch the Colt from its holster, seeing Oates make the same move a split second behind him.

Lizzy looked away, throwing her free

hand over her eyes as the sound of gunfire roared back and forth along the empty street. The two gunmen had made the first move, but effortlessly, in spite of the wound in his chest, Sammy Boy White brought the new Colt up and fired first. Then Lizzy watched both men fall to the dirt as their bullets screamed past him.

"There, Sheriff," said Sammy, smoke curling up from his pistol, "was that clear enough for you to see? Did I give them all the advantage in the world? Did they make the first move?"

"Look out, Sammy!" Lizzy screamed. She didn't have to tell him why.

Turning on his heel, Sammy Boy saw Fat Man Hughes raise a Colt Thunderer from inside the lapel of his loose-fitting black linen coat. Before he got the gun leveled toward Sammy Boy, the young gunman deliberately fanned his new Colt carelessly. "So long, Fat Man!" he yelled as the bullets nailed Hughes in the chest one after the other, each shot slamming him a step backward.

"Lord God!" said Sheriff Neff, seeing the way Sammy Boy handled himself. "Shaw's bullet made a gunman out of you, that's for sure!"

Sammy White twirled the new Colt as if

assessing it. "Yeah, boy! Think what I could have done with my old Colt." He turned the gun toward the sheriff. "Any problems on how this happened, Neff? If so, get it said."

"No, Sammy," said the old sheriff, "I have to admit, those two called the play; so did Hughes. You did it in self-defense."

"That's what I like to hear," said Sammy, stepping over to Hughes's body, bending down, reaching inside his coat, and jerking out a thick roll of money. He stood up holding the money in his hand for the sheriff and the gathering townsfolk to see. "Hughes has no family here, nobody to leave this to. I'm taking it." He turned to the sheriff, the smoking pistol still in his hand, and said, "That is, unless the sheriff here has any complaints about it."

Sheriff Neff saw the wild look in Sammy's eyes, saw the way his thumb slid expertly over the Colt's hammer, cocking it. "Take it and go, Sammy. Don't push this thing too far."

"Too far?" Sammy laughed. "How far is too far?" He turned, giving the town a good look at him as he unbuttoned his shirt. "Look at this, folks. Three men dead in the street! All three of them against one of me! Everybody see this? And look!" he said, spreading his shirt open, showing the bloodstained bandage on his chest, "me with a bullet wound still healing!" He turned back and forth slowly. "Any question who the real gunman is?"

"No, Sammy," said the sheriff, seeing how Sammy Boy White's eyes had glazed in his excitement, "you was faster than anything I've seen in a while; that's a fact."

"Damn right it's a fact!" Stuffing the money inside his shirt, Sammy shouted along the street, "Here's something you can all tell your grandchildren about! You're all looking at the man who's going to outshoot Fast Larry Shaw!"

Mounting his horse, Sammy rode away quickly, Lizzy right behind him, waving back as if telling the whole town good-bye. No sooner than the two were out of town a townsman came forward and, looking at the bodies on the ground, said, "Lord have mercy! There will be hell to pay when that boy catches up to Shaw!"

Still staring in the direction of the rising dust, Sheriff Neff replied, "Aww, that boy ain't going to catch up with Fast Larry. . . . Hell, didn't you notice? He ain't even headed in the right direction. I expect he'll run that little whore ragged going from town to town, telling his gunfight story, showing that wound off till he gets another one or runs out of steam."

"I don't know, Sheriff. . . ." The townsman rubbed his chin, still looking at the bodies in the dirt. "He is a terror with a gun."

"Yep, he is," said the sheriff. "He's fast enough that nobody is going to put another bullet in him for a while. He's learned to pick his fights wisely. But take my word for it; he won't go *looking* for Lawrence Shaw . . . he'll just spend the rest of his life *pretending* he is. Shaw gave him a reason to live." The sheriff smiled. "What happened here will keep him fueled for a long time to come."

"Then I worry about that poor girl, Lizzy," said the townsman.

"I do too," said Neff with a trace of a grin, "for all the times she's going to have to listen to Sammy's gunfight over and over. But other than that, she'll be all right. I was riding Sammy a little, hoping some of it will get through to him. Maybe it will someday, if he'll ever stop running long enough to remember any of it." He nodded at Sammy and Lizzy's dust. "If they're lucky they'll both fall in love with each other along the way, make some kind of life they can live with." Dismissing the matter, he looked around the street, then said aloud to anyone along the boardwalks, "All right, come on; let's get Fat Man and his cronies out of the street. It's already getting hot out here."

PART
Three

Chapter 17

"What can I do for you, Mayor Bland?" Barton Talbert asked the stoop-shouldered man standing before him. The mayor fidgeted with the brim of his worn derby hat, taking a moment to summon up his courage before raising his eyes to Barton Talbert, who sat tilted back in a wooden chair with a boot hiked up on the tabletop. The rest of the outlaws lounged along the bar, watching in curiosity. Bo Kregger stood rigid beside Barton Talbert's chair with his arms folded, a scowl on his face.

"Mr. Talbert, sir," said Mayor Bland, "I . . . that is, we . . . the town council, that is, have had several complaints about the behavior of your men." He fidgeted in place, his eyes fearful and unsteady.

"No," said Barton Talbert, looking greatly concerned, "tell me it ain't so, Mayor. My men? Misbehaving?" He gave the faces along the bar a stern look, then said to the mayor, "Are these just wild, unfounded rumors, or is there some particular thing you can put your finger on?"

The mayor ventured a nervous look around the saloon. Both bat-wing doors lay broken on the floor. The saloon's large windows were a pile of broken glass shards. A wall stood blackened and charred by flames. In a rear corner stood a horse with Gladso Furlin sitting passed-out drunk in the saddle. "Nobody is blaming anything on anyone in particular," the mayor said. "I think it's more of an overall rowdiness that this town can't abide." He cleared his throat and wiped a hand across his wet brow. "They have asked me to come and point this out to you and to . . . well . . ." He hesitated. "To ask you and your men to leave."

As the mayor spoke, Denver Jack Fish walked through the open doorway dragging two freshly slaughtered goats behind him, blood smearing behind them. "Leave?" said Barton Talbert in stunned disbelief, gesturing toward the dead goats. "My goodness, Mayor, we was just getting prepared to invite this whole town to an old-fashioned fiesta!" He grinned broadly. "Compliments of me, of course."

"And me," said Bo Kregger in a low growl.

"Yes, excuse me, Bo," said Talbert. "Compliments of me *and* my *good friend* Bo Kregger."

Seeing the outlaws were in a better mood than they had been since their arrival in Brakett Hats, the mayor pressed on. "I . . . that is, *we* appreciate your offer, Mr. Talbert, but I'm afraid there have just been too many complaints."

"And they decided that since you *are* the mayor, it would be only fitting that you be the one to ask us to leave?" Talbert chuckled. "You are one game peckerwood," he added. "I have to give you that."

"Mr. Talbert, we're just a peaceable little town here . . . we like to welcome everybody. But you have to admit, this is a pretty unrestrained group of men you have riding with you."

"*Unrestrained?*" blurted Jesse Turnbaugh through his thick, tangled black beard, jumping out from the bar as if prepared for a gunfight. "Nobody calls me *unrestrained* and lives to tell about it!"

"Easy there, Jesse!" said Talbert, raising a hand toward him as if to hold the outlaw back. "I don't think the mayor meant to single you out, did you, Mayor?"

Mayor Bland looked terrified. "Oh, no! No, indeed! I'm referring more to an overall disruptive attitude!"

"Disruptive *attitude!* Now you're stepping

on *my* toes," said Denver Jack Fish, dropping a rope he was using to string up the goat carcasses. He stepped forward, wiping his palms on his trousers.

"Boys, boys," said Talbert in a mock show of trying to calm the men. "Let's not allow the mayor's fit of cruel name-calling drive us to rash violence."

"I certainly didn't mean to call anyone a cruel name," said Mayor Bland. His face had turned chalk white beneath a deep layer of sweat.

"Of course you didn't," said Barton Talbert. "I can see this is not exactly your area of experience." Then he said to the men, "I'm sure the mayor is new at this sort of confrontation."

"Well . . . yes," the mayor said, sweating heavily, rounding a finger in his white shirt collar. "If we had a sheriff, I believe he could better express what I'm trying to commun—"

"There's the problem, all right," Talbert butted in. "There's no sheriff here! Had I known that to begin with I ain't sure we would have stopped here. I don't mind telling you, Mayor, a prudent man wants the comfort of law and order anywhere he goes these days."

"Please, Mr. Talbert," the mayor said,

seeing how he was being strung along by the outlaws and their leader, "I'm only trying to get along with you, see if we can come to some sort of —"

"I know what!" said Talbert, cutting him off again. "We'll elect you a sheriff right here and now! All these men, all these guns . . . !" He thumped his palm soundly on his forehead. "Why the hell didn't I think of this before?"

"Mr. Talbert," said the mayor, almost pleading, "I don't want any trouble; this town doesn't want any trouble."

"Nonsense, Mayor Bland!" Talbert boomed with a grin. "It's no trouble at all." He turned to the men, saying, "Boys, which one of you would like to make a bid for the office of sheriff in this small but, I feel, very promising community!"

Bobby Fitt spit on the floor in disgust and said, "Brakett Hats is the worst shithole I ever stepped foot in. I'd like to see everybody who lives here fall over and choke to death!"

"Well, there, Bobby," said Barton Talbert, "I can see we won't be calling upon you for any campaign speeches, will we?" Grinning up at Bo Kregger, he said, "Make a note, Bo, no goodwill speeches from Bobby Fitt."

From the doorway Blue Snake Terril called out through the roar of laughter from the men, "This ain't no child's game here, Barton! We've got some hard killing coming our way."

The laughter fell. Mayor Bland looked sick to his stomach, sweat running down his cheeks. Barton Talbert looked over at Blue Snake and said, "I know it ain't no child's game, Snake, damn it. But I don't see where we've got much to worry about now that Bo Kregger is guarding our flank. Ease up; have a drink. Where have you been, anyway?"

"I rode back a ways with Curley and Stanley, making sure they'll do what they're supposed to when Shaw shows up."

"Don't you worry about those two ol' long riders; they're both tougher than pine knots," said Talbert.

"I know," said Blue Snake, "but I spent most of the day firing this baby." He patted his holstered pistol. "When Shaw gets here, I don't plan on leaving my fate in anybody's hands but my own." He shot Bo Kregger a look, saying, "No offense, Kregger."

"None taken," said the surly gunman.

"Lawrence Shaw?" the mayor said, his eyes widening even more. "Shaw is coming *here?* To Brakett Flats?"

"That's right," said Barton Talbert. "Now you see why we need a sheriff so desperately?"

Mayor Bland only stared, unable to respond for a moment. Finally he said, "Fast Larry Shaw isn't a troublemaker. I've never heard of him having any trouble with the law."

"Not yet, you haven't," said Talbert, standing as he spoke and walking over to where Gladso Furlin sat in his saddle in a drunken stupor, a whiskey bottle standing between his thighs. "But then Shaw hasn't yet met our new sheriff here."

He gave Gladso's horse a slight nudge on the rump, sending it forward with Gladso wobbling in the saddle. A new roar of laughter rose up from the men as the horse walked calmly out the door, Gladso tilting dangerously to one side. "I better go get him before he breaks his damned neck," said Gladso's brother, Harper, hurrying from the saloon.

Turning to Mayor Bland, Barton Talbert said, "He ain't looking too spry right now, Mayor, but once he sobers, he'll be a sheriff this town will be proud of!"

Laughter erupted again. At the bar, Blue Snake poured himself a shot of rye and tossed it back, saying under his breath, "Damned fools! Fast Larry Shaw is going to walk right through the lot of them."

Seeing the look on Mayor Bland's face, Barton Talbert looped an arm over his shoulders and said, "You think you've seen some *unrestrained* behavior? Hell, Mayor, this little fiesta wingding ain't even started yet!" He drew the mayor closer, saying into his ear, "I know there's some young women lives in this town . . . now where have you got them hiding?"

"No, honestly, there are no young women here . . . only the ones you've seen!" said Bland. "I'm afraid you're mistaken! We're not hiding anyone!"

The mayor winced at the feel of the cold metal gun barrel suddenly pressed against his ear.

"Don't lie to me again, Mayor!" Talbert growled, "or I'll clean your ears with this forty-five; then we'll *all* go ask your wife. I bet she'll tell us if we ask her polite-like, don't you think so?"

At the crest of a dry creekbed, Cray Dawson stood up in his stirrups for only a second and gazed up across the higher edge of broken land on the far side of a wide, sandy basin dotted with mesquite and creosote brush. When he sat down Jedson Caldwell started to rise up and take a look for himself, but Shaw said, "Stay put, Caldwell," causing him to sit back down in his saddle.

"I didn't see anything worth seeing," said Dawson, as if to satisfy Caldwell's curiosity.

Jedson Caldwell waited, hoping someone would explain why he shouldn't rise up and take a look. Shaw poured a thin trickle of water onto a wadded-up bandanna and pressed it to the back of his neck.

"That's known in these parts as Sidewinder Ridge," he said, nodding toward the distance where a white, piercing glare of sunlight mantled a long ledge of jagged earth. "Years ago, one Texas Ranger held back a band of Comanche for three days from a position along that rim. He had a Henry rifle and a Patterson Colt. It's an easy place for a good rifleman to pick your eyes out."

"Oh!" Caldwell seemed to sink lower in his saddle. "So you think there's some of Talbert's men waiting up there?" he asked, squinting as he studied the harsh land through the sun's glare.

"If they're not, they're damned fools," said Shaw. "They know I'm coming. We know the Devil ran to them in this direction. Barton Talbert left somebody up there to ambush me; you can count on it."

"Then what are we going to do?" Caldwell asked, looking back and forth between his two companions.

"What are we going to do, Dawson?" Shaw asked, his way of passing Caldwell's question off to Cray Dawson.

Dawson turned his horse slightly. "All they've seen so far is our dust," he said to Caldwell. "We're going to follow this creekbed around them as far as we can. Then we're going to wait until dark and come up behind them." Dawson looked to Shaw to see if he agreed.

"Sounds good to me," Shaw said. He held his horse back for a moment and let Dawson take the lead.

A mile across the basin, Curley Tomes and Stanley Little lay at the edge of the rim gazing out to where they'd seen the thin rise of dust only moments earlier. "Think it might have just been some elk or whitetail crossing in a hurry?" Stanley Little asked, keeping his voice down even though a mile of sand and brush lay between them and the veil of dust lying sidelong on the hot, dry air.

"Could be, I reckon," Curley Tomes

said, reaching up under his hat brim and scratching his moist forehead.

"Think it might just be some other travelers coming this way? Maybe someboJy leaving Texas, heading up to Colorado? I heard there's lots of folks have been doing that lately."

"Stanley," said Curley Tomes, taking a deep breath, "who the hell did you ask all these questions before I came along?"

"There's no need getting belligerent about it," said Stanley. "I was only asking to make conversation."

"Go somewhere and make conversation with yourself," Tomes growled, levering a round up into his rifle chamber. "You're starting to get on my nerves something awful."

"Think it'd be all right if I boiled some coffee?" Stanley asked meekly, as if not to impose on his partner.

"Boil some *coffee?*" Curley said in disbelief. He gazed up at the blistering sunlight and shook his head. Then he looked back at Stanley Little. "I don't give a damn if you boil your head!"

"I won't cause no smoke," said Stanley, scooting back from the edge before standing up and dusting his trousers.

"See that you don't," said Curley. "From

what I hear, Fast Larry Shaw is like a panther. He can sniff trouble on the turn of a breeze."

Stanley Little moved about the area behind them, gathering small dried twigs and kindling. In moments he'd built a small fire and boiled some coffee; then he immediately put out the fire and carried the pot over to where Curley still lay in the same spot watching evening shadows spread long across the earth. "Here we go," he said, setting the pot down beside Curley Tomes. Having used his hat as a pot holder, he shook it out and set it back atop his bald head. "By dark it ought to be simmered to about the way we like it."

"Good," said Curley, concentrating on the land without turning to face him, "now see if you can sit there real quiet-like for a while."

Chapter 18

In the moonlight, Jedson Caldwell held the horses while Lawrence Shaw and Cray Dawson worked their way silently through the brush toward the edge of the basin they had circled in the darkness. Against a short rock sticking up from the sandy earth, Shaw lifted his Colt from his holster and checked it as he said almost in a whisper, "Do you think we ought to send Caldwell on his way before we catch up to the whole Talbert gang? It might keep him from getting killed."

"I think Caldwell has to make up his own mind," said Dawson, also raising his pistol and checking it in the clear moonlight.

"I don't know why he rode with us to begin with," said Shaw. "I can't figure the man out . . . and I don't like riding with a man I can't figure out." He kept the Colt in his hand after checking it, instead of slipping it back into his holster.

Looking at Shaw as he finished checking his gun, Dawson said, "Then I reckon that means you've got me figured out pretty good?"

"You never was hard to figure out, Cray Dawson," said Shaw. "Besides, you and I was good friends years ago. There's some people who don't change much over the years."

"Maybe I haven't changed much since we were friends chasing brush-tailed mustangs together," Dawson offered, also keeping his Colt in his hand, "but things have happened in my life. Things that were just as important as you going off and making a big reputation for yourself."

"I didn't mean it like that," said Shaw. Trying to dismiss the subject, he said, "Come on, let's get on up there, see how many there are."

"Shaw!" Dawson said, not allowing himself to be put off, "we still ain't talked things out."

"Keep your voice down," Shaw said, hearing Cray Dawson speak above their whispered tone. "They'll hear you."

Lowering his voice again, Cray Dawson said, "All right, but I want things straight between us, Shaw."

"They are," said Shaw bluntly. "You might not realize it, but things *are* straight between us."

"Damn it, no, they're not," Dawson hissed to himself. Seeing Shaw had already started moving away through the cover of brush, he arose from against the rock in a crouch and hurried along silently behind him.

When Shaw stopped again, this time behind a stand of creosote and the bone-dry remnants of a juniper bough, they were too close to the outlaws for Dawson to risk saying a word. Less than ten yards from them, they could see well enough in the moonlight to know that there were only two men lying along the rim looking out onto the sandy basin. Shaw inched forward; Dawson followed until they were close enough to hear the two men talking quietly.

"I wouldn't say so to his face," said Stanley Little, "but to me, Barton and Blue Snake are going about this thing with Shaw the wrong way."

"Yeah?" said Curley Tomes with a trace of sarcasm. "I suppose you would have a better way of handling a big gun like Fast Larry Shaw?"

"Yes, I think I would," said Stanley. "If I was Barton Talbert, I would look up Fast Larry Shaw face-to-face, tell him how it all happened, and let the chips fall where they will, so to speak . . . take my punishment, if I had any coming."

"Sure you would, you lying dog." Curley chuckled. "You was there when it happened; so was I. Why don't we go find Shaw and explain it? Let the chips fall where they will, so to speak. That would be about the same, wouldn't it?"

"No, it wouldn't be," said Stanley, "because Talbert and Blue Snake are the ones running this bunch; they're the ones responsible for what happened."

"You're wrong there, pard," said Curley. "If the woman hadn't put up such a fight, she'd be alive today. That's the fact of the matter. All she had to do was keep her mouth shut about everything; who would ever know any of it —"

"Freeze!" Cray Dawson shouted, cutting the outlaw off. Beside him he could see that Shaw was on the verge of killing them without another word.

"What the . . . ?" Both faces turned toward Dawson's shadowy figure standing close behind them, covering them with a cocked Colt in his hand. Stanley Little's hands went up immediately in submission. But Curley's hand tightened on the rifle lying beside him on the ground.

"Any move you make will be your last," said Dawson. As he spoke he reached down and placed his free hand on Shaw's shoulder as if to hold him in place. "Easy," he said to him, "we need them alive for now."

"Is that you, Fast Larry?" asked Stanley Little. "I reckon you got the drop on us fair and square. But I had nothing to do with that woman getting killed. I tried to stop them. I fought for her like a wild man! But it done no good!"

"Shut up, Stanley," said Curley Tomes, lifting his hand slowly away from his rifle and raising both hands over his head.

"I'm not Shaw," said Dawson. "But he is."

Lawrence Shaw stood up slowly, taking a deep breath, knowing that Dawson was right; they needed to find out how many of the same men riding with Talbert now were there the day of Rosa's death. Not that it would mean anything except to him and Dawson. Whoever was with Talbert now would know what had happened and they would have already made their decision to stay and fight. Turning slightly without taking his eyes off the two men, Dawson called out, "Caldwell! Bring the horses on up!"

A short silence passed; then Caldwell replied, "I'm coming."

Stanley Little and Curley Tomes stared wide-eyed as Lawrence Shaw stepped forward, his Colt cocked and pointed at them.

They found no comfort in his uncocking the gun and lowering it into his holster.

Stopping a few feet from them, Lawrence Shaw stooped down, carefully laid his hand against the coffeepot, judging the heat of it, then said as he raised the pot by the handle and shook it gently, judging its contents, "Looks like we're down to grit and grinds," he said, controlling the rage that had begun to boil inside him as he'd listened to their words.

Dawson walked forward, keeping his gun on the two men, saying, "I'll get up a fire and boil some fresh, soon as Caldwell gets here with the horses."

"We've got plenty more fixins," Stanley Little volunteered, as if having coffee might save them.

"We brought our own," Shaw said grimly. "You sit real still. I want to ask you some questions."

"You want to take our guns?" Stanley asked, being overly obliging.

"Why?" Shaw asked bluntly.

"You know, in case we was to make a grab for them?" said Stanley.

"Anytime you feel the urge, feel free to make a grab," said Shaw. "This is not a social call."

Moments later Caldwell appeared

cautiously on the sandy slope as if rising up out of the land. He led the three horses over to one side and ground-tied them to a stand of mesquite near the two horses already there. "Did everything go all right?" he asked timidly, stepping over beside Dawson as he stared at the two men with their hands raised.

"Get some coffee from the saddlebags," Shaw said, not answering his question.

Dawson worked up a small fire while Caldwell cleaned out the pot and poured water in it from Stanley Little's and Curley Tomes's canteens. A few minutes later as the coffee began to boil, Dawson stepped in and picked up both men's guns from the ground and laid them a safe distance away.

"Tell me the whole story," Shaw said to Stanley Little, "just the way you said you would if you were with Barton Talbert."

"You're going to kill us, ain't you?" Stanley ventured.

"What do you think?" said Shaw.

"I think it was all one terrible mistake," said Stanley. "Like I said, I tried to stop them. Tried to talk sense to them."

"Hell, shut up, Stanley!" said Curley Tomes. "He don't give a damn. He's going to kill us anyway!" He turned to Lawrence Shaw. "Here's the truth of it, Shaw, for the better or the worse. We never went by your place to cause any trouble. The fact is, Barton Talbert wanted to meet you . . . wanted to be able to say he shook hands with the fastest gun alive." An expression of pained irony came upon his face. "Damn it all! He idolized you, to tell the truth. Said he was honored that you came from the same part of Texas where he was born. Said every Texan ought to be proud of you!"

"That's the truth, so help us God!" Stanley interjected.

"Go on," Shaw said to Curley, "tell me all of it."

Dawson cut in, saying, "We don't need to hear the details; tell us who was there, the ones who took part in it!"

"No," said Shaw to Curley Tomes, "tell us everything that happened that day."

"Everything?" Curley asked cautiously.

"Everything," said Shaw. "Leave nothing out."

Dawson stepped away and stooped down beside the fire. He stared into the flames as Caldwell raised the coffeepot and poured steaming coffee into three tin cups sitting on the ground.

"We got there to your house," said Curley Tomes to Shaw. "At first it looked like nobody was at home. Sidlow knocked and knocked but nobody came to the door. We were all still mounted except Sidlow, Blue Snake, and Barton. They had already turned to get back on their horses when the door opened, and there was your wife." He swallowed and said in contemplation, "Damn it . . . if she just would've waited another minute or two we would have been gone. None of this would have happened."

"I don't want to hear any more of it," Dawson said in a tight, low voice.

"Then step away from the fire," Shaw said to him.

"No," said Dawson, "I'll stick. If you're here, I'm here."

"Go on," Shaw said to Curley Tomes. Without turning, Shaw reached out with a gloved hand and took the cup of coffee Caldwell held out to him.

"All right, I'll try." Curley rubbed his forehead with both hands as if the memory troubled him. When he'd drawn a deep breath and let it out slowly, he continued, saying, "She . . . she was a real pretty woman, Shaw . . . and she came to that door smiling, just as friendly as can be, like she might have been expecting somebody."

Shaw bit the inside of his lip, recalling how in his last telegram he'd told her he was on his way home. "Go on," he said again.

"Anyway, her expression changed the minute she saw Barton Talbert and us," said Curley. "Barton tried to explain to her that he was just there to meet you, and nothing else. But she was real suspicious. Told him it wasn't the first time somebody came by there looking for you. Said she was telling him the same she told all the others, to get off the place and stay off. Then she tried to slam the door, but Sidlow shoved his boot into it and kept it open. Then the woman — your wife, that is — she got hard to handle. Started screaming at Sidlow and Barton. She wouldn't shut up long enough for Barton to even apologize!"

Stanley Little cut in, saying, "That's when Barton and Sidlow went nuts. Sidlow hauled off and kicked the door in! I hollered and tried to stop him, but he didn't listen to me!"

"That ain't true," said Curley. "Well, most of it is, except you didn't say a damn word. Neither did the rest of us. We let that poor woman die, never done a thing. Some of us even took advantage —"

"Stop it, damn it to hell!" shouted Cray Dawson, slinging his coffee cup away, coming to his feet.

"Get back, Dawson," said Shaw. He held out a hand as if to stop Cray Dawson from going past him to attack Curley Tomes.

"I'm just telling you the truth, like you asked!" said Curley, looking concerned about Dawson.

"I know," said Shaw, "go on." He shot Dawson a flat stare that told him to get back and stay back. Dawson relented, stepped back, and stooped down beside Jedson Caldwell near the fire.

Curley swallowed again, then said, "She . . . she took off running through the house, but Sidlow ran after her. I swear, Barton and Blue Snake tried to stop him but it was too late! There was a gunshot; then Sidlow hollered out that she had a gun and shot at him. Well, that's when Barton and Blue Snake ran inside and the rest of us got down off our horses and ran over to the house. There was another shot; then Sidlow or Blue Snake, one, got the gun away from her and dragged her outside. She was kicking and screaming like a wildcat. Barton tried to calm her down but she scratched his face."

"I didn't see that," said Stanley. "I was looking away."

Shaw ignored him and stared at Curley Tomes.

"Well, that set Barton off," Curley said. "He hit her, hard . . . I mean with his fist." He stopped for a second and drew a breath, having trouble with the picture of it in his mind. "From there on things just got worse, until finally . . . well, you know." His voice fell lower, softer. "Then she was dead."

"What's their names?" Dawson asked, his voice trembling. "I saw their faces; I want to know their names."

Shaw and Caldwell just looked at him, seeing him stare into the low flames, his eyes glistening with tears.

"Tell us," Shaw said, his voice sounding calm and unaffected compared to Cray Dawson's.

Curley Tomes nodded. Then he took a minute to think about it and said, "There was Denver Jack Fish . . . Jesse Turnbaugh, Bobby Fitt . . . the Furlin brothers, Harper and Gladso, Blue Snake Terril, and of course Talbert and Sidlow."

"And us," said Stanley. "Don't forget us."

"Shut up, Stanley," said Curley. "You ain't gaining nothing for yourself." He considered it, then with a puzzled look he asked Shaw, "Is he?"

Shaw shook his head no.

"I didn't think so," said Curley with finality.

"Who else has joined them besides the Devil and his new partner?" Cray Dawson asked.

"That's about all," said Curley Tomes, addressing Shaw. "Willie the Devil came riding in the other day with that scarecrow-looking fellow. Said Shaw had killed Donald Hornetti and was on a rage . . . coming our way."

"I never liked Donald Hornetti much anyway," said Stanley. As they'd all talked, Stanley had managed to scoot a bit closer to Shaw, as if they were old friends who hadn't seen each other for a while.

Ignoring Stanley, Shaw asked Curley, "Are they still in the same place where the Devil met them?"

"Yep, they're still in Brakett Flats," said Curley. He shrugged. "You can be there by morning if you've a mind to."

"Who's their gun?" Shaw asked pointedly, studying Curley's eyes to see if he was telling the truth.

"Their gun? I don't know what you mean," said Curley.

"They wouldn't be there waiting unless they had somebody who thought they could take me . . . who is it? Mad Albert

Ash . . . Teddy Roach?" He continued to search Curley's eyes.

"Hell, what's the use . . ." said Curley. "Barton's got Bo Kregger siding with him and Blue Snake."

"Bo Kregger," said Shaw, trying to pull up the name and face from his memory. "He shot a man once for calling him 'Slick,' didn't he?"

"Damn!" said Curley, impressed by Shaw. "I'd plumb forgot about that, but yes, he did, now that you mention it. He sure hated that name!"

"Slick Bo Kregger," said Shaw. "He carries a pair of Colts instead of just one like everybody else, right?"

"No, he only wears one," said Curley, seeing that Shaw was testing him, "unless I miscounted."

Shaw only nodded.

Stanley said quietly, "I don't suppose you'd be willing to let us go, since we never really laid a hand on your wife?"

"Not a chance," said Shaw. "You wasn't waiting here to enjoy the sunrise."

"But we told you everything you asked . . . that's worth something, ain't it?" Stanley persisted.

Caldwell stood up and stepped over closer, interested in what Shaw might have to say at this point. But Shaw didn't answer.

"You could at least give us a fighting chance," said Stanley.

"What good would it do?" Shaw shrugged.

"You've got a point there," said Stanley.

Caldwell said to Shaw, "Excuse me! But you're not going to actually kill these men, are you?"

"What did you think I was going to do with them, Undertaker?" Shaw asked, turning his attention slightly toward Caldwell.

"I don't know, but my goodness!" Caldwell exclaimed. "I never thought you would just execute them! That's not human!"

"But squaring off in the middle of a street is?" Shaw inquired. "How about a hanging? Tying a man's hands behind his back? Smacking his horse on the rump? Leaving him swinging with his toes pointed to the ground? Does that work better for you, Undertaker?"

"Wait a minute," said Curley Tomes, "why do you call him Undertaker?"

"Because that's what he is," said Shaw.

"Hot damn! That gives me the creeps," said Curley, shivering and rubbing his hands up and down his arms. "I wish nobody had brought that up, not at a time like this, for God's sake!"

While Curley talked, Stanley Little had managed to slip his hand down to his boot, where he kept a small hidden derringer. "Now!" shouted Curley Tomes, giving his partner the signal to make a move as he rolled toward the spot where Dawson had laid their rifles.

Before Caldwell or Dawson made a move, Shaw's Colt came up cocked and sent a bullet through Stanley Little's heart. As Curley Tomes came up onto his knee leveling a rifle toward him, Shaw's second shot turned him a backward flip and dropped him dead on the ground.

"Jesus!" Caldwell shouted in surprise.

Shaw stood up, and walked over to where Curley lay dead at his feet. Looking back at Caldwell as he cocked his Colt, he said, "Feel better now, Undertaker?" He fired a shot down into Curley's upturned forehead.

"My God, he's already dead!" said Caldwell. "Why are you doing this?"

Shaw walked over to Stanley Little's body, rolled him faceup with the toe of his boot, and aimed the Colt down. Seeing what he was going to do, Caldwell turned his face away and held his breath until the shot resounded. Then he turned to Dawson, who had sunk back down beside the fire now that Shaw had killed the two men. "Why is he shooting them? I can't believe this! They're both dead!"

"Shut up, Undertaker," Cray Dawson said bitterly. "He knows what he's doing."

"I can't live this way!" said Caldwell. "How can *any* sane man stand to live like this?"

"If you can't stand it, you might want to think about pulling out now," Dawson said quietly. "Things are going to get awfully bloody from here on." He stared into the low flames with a dark expression in his eyes.

Chapter 19

Willie the Devil sat upon the edge of the bar, writing down bets on strips of paper with a pencil stub. He looked at the short line of townsmen who had ventured out of their homes once they'd heard that Lawrence Shaw was on his way to town. Willie the Devil wasn't about to mention that it was all speculation at this point. If Shaw showed up in Brakett Flats things would start happening pretty fast. The Devil wanted to make sure he had all bets covered.

"I think it speaks well for this town, these gentlemen participating in our little fiesta get-together, which will be getting under way shortly!" Willie the Devil said, raising his voice for all to hear as he spoke to Elton Minton. Elton stood at the bar, taking money and stuffing it down into a tin cash box. Then, speaking directly to the townsmen, Willie said, "Everybody tell us clearly who you intend to bet on. We want no mistakes. We want nothing but satisfied customers!" In the front corner of the saloon a small Mexican band had quickly formed. Racy guitar and accordion music swelled in the ceiling rafters amid a cloud of cigar smoke.

Most of the townsmen looked frightened at being there among members of the Talbert gang. They left as soon as they had their bets placed. At the far end of the bar a fight erupted between the Furlin brothers and Denver Jack Fish. A couple of townsmen left their place in line and scurried from the saloon, one leaving his hat behind when it sailed off his head. A deathlike silence fell over the place when Denver Jack Fish drew his big Russian forty-five and blasted a hole through Harper Furlin's foot.

Before Gladso could respond on his brother's behalf, Denver Jack Fish backed away with his pistol aimed at the tin sheriff's badge on Gladso's chest. No sooner had Fish disappeared out through the doorway and Gladso began attending to his brother's wounded foot than Willie the Devil waved his arms frantically to get the band playing again, shouting, "Nothing to worry about, gentlemen! Just a little glimpse at the kind of action we're going to see between two top gunmen once Fast Larry Shaw arrives!"

"That dirty son of a bitch blew my toe

off!" Harper Furlin shrieked. But the end of his words was drowned out by the boom of a big bass guitar and the squeal of the accordion.

Willie the Devil stepped along the bar quickly and said to Gladso, "Get him out of here before he drives off the bettors!"

"Go to hell, Devil!" Harper shouted as Gladso pressed a wet bar towel on his bleeding foot.

"Yeah, get away from here, Willie," said Gladso. Thumbing the badge on his chest he added, "One word from me and your betting is over!"

Willie the Devil shook his head in disgust and turned back to his end of the bar, saying to himself, "The stupid bastard thinks he really is a sheriff!"

Outside the saloon, Barton Talbert, Blue Snake, and Bo Kregger looked on as Denver Jack Fish left the saloon looking back over his shoulder, shoving his big Russian down into his holster. He stopped at the corner of an alley within hearing distance of Blue Snake, Kregger, and Talbert.

"Sounds like he must've shot Harper," said Blue Snake, looking over at Denver Jack, who nodded in affirmation.

With no further comment on the matter Blue Snake went back to polishing a painted thumbnail against the back of his glove. Beside him Bo Kregger only nodded and stood watching until his curiosity got the best of him. Finally he asked, "Why the hell is both your thumbnails painted? Are you wanting to be a woman or something?"

Blue Snake bristled but held his temper, knowing better than to get sharp with a big gunman like Kregger. "I like a little flare of color," said Blue Snake, getting a glimpse of Denver Jack Fish, seeing the grin on his face caused by Bo Kregger's words. "I learned it from a Frenchwoman back in Waco . . . she had lots of style." He jutted his chin. "It looked damn good on her."

"Maybe on *her* it did, but *damn*, son!" said Bo Kregger, chuckling under his breath.

"What are you trying to say, Bo?" Blue Snake asked, his jaw tightening. Big gunman or no, there was only so much he could take.

"I ain't *trying* to say it," said Bo Kregger. "I *am* saying it. Your thumbs look plumb whorehouse sissy to me. I'm wondering if you ever find yourself feeling all giddy and out of control."

Blue Snake snarled, "There ain't a damn thing giddy about me —"

"Hold it, what this?" said Barton

Talbert, cutting him off. From the far end of town two horses came walking in slowly from the sand flats. Across their back lay two bodies, their arms hanging stiffly down the horses' sides.

"I'll be damned," Blue Snake whispered in awe, already getting the message.

"That's Stanley's and Curley's horses," said Barton Talbert.

"Then I'd say it's a good possibility that's Stanley and Curley across their backs," Bo Kregger offered with a slight smile. "Looks like Fast Larry Shaw is letting us know he's here." Kregger stepped forward with his shoulders leveled, as if facing Shaw in the middle of the dirt street. "I'm here, Shaw," he called out loudly along the street, his voice resounding out toward the sand flats. "You hear me, Shaw? I'll be right here waiting. Anytime you're ready!"

The street fell silent. From the edge of an alley, Denver Jack Fish ventured forward and looked out in the direction the two horses had come from. Along the boardwalk people appeared one and two at a time, looking at the two horses and their gruesome cargo. Meeting the horses, Blue Snake and Barton Talbert stopped them and pulled them out of the middle of the street. Blue Snake reached out, took a handful of Stanley Little's hair in his gloved hand, and tried to lift his head for a look at his face.

"Stanley's stiff as a board," said Blue Snake. Catching a glimpse of Bo Kregger watching him with a smug grin, he jerked harder on the dead man. But instead of Stanley's head rising, the whole body slipped upward, then toppled off onto the street. The horse neighed and jumped aside.

"What sort of message is this?" asked Talbert, looking down at Stanley's body. Rigor mortis had set in and Stanley's body lay on its back in the same shape it had lain in across the saddle. His arms lay flat, extended above his head. Lying jackknifed at the waist, Stanley stared up blindly from between his boots, a bullet hole showing raw and red between his wide eyes.

"If it was Stanley's message" — Bo Kregger chuckled — "I'd think he was telling the whole world to kiss his ass." He looked all around the sand flats just beyond the town limits. "But this is Fast Larry Shaw just wanting to rattle somebody. He's telling your men this is what they've all got coming. He figures if you tell some men they're trapped in a place, they'll try to run, sure as hell."

"It makes sense to me, Bo," said Talbert. "You sure seem to have Fast Larry figured out."

"It ain't hard for one gunslinger to figure another one out," said Bo Kregger with a thin smile of satisfaction. "Staying one step ahead of the competition is what's kept me alive . . . Fast Larry too."

"Nobody here is going to run from any-body," said Blue Snake with determination in his voice.

"Now that's the spirit," Kregger said with veiled sarcasm. Taking a step forward toward the far end of town, he shouted, "Shaw! Your game ain't working! You hear me? I just been told nobody here is going to turn tail just because you shot a couple of saddle tramps! You've got to face *me* to get to Barton Talbert!"

"Saddle tramps?" said Denver Jack Fish, turning to Jesse Turnbaugh, who had walked along the boardwalk with his pistol out, scanning the sand flats. "Hell, Stanley and Curley was no saddle tramps! They were damn good men. Good thieves, good rustlers! What does he mean, saddle tramps?"

"Hell, I don't know." Jesse Turnbaugh shoved his pistol down into his holster and replied quietly, "I reckon to Bo Kregger we're all nothing but saddle tramps."

"I reckon so," said Denver Jack, also holstering his pistol, having kept it in his hand since shooting Harper Furlin in the foot. "Then just between you and me, I ain't going to be real eager to back him up if it comes down to it."

"Bo Kregger ain't interested in you and me backing him up," said Jesse. "Can't you see by his attitude? He ain't concerned about handling Fast Larry Shaw. He ain't concerned about *nothing*, far as I can tell."

"Then maybe he won't mind if I just saddle up and skin out of here," said Denver Jack Fish. "Looks like I've already got the Furlin boys madder than two red-assed apes."

"Bo Kregger might not mind," said Jesse Turnbaugh, "but I bet Talbert and Blue Snake wouldn't be too happy about it."

"Well, the fact is," said Denver Jack, "I'm getting to where I don't much give a damn what they think either. This whole thing with Fast Larry Shaw never should have happened, and we both know it."

"I have to admit," said Jesse, "it was the worst thing I ever took part in. I don't know what the hell came over all of us. Seemed like once it all started there was nothing could stop it."

Denver Jack Fish looked him up and down. "How do you feel about sticking here and maybe having to fight Fast Larry Shaw?"

"If that's what it comes to I reckon I can give him a showing," said Jesse. "I can't say I like my odds at beating him if it came down to a straight-up shoot-out, just him and me. But I don't look for that to happen."

"Neither do I," said Denver Jack, "but how do we know?"

"Bo Kregger is awfully fast," said Jesse Turnbaugh.

"But so is Fast Larry Shaw," said Denver Jack. He looked out on the street to where Blue Snake, Barton Talbert, and Bo Kregger stood looking out past the south end of town. Then, lowering his voice, he said, "I saw Fast Larry Shaw kill Orville Dupre in Brownsville."

"But that was over four years ago, wasn't it?" said Jesse. "A man ages in four years in the gunslinging profession."

"Yeah, Shaw might have aged, but Orville Dupre didn't, not after that. He's as dead now as when Fast Larry left him facedown in the Texas dirt." Eyeing Jesse closely, he added, "As dead as *we'll* both be if we end up facing the man. I ain't no coward, but damn, there's such a thing as good sense."

Jesse Turnbaugh stood in silence for a moment, looking at the two bodies, one in the dirt, the other across a saddle. Finally he said to Denver Jack, "You've got a point there. I ain't no coward either. . . . When are you thinking about leaving?"

"I'm long past thinking about it," said Denver Jack. "Shooting Harper just has cinched it for me. I'm gone just as soon as I can saddle up and slip away." He grinned shyly. "If you look for me an hour from now, you best look ten miles north of where I'm now standing."

"I hear you," said Jesse. "And I'll be right beside you, laying down hoofprints and kicking up sand."

"Hey, over there, you two," Barton Talbert called out.

"Uh-oh!" whispered Denver Jack. "Think he heard us?"

"I don't see how he could," said Jesse.

"Both of you come help us get these men off the street," said Talbert. "Stanley and Curley deserve better than this. Go get some shovels, dig a hole, and drop them in it."

"As hot as it is out here?" Denver Jack

whispered to Jesse Turnbaugh. "He's out of his mind!" But then to Barton Talbert he called out, "Sure thing, boss; we're on our way."

"This could be a good thing for us," said Jesse under his breath as the two started toward the middle of the street. "It'll give us a reason to be gone for a couple of hours. You can't believe how far gone I can get in that amount of time."

"Oh, yes, I can," said Denver Jack Fish.

Five hundred yards out on the sand flats, Cray Dawson had swung around town and headed north to where Lawrence Shaw and Jedson Caldwell were waiting. When he slowed his horse and cut around and down into a natural land fault he found Shaw and Caldwell sitting atop their horses in the shade of a rocky ledge. "I sent them in at a walk," said Dawson. "Bo Kregger was shouting out at you all the while I was riding wide of town."

"Good," said Shaw. He lifted his canteen strap from around his saddle horn and pitched it to Dawson. "Looks like you could stand watering. Help yourself."

Unscrewing the cap, Dawson gave a thin smile, saying, "I don't need to sniff this first, do I? Make sure it's what it should be?"

"It's water, Dawson," Shaw said flatly. "Although right about now I could do with a stiff shot of rye." Seeing Caldwell give him a look, Shaw added, "Oh, not to settle my nerves, Undertaker. Just to cut a couple of pounds of this Texas landscape from my throat. I'm off the whiskey." He thought about it for a moment. "For the time being, anyhow."

"What makes you so sure some of the Talbert gang will try to slip out of town and make a run for it?" Jedson Caldwell asked.

"Somebody always does," said Shaw.

"But what if this time they don't?" asked Caldwell. As he spoke he lifted the big Colt from his holster and began twirling it on his finger, still awkward but getting better at it, having been practicing anytime he could when Shaw and Dawson weren't watching.

When he heard no answer but rather felt the silence from Shaw, Caldwell looked up and saw Shaw's cold green eyes staring at him. "Sorry," he said, immediately stopping the Colt and slipping it back into his holster.

Now Shaw answered him, saying, "If nobody tries to make a run for it I haven't lost a thing, Undertaker. I've still got them surrounded." He offered a thin smile. "I can go in anytime I feel like it. But the less of them I have to face in the confines of a town, the better I like it. Everyone who leaves betters my odds that much more."

"Betters *our* odds," Cray Dawson put in.

"That's right," said Shaw, "betters *our* odds." Taking the canteen back from Dawson, he said as he capped it and looped it on his saddle horn, "You'll have to excuse me, Cray Dawson; you can see I'm used to working alone."

"I understand," said Dawson. He turned his horse in beside Lawrence Shaw, and the three of them sat quietly for the next fifteen minutes, hearing nothing but the low whir of hot wind across the sand flats.

Finally Shaw said, "Here comes somebody already." He tuned his hearing toward the trail coming north out of Brakett Flats. "Sounds like two riders, moving fast."

"How could you possibly tell that?" said Caldwell, greatly impressed. "I can't hear a thing!"

"Spend a few years knowing there's somebody coming any minute to try to kill you, Undertaker," said Shaw. "After a while you get to where you can almost hear their shadows." He nudged his big buckskin forward to the edge of the rock shade and looked back toward Brakett Flats at the high-spiraling rises of dust. "Let's get into position, pards. They're going to shoot through here like a train on fire."

"Mr. Shaw, do you suppose . . . ?" Jedson Caldwell started to ask Shaw something, but then he stopped in reluctance.

Turning in his saddle, Shaw said, "Do I suppose what, Undertaker? Come on, spit it out; we've got company coming."

Caldwell let it drop, saying, "Nothing, never mind."

As if reading Caldwell's mind, Shaw said, "I gave you that gun to use. When you see fit to use it, you don't need my permission." He started to turn and nudge his stallion forward, but on second thought, he added, "Just don't shoot me with it again. I couldn't overlook it a second time."

"I won't, Mr. Shaw," said Caldwell, "and thanks."

A thousand yards north of Brakett Flats, Jesse Turnbaugh and Denver Jack Fish slowed their horses to a trot and looked back over their shoulders through their wake of dust. "Yeehiii!" shouted Denver Jack, yanking his hat from his head and waving it in a high circle. "*Adios!* And good riddance, you stupid bunch of peckerwoods! So long, Harper, you bloody-foot idiot, you! So long, Bobby Fitt and that seven dollars I owe you!"

"Yeah!" shouted Jesse Turnbaugh, looking back also, extending a long, exaggerated salute toward the distant outline of Brakett Flats. "*Adios,* Bo Kregger! *Adios,* Barton Talbert and Blue Snake, you painted-thumb son of a bitch! *Adios,* Fast Larry Shaw, fastest gun alive! You played hell getting us!"

They laughed as they turned back in their saddles to attend to the trail lying before them. To their surprise, ahead of them fifty yards, in the middle of the beaten trail, sat a single rider atop a big buckskin. "Uh-oh!" said Denver Jack Fish, placing his crumpled hat back down on his head. "Was we being too loud?" They drew their horses to an abrupt halt.

"I believe that's Fast Larry Shaw!" said Jesse Turnbaugh. As they looked, to their right they saw another rider closing in slowly, to their left another. All three had Colts in their hands.

"Damn!" said Denver Jack Fish. "Fast Larry has put us both in his Denver jackpot, bigger than hell. He was expecting us to come running this way!"

"What are we going to do?" asked Jesse Turnbaugh, getting a little shaky about being surrounded.

"I don't know," said Denver Jack. "I ran out of any good ideas once we got out of Brakett Flats."

"I ain't going down easy," said Jesse. His hand crept toward his pistol butt as the three riders closed in around them.

"Get your hand away from your gun, mister," said Jedson Caldwell, to both Shaw and Dawson's surprise.

Seeing the outlaw raise his hand quickly away from his gun gave Caldwell a strange feeling, knowing that it was his command that had initiated such obedience. He continued, saying, "Both of you raise your hands and keep them raised." Then he stared, almost bemused by the fact that both of these hardened gunmen actually did as he told them to do. "Now both of you —"

"All right, Undertaker," said Shaw, "don't get carried away with yourself."

The two men looked back and forth among Shaw, Dawson, and Caldwell, their hands held chest-high. "You must be Fast Larry Shaw," said Denver Jack Fish, looking Shaw in the eyes as Shaw rode up to within ten feet and stopped.

"That's right, I'm Fast Larry," said Shaw. "What's your names?"

"I'm Denver Jack Fish . . . hell, you must've heard of me, as much as I've done over the years?"

"Can't say that I have," said Lawrence Shaw, the Colt lying poised comfortably in his hand.

"We know this is all about the woman, Shaw," said Jesse Turnbaugh. "But if you kill me you're killing an innocent man."

"Me *too,* damn it!" said Denver Jack Fish, giving Turnbaugh a harsh stare. "What about me?"

"Well, him too," said Turnbaugh. "That's why we headed out when we heard you was coming. Talbert, Blue Snake, and the others have to answer for this, not us!"

Shaw looked at Dawson. Looking them up and down closely, Dawson gave Shaw a nod, telling him he recognized these two men.

"What's going on back in Brakett Flats?" Shaw asked them both.

"How do you mean?" asked Denver Jack Fish.

"I mean, what's going on? Is Bo Kregger anxious to get this thing over with? Are the rest of the men ready? Tell me what it's like in town about now."

Jesse and Denver Jack looked at each

other; then Denver Jack said, "Well, Bo Kregger is cool as can be. I don't think he's human. Last I saw he had Blue Snake riled, shaming him over his thumbnails being painted. I just had shot one of the Furlin brothers in his foot. I heard Bo and Blue Snake arguing about his painted nails . . . then those two horses came in carrying Stanley and Curley." He shook his head. "*Whew!* What made you send them in like that, bullet holes in their foreheads? Did you execute them? Them on their knees pleading for their lives?"

"What do you think?" said Shaw coldly.

"I never heard of you being that kind of man," said Turnbaugh. "But then I reckon somebody kills your wife . . . it's understandable."

"What about the painted thumbnails?" Shaw asked, dismissing the matter of whether or not he had executed Stanley Little and Curley Tomes.

"Aw, that's just how Blue Snake is," said Denver Jack. "He's what you might call flamboyant. Ain't nothing wrong with him, though. We all got used to it. Bo Kregger seemed to be looking for something to ride Blue Snake about."

"Blue Snake don't take well to anybody questioning his manliness," said Jesse

Turnbaugh, "not that they should."

"He likes colorful thumbnails, what the hell?" said Denver Jack Fish with a tight shrug.

"How's the town laid out?" Shaw asked.

"You mean for street fighting?" asked Denver Jack.

"Yeah, for street fighting," said Shaw.

"About like every other town," Denver Jack said, "a big ol' street running north and south through its belly, a saloon on the west side, a vacant sheriff's office. . . . There is one thing different, though — a big gallows out front of the sheriff's office."

"It used to be a county seat," said Cray Dawson. "Judge Roscoe Perls had a gallows built there."

"What's along the east side of the street, opposite the saloon?" Shaw asked.

"Let's see," said Denver Jack, "there's a barbershop, a vacant apothecary shop, a woman's hat shop. That's as much as I remember."

"That's enough," said Shaw.

"What about us, Fast Larry?" Jesse Turnbaugh asked, looking hopeful. "Are you going to kill us?"

"How many men are there in town with Talbert and Blue Snake now?" asked Shaw, his expression revealing nothing.

Taking a second to figure it up, Jesse Turnbaugh said, "There's six men with them now, if you count the Devil and that scarecrow that rode in with him. Me and Denver Jack couldn't stand it any longer . . . we cut out. So what do you say? Are you going to kill us or what?"

Shaw noted how both men had dropped their hands slightly more each time they asked that question.

"If you were me what would you do?" Shaw asked flatly.

"If I was you," said Denver Jack Fish, "I believe I'd at least give us both a fighting chance."

"The way you gave Rosa a fighting chance?" said Cray Dawson, who had been sitting silent until now.

The harsh bite in his words caused both men to turn toward him, a bit surprised. Shaw just watched and listened. When the two men turned back to face Shaw as if for some guidance, he said, "You heard him. Answer his question."

Chapter 20

In the streets of Brakett Flats, Barton Talbert had called his remaining men together in a rally of support. But when the gunfire resounded in the distance north of town, he immediately looked all around and said, "Where the hell are Jesse and Denver Jack?"

"You sent them to bury Stanley and Curley," said Gladso Furlin.

"I know damn well I sent them to bury Stanley and Curley," Talbert snapped at him. "But that was a long time ago! Ain't they back yet?"

Bobby Fitt looked all around. "I haven't seen them. Want me to look for them?"

"Go check the barn," said Bo Kregger. "If their horses aren't there, they've turned tail and run."

"Denver Jack and Jesse Turnbaugh ain' the kind to turn tail," said Blue Snake with a bitter twist to his voice.

"It happens to the best of us," said Bo Kregger. "Take yourself." He grinned. "Do you ever get the urge to just scream out loud? Go into some crying fit?"

Blue Snake started to take a step toward Bo Kregger, but Talbert stepped in quickly and blocked his way. "Both of you, try to get along! I've got a feeling Jesse and Denver Jack have met up with Shaw out there!"

"Those shots came from a long ways off," said Bo Kregger. "Why would they go so far to bury those two?"

"I don't know," said Talbert, studying the sand flats in the direction the shots had come from.

"I do," Bo Kregger said with a smug grin, giving Blue Snake a slight wink.

"Both of their horses are gone, boss!" said Bobby Fitt, hurrying back from the livery barn.

"Told you," Bo Kregger said in almost a whisper.

"Damn it, I'm losing men!" said Talbert. "I can't afford to lose any more!" He turned to Gladso Furlin. "Take that sheriff's badge off your chest, Gladso! How's your brother's foot doing?"

"It's wrapped up and stopped bleeding," said Gladso, unpinning the badge from his chest and handing it to Talbert. "I'm keeping him drunk till the pain eases down some."

"No," said Talbert, "don't keep him

drunk! We'll need every gun we've got once Shaw gets here! Get him sobered up. Get some coffee down him!" He looked around nervously. "Let's all get some coffee! Get ourselves ready for a serious gunfight!"

On the boardwalk out front of the saloon, Willie the Devil stood with a handful of money and betting slips. "What about the fiesta? It'd be good for business. There's goats roasting out back right now."

"Damn the fiesta! And damn your business!" shouted Barton Talbert. "Did you hear those gunshots? Fast Larry Shaw is killing our pards quicker than we can get them buried!"

Bo Kregger chuckled and said, "Why don't you settle down, Talbert? Between you and this man with the shiny thumbnails I don't know why Shaw wants to waste a bullet on either of yas. Looks like he might just scare you to death."

"That's it! I've taken all I'm going to from this smug bastard!" shouted Blue Snake Terril, his hand going down to his gun butt. "Fill your hand, Bo Kregger!"

But before Blue Snake could even reach his Colt, a shot from Bo Kregger's gun sliced the holster from his hip and sent his gun, holster and all, spinning in the dirt.

Blue Snake stood dumbstruck. The other men on the street stood gripped in a deathlike silence until they saw Bo Kregger tip his gun barrel up slightly and say with a short laugh to Blue Snake, "Oops, looks like you dropped something."

A sigh of relief rose among the onlookers. Barton Talbert stepped in between Blue Snake and Bo Kregger now that it looked like the danger had passed.

"I can't be humiliated this way," Blue Snake seethed under his breath to Talbert.

"My God, Snake," said Talbert, his voice a harsh whisper, "swallow your pride long enough to see what we've got on our side here! A man who can do something like that can shoot the eyes out of Fast Larry's head! I think Bo is just doing this to show everybody here they've got no reason to turn and run! Can't you see that?"

"I'll try to go along with you, Talbert, but the minute this is over . . ." He left his words hanging, both he and Barton Talbert knowing that there was nothing he could do to a gunman like Bo Kregger; they'd both just seen that.

"Folks, there you've seen it!" said Willie the Devil, turning the situation to his advantage. With both arms in the air he shook the money and the betting slips.

"Anybody who wants to make some last-minute wager after seeing this fine shooting exhibition better do so right away. The fiesta has been cut short! This gunfight could occur sooner than we expected."

"Do you care if I shoot the Devil dead right here and now?" Bo Kregger asked Barton Talbert. "You don't need men that bad, do you?"

Hearing Kregger, Willie gave a frightened look and slunk back toward the saloon, Elton Minton right behind him.

"To give the Devil his due," said Talbert, "in a pinch he is the sneakiest son of bitch you ever saw with a shotgun."

"But we ain't going to *be* in no pinch," said Bo Kregger. "In spite of all I've shown you, I still don't think you realize just how god-awful fast I am." He grinned smugly, twirling his Colt back down into his holster. Then, looking at Blue Snake Terril, who stood dejectedly on the same spot, his gun and holster behind him in the dirt, Kregger said without mercy, "You can get any ol' cobbler to fix that real cheap . . . send me the bill."

When Talbert and Bo Kregger had walked away, Blue Snake stepped back, snatched up his gun and holster, and walked rigidly away toward the livery barn.

"Bo," said Talbert, looking back, "I need every man I've got. I don't think you realize how good a man Blue Snake is at what he does."

"At what he does?" said Bo Kregger. "If you mean changing brands on cattle or throwing a gun in somebody's face and taking their money, maybe so. But if he was any gunman at all, I'd be lying dead back there right now."

"All right, maybe he ain't the gunman you are . . . but who is?" said Talbert, offering a little flattery. "Nobody is!" Talbert said for good measure, throwing up his hands. "I never seen anything like it."

"That's what I like to hear," said Kregger, "a little brownnosing before a big gun battle." He stopped out front of the saloon and looked west toward the fading afternoon sun. "I'm going to get a couple quick drinks, and a hot meal; then I'm going to clean my gun and get myself a good night's sleep."

Barton Talbert looked at him with an air of respect. "Now that takes some cool, calm nerve! What do you want me to be doing?"

Seeming to have to give it some thought, Kregger said, "Well, you could go count out the rest of my money and stack it real neat-like."

"No, I mean as far as how you might want me to set up my men . . . you know, in case things don't go the way we all know they will?"

"Since we *all know* they will," said Kregger, "I don't give a damn how you set your men up, so long as they don't all piss themselves and muddy up the street." He started to walk on into the saloon.

"But don't you want some say-so in how I set them up? Don't you want to know what's going on?"

"Put a couple on the roofs, one in an alley," said Kregger as if bored with the mundane details of killing. "As far as knowing what's going on, I already know when Shaw will get here, and where he'll be standing. Now if you'll excuse me."

"Damn it, Bo, wait a minute," said Talbert. "Let me in on it! Tell me something! You know this is driving me nuts. Not that I'm afraid; just that I can't stand waiting and wondering."

"All right," said Kregger, stopping again and taking a deep breath, looking put-upon by Talbert. "Once Fast Larry Shaw sees there's no more runners among your men, he'll come on in. It will be right at the time the sun comes glaring up in the east. He'll come in from that direction."

Kregger pointed to where the main street, which ran north and south, intersected with another wide street to the east. "He'll stop right there, at that corner, where the sun is going to make him hard to see. Anybody riding with him will come straight down along the boardwalks, watching the alleys, the rooflines, and so forth."

Kregger stopped for a moment in contemplation.

"All right, then what?" Talbert asked anxiously.

"Then what?" Bo Kregger said, teasing him.

"Come on, Bo, what next?" Talbert asked.

Bo chuckled, then said, "All right. Then, if none of your men has made a move on him, or even if they have, for that matter, Shaw is going to call out my name. 'Bo Kregger,' he'll say, just like that. I've done the same thing many times," he reflected as he spoke.

"All right, then you'll step out? Let him have the advantage of the sun being at his back?"

"Hell, no! Do I look like a fool to you, Talbert, giving a big gun like Shaw that kind of an edge?"

"No, no, of course not!" Talbert shook

his head briskly. "But what will you do to take that edge away from him?"

Bo Kregger smiled again. "I just won't come out from where he'll expect me to. I'll come out from over there." He pointed past where he predicted Lawrence would step out and call his name. "I'll come from that little bonnet shop behind him along the same street. It'll keep us both in the same position of sunlight. There went Fast Larry's edge." He tapped himself on the temple. "See, this ain't all about shooting each other down. There's a lot of thought goes into staying alive in this business."

"I got to admit," said Talbert, "you gun-slingers know how to read one another like penny dreadfuls. Sounds good as long as he does it the way you say he will."

"Ha!" said Bo Kregger. "I figured Fast Larry out a long time ago. He's got to do it this way. Don't forget, the fastest gun alive has a reputation he has to keep no matter what."

"I'm counting on it," said Talbert, looking relieved now that he'd heard Bo Kregger's keen insight into Fast Larry Shaw.

"*Counting* on it?" Kregger chuckled confidently. "Talbert, you can *bet* on it — in fact, I hope you already have." He gave a knowing nod toward the saloon, where Willie the Devil was back to work promoting the upcoming gunfight in a huckster's voice.

"It looks like we've got all we're going to get out of Brakett Flats," said Cray Dawson, stepping down from the rise of rock and back over to where Lawrence Shaw and Jedson Caldwell had sat down on the dirt beside the horses. In the west the sun had moved down along the horizon and spread boiling red across the low sky. "What's our next move, Shaw?"

Lawrence Shaw stood up, dusted the seat of his trousers, and looked off across the sand flats toward town. "It's time I get prepared to go on in and get it done."

"How will you want us to play it?" asked Dawson. As he asked, Caldwell stood up too and stepped in closer to hear what would be expected of him.

"Things are going to start happening pretty quick from here on," said Shaw. "Bo Kregger will be expecting me at sunrise, just as the sunlight streaks in."

"And we'll be backing your play," said Dawson. "Where will you want us positioned?"

Shaw didn't answer him. Instead he went

on as if Dawson hadn't said a word. "Bo Kregger already has an idea where I'll come from and where I'll be standing. Talbert will have a couple of his men on the roof somewhere in case things don't go well for him."

"So Caldwell and I will be across the street, covering the roofs and the alleys?" Dawson asked.

With no expression in his cold green eyes, Shaw continued speaking flatly, as if Dawson weren't there, "Right about now Kregger has me pegged, my every thought, my every move. To hear him tell it he could tell you my tone of voice when I call out his name."

"Can I say something, Shaw?" said Dawson.

Shaw just stared at him.

"What about Caldwell and me? Where are we going to be positioned? I want to be in the thick of it when these rats hit the ground."

Shaw looked back and forth between the two men. Then he said calmly and with resolve, "Both of you go on home. I'll take it from here."

"Well, all right then, if you say so," said Jedson Caldwell meekly. He took a step back out of the way.

"Wait a minute! Are you *loco*, Shaw?"

said Dawson. "You've got seven gunmen, plus Bo Kregger, waiting in there to shoot your eyes out! You've got a shoulder wound still healing where Caldwell shot you! No way I'm going home, huh-uh! Not until this is finished!"

"You're going home now, Dawson," Shaw said in a strong tone. "I no longer want you with me." He turned a harsh look to Jedson Caldwell. "Same goes for you, Undertaker. Both of you drag up and ride away. The matter is not even open for discussion."

"The hell it's not!" said Dawson. "If you're cutting me out I've at least got a right to know why! I've rode with you long enough . . . spilled enough blood for you! You owe me that much!"

"I don't owe you a damn thing, Dawson," said Shaw in a low, even tone. "You came along for Rosa's sake, remember? Said how much you loved her? Said how you would have married her if it hadn't been for me coming along? Well, I came along. She was my wife. I stood over her grave imagining what those killers put her through. Now it's time they pay up, and it'll be me that sets things straight, nobody else!" He stared pointedly into Cray Dawson's eyes, then said, "Unless there's some reason why things should be otherwise."

A nerve twitched in Cray Dawson's jaw for a tense, silent moment. Caldwell stood staring in breathless anticipation. Then Dawson broke the silence, saying, "All right, Shaw, I've been trying to tell you all along but you wouldn't listen to me. This is what I meant when I kept saying things still needed to be talked out between us."

"I knew what you had to say then, Dawson," said Shaw, "and I know what you've got to say now. The problem is, I don't know whether or not I can keep from killing you after I hear you say it. Do yourself, me, and Rosa's memory a favor: Keep your mouth shut and get out of here."

Caldwell stood frozen in place, not sure he could trust his own senses. Cray Dawson swallowed hard. "All right, Fast Larry Shaw," said Dawson. "As always, you get your way. I'll leave. There's no arguing with the fastest gun alive." He took a step back toward his horse, then he stopped and pointed his finger at Lawrence Shaw. "But tomorrow morning at sunrise, I'm going to be there in Brakett Flats! If you think you have reason enough to kill me, that's up to you. I'll be there whether you like it or not." He turned, stepped up into his saddle, and started to turn his horse away.

"Damn it to hell, Dawson, wait a

minute," said Shaw, his demeanor softening. "I don't want things to end like this between us. I know you're a good man. Things being the way they were, Rosa must've cared an awful lot for you. Let's just ride away from one another and stay away from one another. We loved the same woman. Everything else about her is gone. Let's keep her memory good."

Dawson stared at him for a moment longer. "I say the same, except it ain't easy for me to forgive myself the way it is for you, Shaw. I've tried every way in the world to admit it to you; it just never got said. I wish to God they'd buried me in Somos Santos instead of her. Dying has got to be easier than this!" He jerked his horse around without another word and gave it his spurs. In a moment all that remained was his wake of dust on a passing breeze.

"Well, what about it, Undertaker?" said Shaw. "Hadn't you better catch up to him? You don't want to be left out here all alone, do you?"

"Mr. Shaw, can I say something too?" said Jedson Caldwell.

"Well, I don't see why not; you're the only man who ever shot Fast Larry Shaw and lived to tell about it," Shaw said with a trace of sarcasm.

Caldwell said in a shaky voice, "I'm not sure what I just heard here . . . and believe me, it's none of my business. But I think Cray Dawson is by far one of the most decent, loyal, straightforward men I've ever had the honor of meeting in this godforsaken land. It's rare to find a friend like that; I think you would do well to value such a friendship."

"Is that all?" Shaw asked.

"Well, yes," said Caldwell.

"Then get a saddle under you and get your knees in the wind. I've got more to do than listen to you give me a sermon on friendship."

"Yes, Mr. Shaw, I'm going now," Caldwell said nervously. "But I want you to know that when Cray Dawson shows up in town tomorrow at the stroke of sunrise, I plan on being there beside him."

"Do you now?" Shaw asked with a scowl. "Right at the crack of sunrise?"

"Yes . . . indeed I do," said Caldwell.

"Well, then, you and Mr. Dawson just be my guests," Shaw said with a bitter twist to his voice. "Show up at sunrise; I won't try to stop you. Now *adios*, Undertaker. Get out of here before I give this shoulder wound back to you!"

Chapter 21

It was dark by the time Jedson Caldwell caught up to Cray Dawson. The two rode on without talking until they made a camp without a fire only five miles from Brakett Flats. In the moonlight they shared a cold meal of stiff jerked meat and tepid canteen water. After a while Dawson broke the tense silence, saying, "I suppose you heard enough to figure what had been going on between Rosa Shaw and me?"

"If you don't mind me saying, I've been seeing that for some time. I had even wondered if Shaw could see it . . . apparently he did." Caldwell stopped for a moment, thinking it over; then he said, "She must've been a remarkable woman, if two men loved her so much they're willing to share the memory of her."

"She was a remarkable woman," said Dawson. "I just wish to God I could have known what was going on that day. *I* would have been there even though Lawrence Shaw *wasn't!*"

"You really do blame yourself, don't

you?" Caldwell asked carefully.

Dawson hung his head. "I actually saw them on their way along the road after they left the Shaw home. I had no idea where they had been."

"Even if you had, it wouldn't have saved her," said Caldwell. "It would only have meant that you would have found her killers sooner." He shrugged. "I call that little comfort for so great a loss."

"That's all I get," said Dawson. "But tomorrow I will be there at sunrise, and even if it means I have to fight Lawrence Shaw, I'm taking vengeance on Rosa's murderers."

"You won't have to fight him," said Caldwell. "The last thing he said was that he wouldn't try to stop us if we showed up."

"He said that, huh?" said Dawson.

"Yes, he did," said Caldwell, nodding. "He said, 'Show up at sunrise; I won't try to stop you.'"

Dawson let out a tired breath. "Then something I said must've changed his mind after he took time to think it over. That ain't like him," he said. He shook his head, then added, "Never fall in love with another man's wife, Caldwell; it'll bring you and everybody else nothing but misery. I expect I am lucky Shaw didn't put a bullet in me. The plain truth is, I hurt so bad I just didn't really care." He stood up, dusted his trouser seat, and took down his saddle and blanket roll.

Caldwell did the same, saying, "So tomorrow we'll meet Shaw there first thing, at sunrise?"

"Yep," said Dawson. "I will, anyway. If you want to ride on, nobody will ever blame you."

Taking down his own saddle and blanket roll, Caldwell said, "I know . . . but if it's all the same, I want to be there."

Dawson just looked at him.

"Call it a test," said Caldwell. Then without another word on the matter he shook out his blanket and spread it on the ground at his saddle.

Dawson nodded and did the same.

Caldwell lay awake in restless anticipation of the upcoming events, while Cray Dawson soon fell fast asleep. But at midnight, as Caldwell still wrestled with his blanket and tossed and turned, he was suddenly startled by the sound of Dawson's voice, saying to himself, "Damn you, Shaw! I should have known better!"

Jedson Caldwell sat up quickly, leaning on both palms, looking around as if expecting to see Lawrence Shaw in their midst. "What's going on, Dawson?" he asked, bewildered.

"Shaw just jackpotted us, that's what's going on!" said Dawson. "It just came to me in my sleep what he's trying to do, only it's not going to work! No, sir! Not if I can help it!"

"What is he trying to do?" asked Caldwell.

Cray Dawson snatched his saddle and blanket from the ground and hurried over to where the horses stood at rest. "Come on, Caldwell, if you're coming! We've got to get a move on!"

"But it's the middle of the night!" Caldwell protested, even as he grabbed his boots in one hand, his saddle and blanket in the other. "Where are we going?"

"Shaw told you it was all right for us to be there at sunrise because he knew damned well he was going into Brakett Flats *tonight!* He's deliberately trying to get himself killed!"

Bobby Fitt stood guard until midnight, until Harper Furlin limped over to the abandoned gallows to relieve him. "I don't see the damn point in us standing guard like this," Harper said, feeling cross and testy from the pain in his swollen, wounded foot. "If I wanted to stand guard

I'd have joined the army."

"I know," said Bobby Fitt. "I've never seen Talbert so worried about anything since I've been riding with him." He looked Harper up and down. "How's the bad foot doing?"

"No good at all," said Harper Furlin. "The only thing would help it is if I could stomp it up and down on Denver Jack's face."

Bobby Fitt chuckled slightly under his breath. "It's a well-known fact that Denver Jack Fish will shoot a man without warning, and with very little provocation."

Harper only sneered and cursed silently.

Leaving the gallows Bobby Fitt walked over to the saloon, where Willie the Devil and Elton Minton were still drinking, the Devil fervently swapping gunfighting tales with a couple of townsmen who had grown bold enough to drink with what remained of Barton Talbert's men at the bar. "What happens if this fight doesn't take place?" one townsman asked the Devil.

Willie the Devil spread his hands in a gesture of innocence, saying, "Then everybody gets their money back, of course! Look, friend, making book on these gunfights is not something I do for money. This is all done through my love of sporting events."

"I never thought of two men shooting at each other as a sporting event," said the townsman, scratching his head.

"Then you haven't studied much history," said the Devil. "The contest of man against man in a contest of life or death is the oldest sport in the world. The Romans did it with swords and pikes and other assorted cutting and maiming objects. So did the Greeks, the Chinese . . . God knows who else! Shooting a man with a gun is perhaps the most humane way in the world to kill him. I hate even thinking about some of the others." He winced in contemplation.

"I hadn't thought of it, but I reckon you're right," said the townsman, again scratching his head.

"You bet I am," said Willie the Devil, smiling broadly. "The Devil wouldn't steer you wrong! Right, Elton?"

"Right you are, Devil," said Elton Minton, who stood farther down the bar. Elton had taken up with a young woman who had been drinking and consorting freely with the outlaws ever since Talbert had convinced the mayor to allow the young women of the town out of hiding. The young woman raised her dress hem slowly and smiled as Elton stuffed a dollar bill under her garter.

"Why do most of the men call you Scarecrow?" she asked Elton, taking her slow, sweet time lowering her hemline.

"I didn't know they did," said Elton with a dumb look on his face.

As Bobby Fitt poured a glass of rye and raised it to his lips, Blue Snake walked through the open doorway with a sour scowl on his face and his eyes blurry and red-rimmed from both whiskey and sleep. "I ate another polecat in my sleep," he said, walking to the bar. He looked back and forth, seeing the line of empty bottles, glasses, and stubbed-out cigar butts along the whiskey-stained bar top. Flies swirled. "What happened to that peckerwood bartender?" he asked, swiping a hand to shoo the cloud of flies away.

"He's been gone three days," said Bobby Fitt, "ever since Denver Jack wanted to shoot a bottle off his head."

"Yeah, I remember," said Blue Snake. Then, as if remembering something important, he asked, "Ain't you supposed to be standing guard?"

"Just till midnight," said Bobby. "Harper relieved me a few minutes ago."

"Harper? Hell," said Blue Snake, "the shape his foot's in, he ain't going to pay attention to what's coming or going. Talbert ain't going to like it." He jerked his head toward the street. "Get over there and send Harper to bed."

"I don't know why," said Bobby Fitt, throwing back his drink of rye. "There ain't nothing going to happen till sunrise anyway. You heard what Bo Kregger said about gunfighters like Shaw."

"That's right, I heard him," said Blue Snake with finality. "Now go send Harper to bed. Talbert is jumpier than a squirrel."

Bobby Fitt grumbled under his breath but did as he was told. He left the saloon, but was back inside of a minute, a stunned look on his face. "Blue Snake, you better come see this! Ol' Harper has committed suicide!"

"Like hell," said Blue Snake, hurrying past him out the door. "Come on, all three of you!" he shouted over his shoulder.

But as Willie the Devil ran out the door, Elton acted as if he hadn't heard Blue Snake's command. "Aren't you going with them, *Scarecrow?*" the young woman asked playfully.

"No," said Elton, "I'm strictly here for the sporting event." Taking the woman by her arm, he headed for the stairs leading up to the second floor. "Come on up to my room; I want to show you my betting slips."

"Oh, goody!" said the woman, going along with him.

But as the two townsmen stood peering out the open doorway, before Elton and the woman reached the stairs, Lawrence Shaw stepped out of the shadows from the rear of the saloon, his Colt raised and cocked in Elton's face.

"Fast Larry Shaw!" Elton Minton gasped, seeing the big open gun bore staring him in the eye.

"Fast Larry?" said one of the townsmen in disbelief. Seeing both townsmen snap around in the open doorway to get a look at him, Shaw said, "Gentlemen, keep your eyes turned to the street. Don't draw attention to me."

"Oops! No! We won't do that!" said a townsman, grabbing his companion and turning him back toward the street.

"You . . . you remember me, don't you?" said Elton in a shaky voice. The young woman, who had been shocked at first, now looked Shaw up and down with an inviting smile.

"Should I?" Shaw said to Elton.

"I'm the one who took care of the bets on you and Mace Renfield. Remember me?" said Elton.

The young woman cut in, saying, "The

men call him Scarecrow."

"The one who stole all the betting money?" Shaw said.

Elton fell silent, his eyes seeming transfixed on the gun barrel.

"I'm not here to kill you, *Scarecrow*," said Shaw. "And I don't care about the betting money you stole. I want you to go tell those boys out in the street that I'm up there" — he gestured a nod toward the rooms upstairs — "having a drink with this young lady. Tell them I'll be right down . . . I'm here to kill them."

"All *right!*" One of the men in the doorway said, raising a fist in a cheer without turning around. "I've got three dollars bet on you, Fast Larry! I just want you to know!"

Shaw didn't answer. Taking the woman by her forearm, he directed her toward the stairs. "After you, ma'am," he said.

"Well, thank you, Mr. Shaw," the woman said. "My name is Florence, by the way."

"Lawrence Shaw, ma'am," Shaw replied, "at your service."

"Oh, my, I hope so!" Florence whispered suggestively.

Shaw said to Elton, who stood stunned, "Well, are you going, or do I have to clip your toenails?" He lowered the barrel toward Elton's feet. Elton jumped back as if a snake had nipped at his toes.

"Yes, sir, Mr. Shaw! I'm gone!" Elton said.

As soon as Elton was out the door, the townsmen ventured a glance around and saw Shaw and the woman climbing the stairs, Shaw escorting her with her hand lying on his forearm. But when they reached the top of the stairs and turned a corner out of sight, Shaw said, nodding toward a door at the far end of the hall, "I suppose that's the way out of here?"

"I don't know," said Florence, not as seasoned and seductive now that she thought they were about to enter one of the small rooms. "I've never really been here before. I just thought it would be exciting!"

"And now your stomach is feeling a little queasy?" said Shaw.

"I'm sorry," said Florence.

"Think nothing of it, ma'am," said Shaw. "The fact is, I want you to get out that door and down the back stairs as quick as you can. Get away and stay away. Will you do that?"

"But if there's going to be a gunfight —" Her words stopped short when she saw the look on Shaw's face. "All right . . . yes, I'll go, and I'll stay out of your way."

"All right, get going," said Shaw, giving her a slight nudge.

"Good luck, Fast Larry," she said as she turned away.

Fast Larry . . . "Much obliged, ma'am," Shaw said patiently.

On the street by the gallows, Blue Snake, Willie the Devil, and Bobby Fitt stood staring at the body of Harper Furlin as Elton Minton came running up beside him, out of breath. Elton skidded to a halt at seeing Harper's body twist back and forth slowly on the long gallows rope, his toes only two inches off the ground.

"My, my! Harper hanged himself," Bobby Fitt said quietly. "His foot must've hurt lots more than he let on."

Blue Snake stared at Bobby Fitt. "Damn it, Bobby, Shaw did this! Harper didn't kill himself!"

"He's there!" said Elton, grabbing Blue Snake by the shoulder to keep from falling.

"Who's there? There where?" Blue Snake demanded, throwing Elton's hand off of him roughly.

A cry of pain and outrage arose as Gladso Furlin arrived and saw Harper's body hanging from the gallows. He flung himself forward, raising Harper into his arms.

"Fast Larry!" said Elton, still struggling to catch his breath. "He's in the saloon! Right now! Upstairs with that young woman, Florence!"

Barton Talbert arrived just in time to hear what Elton said. Behind Talbert, Bo Kregger walked along sleepily, shoving his shirt down into his trousers, his gun belt hanging from his shoulder. He gave an unconcerned glance to Gladso and his dead brother and shook his head. "Fast Larry Shaw ain't in the saloon. I told you *sunrise,* damn it!"

"Maybe he forgot to set his watch," said Blue Snake dryly, as he drew his pistol and checked it. "Willie, Bobby, Scarecrow . . . let's go get him."

Barton Talbert turned to Bo Kregger. "If Scarecrow saw him, he's there! What are you thinking, anyway?"

"He ain't there," said Bo Kregger confidently, rubbing his sleepy eyes. "He might have just been there, and he might have taken some woman upstairs, but he ain't there now."

"We can at least check and see!" said Barton Talbert.

"Suit yourself," said Kregger. "He won't be here till morning, just like I said." He turned and started to walk away.

"Bo! Where are you going?" Talbert asked.

"Where does it look like I'm going?" said Kregger. "Back to bed. I've got a busy morning coming."

Chapter 22

Inside the saloon, Blue Snake stood back cautiously, his Colt in hand, poised, looking up at the top of the stairs. "Shaw! He brought us, just like you told him to! Come on down! This is Blue Snake Terril! I'll fight you man-to-man! Nobody will interfere; you've got my word on it!"

Close beside Blue Snake, Bobby Fitt whispered, "Want me to see if there's a shotgun under the bar?"

"Hell, yes, get the shotgun! What's the matter with you?" Blue Snake whispered harshly. "Hurry up!"

"Got it!" said Bobby, hurrying behind the bar, snatching up the shotgun, and waving it to show Blue Snake.

"Shaw," said Blue Snake, "you know that Bo Kregger is here, and he's wanting you awfully bad. But I say first come, first served, don't you?" He paused for a reply, but when none came, he said, "I understand you've got to take vengeance for what happened. But since I had nothing to do with what happened to your wife, I figure you and me ought to treat one another with respect. I'm going to give you a minute to think about it. Then I believe you and me ought to handle this like a couple of honorable men. That's my thinking on it."

"I got the kerosene!" Willie the Devil whispered, appearing from the back stockroom of the saloon.

"It's about damn time!" said Blue Snake, still whispering. "Get some matches and get ready."

"For God's sake! Don't burn the saloon!" one of the townsmen pleaded shrilly, nearing hysteria. He jumped up from where he and his companion had hidden beneath a rough wooden table and screamed toward the top of the stairs, "Mr. Shaw! Please! If there's any humanity in you, don't let them burn the —"

He cut his words short, seeing Blue Snake swing his big Colt toward him. Before Blue Snake could get a shot off, both townsmen turned the table over as they ran from the saloon.

"Never mind them, Shaw!" said Blue Snake. "They're just drunken citizens! What do they know about bold gunmen like you and me, right?"

While Blue Snake spoke to the empty

stairwell, Bo Kregger heard the two townsmen running from the saloon as he made his way to the front of the hotel. Looking back, he said aloud to himself, "You stupid sons a' bitches. No wonder you'll all be dead tomorrow."

Hiking his gun belt onto his shoulder, he started to step onto the front porch of the hotel when something made him freeze. Gooseflesh ran the length of his arms. His back tightened as if a cold serpent had caressed his spine. "Shaw?" he whispered to himself, his gunman's instincts sensing something that his mind had not yet fathomed, let alone accepted. "No, wait!" he said, turning around to face the dark street.

In the blackness of the overhang out front of the women's hat store, Shaw stood, his tall outline somehow even darker than the broad blackness surrounding him. He was invisible, yet Bo Kregger saw him, his hat brim, his long riding duster, his high, upturned collar. Then, in that tight curve of time and air when the sequence of events pile one upon another to become death, Bo Kregger saw the bright orange-blue flash that exposed Shaw for another split second as Kregger tightened his grip on his gun belt and said in disappointment and dread, "Damn it, I never even got to —"

And even as he said it, he heard Shaw reply, or thought he heard him reply, "She was my wife, you understand."

The roar of the bullet sounded short to Bo Kregger as it lifted him up by the heart and flung him backward against the front of the hotel, dead, his eyes staring into the darkness, stuck in rapt awareness, like a man having learned a great lesson too late.

Inside the saloon, Blue Snake Terril continued to speak to the empty stairwell while the Devil poured kerosene all over the floor and walls, shoving bottles of rye into his coat pockets in the process. "Hear that, Shaw? That'd be ol' Bo right now, practicing, I bet, wanting you to meet him in the street. But I say first it's between you and me. What do you say?"

"Blue Snake, you *fool!*" shouted Barton Talbert from the open doorway, a rifle in one hand, a pistol in the other. "Shaw's not up there! He's out here! He's just killed Bo Kregger deader than hell!"

Blue Snake went blank for a second. Then he shook his head as if to get his mind started again. He shot a quick glance at Willie the Devil, who stood striking a match along the edge of the bar top. "Don't, Willie!" he shouted, but not in time. The Devil had already given the match a pitch toward the stairwell. Flames spread quickly upward, following the long, wet stream of kerosene Willie had slung up the stairs. As soon as Willie saw the fire spread he hurried back toward the doorway, hearing Blue Snake, but unable to undo what he'd started.

"Sorry, Blue Snake," Willie said, "but when the Devil starts a fire there's no stopping it from running its course."

"Bo Kregger? Dead?" said Blue Snake, as if he couldn't believe it. He no longer seemed to care about the saloon being on fire.

"Deader than hell!" said Barton Talbert. "Shaw's here, and he'll have to be dealt with before he kills us all!" He stepped inside the burning saloon and looked back out onto the dark street. "I tell you, this man don't act human!"

Blue Snake grabbed the rifle from Talbert's hand and levered a round into the chamber. "He might not act human, but he damned sure is! Once we put a couple of bullets in him, I expect he'll bleed just like the rest of us!" Looking out into the shadowy moonlight, Blue Snake called out, "All right, Shaw, if this is how you want it, here we come!" Then he said to Talbert, "Where is Gladso?"

"Gladso took his brother inside and laid him out on the floor of the hotel," said Bobby Fitt, standing ready with the shotgun under the bar. "If I know Gladso, he's listening to everything right now. He's the sneakiest man I ever saw. He'll pop out on Shaw when Shaw's least expecting it, is my guess."

"Then what are we waiting for?" said Blue Snake. "Bobby, take the shotgun and get around on the far side of the street. Blast Shaw down when he comes past you to get to us." He looked around and saw Willie the Devil, but no sign of Elton Minton. "Where's Scarecrow, Devil?" he asked.

"I don't know," said the Devil, "but forget him; he's no fighter anyway."

Barton Talbert took a deep breath and said with resolve, "All right, let's get out there and kill this bastard. There's still plenty of us, counting the Devil. . . . I'm tired of worrying about Fast Larry Shaw. Whoever kills him gets the other thousand dollars that was going to go to Bo Kregger!" Then, thinking about it, Talbert said, "No, make that five hundred of what was going to go to Kregger." But it made no difference to Bobby Fitt, Blue Snake, or Willie the Devil. This was all about staying alive now, and nothing else.

As they left the burning saloon, Bobby Fitt hurried away along the boardwalk, crouched and ducking into the shadows, where he could lie in wait for Shaw to come down the middle of the street. Throughout the town word had spread about the saloon being ablaze. Townsmen appeared, hiking up their suspenders and buckling their belts, their shirttails flapping loosely. Ghostly flames licked high into the night, streaking upward through boiling black smoke and racing sparks.

Lawrence Shaw sat inside a darkened doorway and watched the fire calmly. He thought of a Fourth of July celebration in Somos Santos back when he and Rosa were still young lovers thinking their lives together were unending. In Shaw's eyes the saloon fire sparkled and shone, and he felt a tear well up until it spilled freely and warmly down his cheek. "Rosa . . . Rosa," he whispered, "look where this life is taking me . . . look where it's taken you."

Then he stood up, seeing the outline of men walking toward him against the backdrop of fire. "Shaw," he heard Blue Snake Terril call out.

Wiping his fingertips through the tear on his face, Shaw said to Rosa under his breath, "I won't be but a minute, Rosa, darling . . . I'll be coming right along."

"Step out, Shaw!" said Barton Talbert, letting go of his fear and taking charge, leading Blue Snake and Willie the Devil down the middle of the dark street. "I had nothing to do with killing your wife! I'm innocent! But if there's got to be some killing to make it right . . . come and get all of it you want!"

Several of the townsmen who had formed a bucket brigade to fight the saloon fire ducked out of sight at the sound of Barton Talbert's words. "We've got a fire going, damn it!" one townsman shouted in anger.

Seeing Lawrence Shaw's dark figure appear before them, Blue Snake and Willie the Devil began firing. But their first shots were wild and unaimed. Barton Talbert stopped and took careful aim. Yet, as he fired, Shaw moved at the last second and the shot sliced through the air past his head. "Damn it, somebody hit him!" Talbert shouted.

Lawrence Shaw drew his big Colt and walked forward, taking quick aim and firing. Shot after shot, the three men felt the bullets punch and cut and drive them to their knees in bloody submission. Once flat on his belly, Willie the Devil managed to lie quietly, a pistol tucked up under him. Blue Snake Terril took a bullet in the chest but still managed to crawl away, leaving a blood trail behind him until he managed to turn and shove upward to his feet. Shaw didn't see him, but as Blue Snake took aim, a bullet came out of the darkness and knocked him dead.

Shaw kept walking, kept firing, knowing that with each shot fired at him his odds of living fell dramatically. "Shoot, damn you, *shoot!*" he shouted. "Can you only kill women?"

But as he stepped closer, he saw only Barton Talbert, on one knee in the dirt, his Colt hanging loosely in his hand. "I just . . . want to say . . . I'm sorry, Shaw," he said in a gasp, blood spilling from his lips.

"Why didn't you shoot?" said Shaw bitterly, the Colt bucking in his hand, knocking Barton Talbert flat onto his back in a spray of blood.

To his right, Shaw heard Cray Dawson's voice call out, "Look out, Shaw!"

Before Shaw could turn to see why, Dawson's Colt exploded, causing Bobby Fitt's shotgun to go off wildly as Fitt fell dead with a bullet through his heart.

"I told you I was going to be here, Shaw," Cray Dawson's voice called out in the darkness. "I got Blue Snake."

With a sigh of resignation, Shaw said, "So you did, Dawson, and I got Barton Talbert." Shaw lowered his pistol and whispered, "Well, Rosa, looks like I'll be a while longer."

"What?" asked Dawson, stepping into the dimly moonlit street.

"I wasn't talking to you," said Shaw.

There was a pause. "Oh," said Dawson, as if he understood.

Just as the tension eased a bit and both men let their gun hands relax, Gladso Furlin stepped out of nowhere with a double-barreled shotgun pointed at Lawrence Shaw's chest. "Shaw, I got you!" he said, pulling the trigger.

"No!" Cray Dawson shouted, lunging into Shaw as the shot exploded, taking part of the buckshot in the back of his shoulder, keeping the bulk of the blast from hitting Shaw full in the chest.

On the ground atop of Shaw, Dawson clung to him, braced for the second blast, knowing that Gladso had them cold. Then Dawson flinched three times in rapid succession as Jedson Caldwell fired without hesitation, each shot driving Gladso Furlin backward until the third one hurled him into a water trough that the townsmen were using to fill buckets to extinguish the saloon fire. No sooner than the shooting had stopped, the townsmen ran forward, rolled Gladso's body from the trough, filled their buckets, and began concentrating on the fire.

Jedson Caldwell ran out of the dark shadows into the moonlit street, shaking out of control, looking over at the wet, dripping body of Gladso Furlin. When he got to where Cray Dawson and Lawrence Shaw lay in a bloody heap, he saw Dawson roll over off of Shaw and struggle up into a crouch, his back covered with blood. "Are you all right, Dawson?" Caldwell asked, his words trembling.

"I'm all right," said Dawson. Then, looking down at Shaw, he said, "What about you, Shaw? Are you doing all right?" He saw the wide spread of blood on Shaw's shoulder, his chest, his face. "Shaw?" he asked, his voice taking on a hushed tone.

Lawrence Shaw lay flat on his back, his eyes staring blank yet serenely upward into the wide, starry sky. "Oh, no, Shaw!" said Dawson, his voice beginning to fail him at seeing the expressionless look on Shaw's bloody face. Jedson Caldwell stepped in quietly beside him, the two of them staring down at Lawrence Shaw.

"That was . . . a damn stupid thing to do, Dawson," Shaw said, reaching a hand up slowly for help to his feet.

Dawson and Caldwell each let out a breath of relief. "You're right," said Dawson, feeling the pain in his wound begin in earnest as he gave his hand to Shaw. "I don't know what I was thinking, doing that."

"Oh, Mr. Shaw," said Jedson Caldwell, "we thought for certain you were dead."

"Dead? No, not dead, Undertaker," said Shaw, "just taking a second there, wondering what it would be like if I was." He looked longingly up at the night sky again and wiped a sleeve across his face, clearing off some of the blood. "I'll probably go from being the fastest gun alive to being the oldest gun alive, the way things go for me." Then he said to Dawson, "You saved my life, Cray Dawson. . . . I'm obliged."

Dawson let it pass him by, saying, "Caldwell saved both our lives."

"That you did, Undertaker, and I'm obliged to you, too," said Shaw. Seeing the Colt still in Caldwell's hand, the barrel pointed at him, Shaw reached out and nudged the barrel down at the ground.

Caldwell was still shaken but highly excited. "I didn't see the Devil or Elton go down. Want me to go hunt them?"

"No," said Shaw. "The Devil had nothing to do with Rosa's death, and Elton just got dragged along by the Devil. It's finished." He sighed. "The killing, anyway. Now comes the hard part for me . . . just living."

"Are you sure you're all right, Shaw?" said Dawson. "You didn't come here tonight to do anything foolish, did you?"

"Foolish?" said Shaw, with a twist of irony in his voice. He looked around at the burning saloon, the bodies on the ground, the blood on Dawson's face, and the blood on his own chest. "Why would you say something like that?"

"Just the way you did this," said Dawson, "trying to get rid of us . . . coming here in the dead of night, one man against all these guns. I wondered if maybe you weren't out to get yourself killed."

Shaw managed a dark chuckle. "Dawson, I suppose I could say I've been trying to get myself killed my whole life. But I'm just too good at staying alive to let it happen."

"You know what I mean, Shaw," said Dawson, not letting Shaw play it off.

"Oh, you mean suicide?" said Shaw, sounding astonished at such a thought. "No way, Dawson. I got too much pride to do something like that," he lied. "You just misread me. I didn't want you two here because . . ." His words trailed; then he shrugged and said, "Well, being the fastest gun alive, I don't suppose I have to explain every move I make, do I?"

"Not to me, you don't," said Cray Dawson. Seeing Shaw stagger a bit, he reached out, took his arm, and looped it across his shoulder. "Here, let's go find a doctor before we both bleed ourselves dry."

A townsman rushed in and looked around at the dead, then said to Shaw, "This was supposed to happen in the daylight! When folks could see it!" He tossed his hands in the air.

"The Devil had a scheduling problem," Shaw said without looking at him.

"But I had money on this!" the man said. "Many of us did! Where is it? Who has it? I demand my money back!"

Caldwell gave him a narrow, blank look and hissed, "Mister, the betting was all put up by Willie the Devil! If you've got a problem with it, go to the Devil!" He stared coldly until the man shied back, turned, and hurried away.

"Getting cocky, ain't he?" Shaw said quietly to Dawson.

"Yeah," Dawson replied as they limped along, "I've been expecting it."

Caldwell picked up Shaw's hat from the dirt and carried it dutifully along behind them. Taking a deep breath, he kept his chest expanded, liking the broad, strong feeling it gave him. When the wounded gunmen had gone a few feet farther, Caldwell dusted the big hat, raised it, and set it atop his head, but just for a moment, just long enough to see what it felt like.

About the Author

RALPH COTTON has been an ironworker, a second mate on a commercial barge, a teamster, a horse trainer, and a lay minister with the Lutheran church. Visit his Web site at www.RalphCotton.com.

The employees of Thorndike Press hope you have enjoyed this Large Print book. All our Thorndike and Wheeler Large Print titles are designed for easy reading, and all our books are made to last. Other Thorndike Press Large Print books are available at your library, through selected bookstores, or directly from us.

For information about titles, please call:

(800) 223-1244

or visit our Web site at:

www.gale.com/thorndike
www.gale.com/wheeler

To share your comments, please write:

Publisher
Thorndike Press
295 Kennedy Memorial Drive
Waterville, ME   04901